MR. SHIVERS

By Robert Jackson Bennett

Mr. Shivers

MR. SHIVERS

ROBERT JACKSON BENNETT

www.orbitbooks.net

Ben

Orbit
Hachette Book Group
237 Park Avenue, New York, NY 10017
Visit our website at www.HachetteBookGroup.com

First Edition: January 2010

Orbit is an imprint of Hachette Book Group. The Orbit name and logo are trademarks of Little, Brown Book Group Limited.

Library of Congress Cataloging-in-Publication Data

Bennett, Robert Jackson.
    Mr. Shivers / Robert Jackson Bennett.
      p. cm.
    ISBN 978-0-316-05468-3
    1. Fathers of murder victims—Fiction.   2. Murder—Investigation—Fiction.   3. Depressions—1929—United States—Fiction.   I. Title.

    PS3602.E66455M7 2010
    813'.6—dc22

                                             2009002150

10   9   8   7   6   5   4   3   2   1

Printed in the United States of America

MR. SHIVERS

CHAPTER ONE

By the time the number nineteen crossed the Missouri state line the sun had crawled low in the sky and afternoon was fading into evening. The train had built up a wild head of steam over the last few miles. As Tennessee fell behind it began picking up speed, the wheels chanting and chuckling, the fields blurring into jaundice-yellow streaks by the track. A fresh gout of black smoke unfurled from the train's crown and folded back to clutch the cars like a great black cloak.

Connelly shut his eyes as the wave of smoke flew toward him and held on tighter to the side of the cattle car. He wasn't sure how long he had been hanging there. Maybe a half hour. Maybe more. The crook of his arm was curled around one splintered slat of wood and he had wedged his boots into the cracks below. Every joint in his body ached.

He squinted through the tumble of trainsmoke at the other three men. They hung on, faces impassive. One of them called to the oldest, asking if it was soon. He grinned and shook his head and laughed.

Ten miles on Connelly felt the train begin to slow and the countryside started to take shape around him. The fields all seemed the same, nothing but cracked red earth and crooked fencing. Sometimes there were men working in the fields, overalled and with faces as beaten as the land. They watched the train's furious procession with a country boy's awe. Some laughed and called to them. Most did not and watched their coming and going with almost no acknowledgment at all.

The old man before him hitched himself low on the train, eyes watching the wheels as one would a predator. He held up three fingers, waved. Then two. Then one, and he dropped from the side of the train.

Connelly followed suit and as he rolled he saw the churning wheels no more than three feet from him, hissing and cackling. He slid away until he came to rest in a ditch with the others. They stood and beat the dust and grit and soot from their faces. Then they crouched low in the weeds and waited until the train's passage was marked only by a ribbon of black smoke and a roar hovering in the sky.

"Think they coming back?" whispered one of the young ones. "Coming back to look for us?"

"Boy, what are you, an idiot?" said the old man. "No train man is going to double back looking for trouble. If we're off then we're off. Done."

"Done?"

"Yeah. Count your limbs and teeth and start using your feet. Maybe your head, too, if you feel like it." He scratched his gray hair and grinned, flashing a crooked mouthful of yellowed teeth.

They shouldered their packs and began heading west, following the tracks.

"Should have held on longer," said one of the men.

"Ha," said the grayhair. "If you did that then I guarantee you wouldn't be looking so hale and hearty right now. Don't want to get caught, caught by the freight boss. He'd whale you raw."

"Not with him, I'd reckon," the man said, nodding toward Connelly, who was a head taller than the others. "What's your name?"

"Connelly," he said.

"You got any tobacco?"

Connelly shook his head.

"You sure?"

"Yeah."

"Hm," he said, and spat. "Still think we should've held on longer."

They took up upon an old county road. As they walked they kicked up a cloud of dust that rose to their faces, turning their soot-gray clothes to raw red. The land on either side was patched like a stray's coat, the hills dotted with corn lying flat as though it had been laid low by some blast. Roots lay half submerged in the loose soil, fine curling tendrils grasping at nothing. In some places growth still clung to the earth and men grouped around these spots to pump life into their crop. As Connelly passed they looked up with frightened, brittle eyes and he knew it would not last.

The two younger men paced ahead and one said, "Why don't these dumb sons of bitches leave?"

"Where they going to go?" asked the other.

"Anywhere's better than here."

"Looks like home to me. This seems to be my anywhere and it ain't much better."

"Things'll turn different in Rennah," the other said. "You just watch."

The grayhair dropped back beside Connelly. "You headed to the same place? Rennah, you headed there?"

Connelly nodded.

The grayhair shook his head, swatted the back of his neck with his hat. "Your funeral. Nothing going to be there, you know that?" He leaned closer to confide a whisper. "These fellas is just suckers. They flipped that ride 'cause they heard there's work here, but there ain't. Further down the line, I say. Maybe south, maybe west. Eh?"

"Not going for work," said Connelly.

"What? What the hell you going for, then?"

Connelly bowed his head and pulled his cap low. The old man let him be.

The sun turned a deep, sick red as it sank toward the earth. Even the sky had a faint tinge of red. It made a strange, hellish sight. It was the drought, everyone said. Threw dirt up into the sky. Touched the heavens with it. Connelly was not so sure but could not say why. Perhaps it was something else. Some superficial symptom of a greater disease.

He counted the days as he walked and guessed it had been more than two weeks since he had left Memphis. Then he counted his dollars and reckoned he had spent a little over three. He was spending at far too high of a rate if he wanted to go much farther. And he would have to go farther. The man had a week's head start on him at least. It was unlikely that he'd even be in Rennah. But he had been there once and that was all Connelly needed.

Closer, he said to himself. I'm close. I'm very close now.

"Town's up that way," said one of the men, pointing to a few lines of smoke on the horizon.

The old man eyed the spindle-like lines twisting across the sunset. "That ain't the town," he said.

"No?"

"No. Those are campfires."

The men looked at each other again, this time worried. Connelly was not surprised. He knew they had expected it, whether they said so or not. For many it was the same as the town they had just left.

Connelly caught its scent before he saw it. He smelled rotten kindling and greasy fires and cigarette smoke, excrement and foul water. It was a plague-stink, a battlefield-reek. Then he heard the cacophony of dogs barking and children crying, a junkyard song of pots and pans and old engine parts and drunken melodies. Then finally it came into view. They shaded their eyes and looked at the encampment before them, saw jalopies lurching between canyons of shuddering tents, people small as dots milling beside them. A wide smear of gray and black among the white-gold of the fields. There had to be at least a hundred people there. At least.

"Jesus," said one of the men.

"Yeah," said another.

"Can't see there being much work here."

"I reckon not, no."

"Told you so," said the grayhair softly. "Told you so."

Connelly and the men parted ways as they approached. The men walked on and came to the camp's ragged border. Some of the people had tents and some had cars and some had nothing at all but still mingled around these tattered constructs like refuse caught washing downstream. They watched the new strangers approach, too tired to hold any real resentment. The men split up and wandered in and were caught among the webs of the encampment, filtering through the grubby people to find some spot to sit in or a fire to stand by. They sat and made talk and waited for night and the following dawn. By now it was routine.

Connelly did not join them. He walked around the camp and into town.

CHAPTER TWO

The town couldn't have been more than five hundred people, at most. Yet the essentials were there: a main street, a post office, a general store, and finally a saloon at the end of the street.

Connelly peered through the yellowed windows of the bar. Dusty bottles were lined up behind an old wooden countertop. Men sat in sweat-soaked shirts with their hats pulled low, staring into their drinks with eyes like muddy ice.

He walked in carefully, stepping like the floor could collapse at any moment. All the men looked at him, for his size caught the eye. He removed his cap and stuffed it in his pocket and sat down at the bar. The others relaxed as he did, seeing that underneath all the miles of travel he was still a man, though no doubt one who had been roughing it for the past months. His hair had grown long and a beard crawled at the edges of his jaw. He could have been thirty, or forty, or even fifty, as his skin was tanned and dark and bore deep lines from the sun.

"What can I get you?" asked the bartender.

"Whisky," Connelly said.

"Ten cents."

"All right."

Neither one moved.

"You don't have whisky?" asked Connelly.

"We have whisky. You have ten cents?"

Connelly reached into his satchel and took out a thin wallet and a dime and slid it over.

"Sorry," said the bartender, taking it. "Got to do that. Lots of folks come in here, order, then run out."

"Wasn't anything."

The bartender poured and placed the glass in front of him. Connelly took the glass and drank it in a single swallow.

"Long time getting here?" asked the bartender.

"Here is just another stop on the road," he said.

An ancient old man stood up and came and sat beside Connelly. He ordered as well, hands trembling. Then he turned to Connelly and studied him, his face fixed in a terrible awe.

"What you doing there, grampa?" asked the bartender cautiously.

The old man did not answer. Instead he said, "West."

"What?" said Connelly.

"West. You're going west, ain't you?"

"If that's where I'm going, yeah," said Connelly.

"You are," he said. "You are. I can tell. I seen enough people heading west to know when one's going that way. And you are."

"Okay."

"You shouldn't, you know. You shouldn't."

"I could go back south or north right after you get done talking to me."

"No. You won't. Certain men, the way they look at things and the way they walk, they're drawn to the west, to the far countries. Even if they turn aside and walk for days on end, soon enough they'll find themselves facing sunset again."

"A lot of people are moving west right now."

"True. That's true. But they should not go."

Connelly fiddled with his glass, ignoring him.

The old man said, "They say the sun kisses the land out there, like a lover. That may be so. I been out there. For years, I been out there. And if that's so then the sun's love is a terrible, harsh thing. Where it's placed its kiss nothing grows, all is burned away, everything is scorched and nothing lives and your heart is the only one of its kind that beats for miles and miles. And all is red. Where the sun and the horizon and the sands meet, all is red."

"Is it?"

"Yes," said the old man. "You should not go. You should turn around. Stop looking. And go."

"You leave me the hell alone," Connelly said.

"Listen," the old man pleaded. "Listen to me. I been out there. I seen the great, red hunger, and where it walks everything aches. From the stones to the skies, everything aches. It's broken land, there. It is broken and lost, like those who live there, and they cannot go back. You should not go out there. You should not."

The bartender scowled. "Get out of here, you damn crazy fool. Stop worrying my customers and get the hell out of here."

"Go back to your home," said the old man.

"I don't have a home," said Connelly. "Not anymore."

"But you still could have another," said the old man. "In the west there is no hope of that. Such things are forfeit there."

"Get out. Now," said the bartender. "I won't ask you again. If you stay here for one more second I'm going to whale you, I don't care how old you are."

The old man stepped down from the seat and staggered out onto the sidewalk. He mumbled to himself, played with the buttons on his overalls, and shambled away.

"I apologize for that," said the bartender. "Damn old coot. He's always causing trouble. I don't think he even lives here. He just drinks when he can and sleeps in whatever alley he finds. There's more and more of them. They're almost like dogs."

"Another whisky," said Connelly.

The bartender poured, gave him the glass, and watched again as Connelly drank in one swallow.

"Well, you don't spend like an Okie and you don't drink much like an Okie, either," said the bartender.

"Probably 'cause I'm not an Okie."

"Oh?"

"No."

"Where you from?"

"Back east."

"Ha. People who're east ought to stay east, I'd say."

"You going to give me another earful like the old man?"

"No. I just don't see why you'd want to come here. Nothing to come for. No one wants to stay here. *I* don't want to stay here. Folks are all heading west or south or wherever they can go that isn't here. Anywhere there's green ground and work."

"I'm not looking for work."

"What are you doing here, then?"

"I'm looking for a man," said Connelly quietly.

"Oh?"

"Yeah. He came this way. Took a train, hitched his way here. I'm looking for him."

"Why are you looking for him?"

"Got some questions for him."

"What sort?"

Connelly didn't answer.

The bartender grunted. "I don't want any trouble."

"I don't mean to give you any," Connelly said.

"Ain't that what they all say."

"You may have seen him."

"I see a lot of men. Too many of late."

"You would remember him," said Connelly. "He was scarred, on his face."

"Any working man is liable to be scarred."

"He had a bunch of them, all over his face. Three big ones, here and here," he said, and drew one finger from each edge of his mouth along the cheeks, back to the angle of the jaw. Then once more, around the socket of his left eye.

The bartender turned to watch. His mouth opened slightly in surprise and he looked away.

"You seen him," said Connelly.

"I haven't."

"You have."

"I said I haven't and I meant it. I haven't."

"Then why'd you almost fall over on yourself when I asked?"

"I didn't. Just... You ain't the only one looking for him," he said.

Connelly's eyes opened wide and he sat forward. "What do you mean?"

"I don't want trouble," said the bartender. One hand reached under the bar. Almost certainly searching for some hidden cudgel.

Connelly sat back down. "I just want to know what's going on," he said.

"I don't rightly know," the bartender said, and sighed. "Three men come in here, just a day or two ago. Came in, asked if I'd seen a man with a scarred face. 'Like he's got a big mouth. Big,' they said, and they drawed on their own faces just as you done now. I hadn't seen him, not a man with scars as such, and I told them the same as I told you."

"Who were they?"

"I don't know. How the hell should I know? Don't know you, either. I don't know you from Adam."

"What else did they say?"

"They didn't say anything else. They just come in here, ask, then when I said no they just go on out."

"Where'd they go?"

"To the camp, I guess. Back out to that camp outside, with all the other people who pitched out there. I guess they came in on the train," he said, and eyed Connelly once more. "Much like you."

"Where are they camping?"

"You got a hell of a lot of questions for a guy who only drank two whiskies."

"I just want to know. That's all I want. Please."

"Little bit northwest of here, I think. At the old tree. Bent tree, big dead tree. You can't miss it."

Connelly thanked him for the drink and walked out.

*   *   *

Outside the sun had fallen until its light was a pale pink halo in the distance. Pools of shadows swept down out of alleys and ditches and into the streets. Miserable fires glowed in the darkness, like mad fireflies or failing stars. Connelly wound through the streets and the camp and out to the hills on the other side of the town.

As he walked through the weeds and the stones he looked but saw no other encampment. Just the growing dark and the faint outline of the country. The chatter of cicadas rose and fell, punctuated by the chirps of the nighthawks circling far overhead. As he mounted the next knoll he saw the greasy spark of a small fire not far away and above it the twisted skeleton of an ancient tree. He stood watching the flame and began to ascend. When he heard the mutter of quiet talk he stopped.

He took off his cap and used it to dab at the sweat on his brow. He knelt to think and as he did the voices ceased. Then a hoarse shout came: "If you're going to come out then come out. We can't wait on you all day."

Connelly hesitated, then tramped up the hill. He saw three men standing before the fire looking down on him, their faces almost masked in the dark. One, the shouter, was very tall, and while not as tall as Connelly just as broad. His face was aged and hoary and was half hidden by a grisly, raw beard. The one beside him was shorter and more slender, his face narrow and handsome and somewhat amused. The third was short and portly. His eyes were runny and frightened and unkempt hair grew around his chin and upper lip. He wore a ragged bowler hat that he could not stop touching and he stayed back farther than the other two.

"The camp is back that way," said the leader. "Plenty of room there."

"I didn't come here to throw down a mattress," said Connelly.

"Then what did you come here for?"

"To ask a question."

"A question, eh? If you want to ask, then ask."

"I came looking for someone."

"Oh?"

"Yes. A...a man. A scarred man. Cheeks all tore up."

They did not answer, did not move or tense or twitch. They stood as statues crowning a hill, eyes placid and blank, faces dark.

"Heard you were looking for him, too," said Connelly. "Came to...to see. Just to see."

The men still did not speak, nor did they glance among themselves to confer. They remained quiet for far longer than any man had the right to.

"Why are you looking for him?" said Connelly. "What's he done? What's he done to you? Who...who is he?"

"The camp is back that way," said the leader, this time quieter. "Plenty of room there."

Connelly looked at them a moment longer, waiting for some answer or at the very least some sign of knowledge. They gave him nothing. He walked back down the hill to the camp. When he glanced back they were still standing, still watching him, unmoving as though part of the hill itself.

It was late when Connelly made it back to the grounds and he could not navigate among the jalopies and the shabby homes.

He picked out the bank of a small stream not far from the camp. Then he unrolled his bedding and threw it down and lay there, looking up at the stars and listening to the worried mutterings of the other travelers. He took out a pint of whisky and drew deeply from it. He grimaced as it went down, then took another draw and watched the sky die and the moon rise above him.

On the cusp of sleep he whispered to himself: "Molly. Molly, I'm close. I'm closer than ever now."

He slept, but not for long. He awoke less than an hour later, his heart beating and his mind screaming, awoken by some nameless animal instinct that told him he was no longer alone.

His eyes snapped open and he sat up and heard a gruff, low shout. Something crashing through the brush to his right. Then a figure barreled through the weeds at him, arm held high, something gold and glittering clutched in its fingers.

Connelly reacted without thinking and threw his arm up to catch the blow. His elbow met with the man's lip and the man grunted and something sprayed Connelly's cheek, hot and wet and thick. His attacker stumbled and collapsed, clutching his face. Another voice cried out in the darkness, "Georgie, Georgie! What you done to my Georgie!" A second man came running out, ready to tackle Connelly, but Connelly outweighed the man easily and tossed him to the ground. He straddled him and struck him once, twice, around the face. He tried to weigh down the man's struggling but still he cried out, "Georgie! Say something! Say something!"

Fingers dug into the flesh at Connelly's neck and the other hand clawed at his armpit. Connelly groped in the dark and found the pipe that had served as the first's weapon and brought it down, again and again. The man yelped and fell silent, his body seizing up and his knees rising to touch his face. Behind Connelly the first attacker struggled to his feet. He roared drunkenly and though Connelly could not see him his ears sought the sound and brought the pipe to it. With a sharp crack the man fell limp and did not move again.

Connelly stood over them, breathing hard, his arm aching and his blood beating so hard and fast he felt it would erupt out of his veins. Yards away voices were shouting, calling out, "What was that? What the hell's going on out there?" Connelly looked at the shapes of the bodies in the dark, not knowing if they were alive or dead, unable to hear any breathing over the rush in his own ears. He hurled the pipe into the stream and felt his hand and knew it was covered in blood, perhaps his or perhaps another's.

He gathered up his satchel and his bedding and ran downstream, across the water and over stones. The keening of birds and insects filled his ears. He threw himself down next to a fallen old oak and looked over the top. He could see nothing, no eyes in the starlight, no hands or glint of metal. Someone shouted, calling to another. He held his breath, then picked himself up and began running again.

He ran until his legs failed and he collapsed beside the stream, lungs and knees on fire. He washed his hands and face, cupped his hands and drank deeply and tried to ignore the coppery taste that he knew was blood, then drank again.

"You sure beat the hell out of those gentlemen," said a voice.

He looked up. Across the stream was the leader of the three men, his hoary face floating above the silvery water and his eyes alight with satisfaction. Before him he held on to a thick walking stick, chin high. He leaned forward on it thoughtfully.

"What?" said Connelly.

"Those men. I saw. They jumped you as you slept. Trying to roll a drunk, I believe. And you beat them. I'll not turn you in," he said as Connelly began to move. "I don't think you could run much further, regardless."

"You saw me?"

"I came down here to refill my canteen. Yes, I saw. Not many men could go from sleep to fighting off two men."

There were more shouts from downstream. Connelly whipped his head to look. The other man did not.

"If you find the scarred man, what will you do?" the man asked.

"What?" said Connelly.

"If you find the scarred man, what will you do? What do you want of him?"

"They're coming."

"Yes. They are. I have nothing to run from, so let them come. They may not know you to be innocent in this affair, however." He leaned into his staff. "If you were to find this man, what would you do, sir?"

Connelly looked at him, then down at the water. He could barely make out his own reflection. It was faceless, formless.

"Kill," said Connelly. "I'd kill him."

The man nodded, satisfied. "Then cross. Come with me. You can stay by our fire. If they come I will say you have been there all along, and avoid any unpleasantness, should God allow it."

He turned and began walking uphill and soon disappeared into the undergrowth. Connelly heard the bark of dogs to the east, then hoisted his satchel over his head and crossed, wading through the water and up to the fire on the hill.

CHAPTER THREE

The other two men were seated around the campfire, the short fat one and the slender handsome one Connelly had seen before. They looked up when he approached and the slender one's hands dipped into his coat.

"Easy," said the leader, striding over to them. "I've brought him here myself."

"Didn't ask us," said the portly one indignantly.

"No, I'm afraid I didn't. It was spur of the moment, brought on by providence." The leader sat down upon a log they had picked up as a crude seat. "Come," he said. "Come and sit. Fire's warm and the night's dropping fast. Come and sit."

Connelly walked over to them, still careful, and sat.

"You look pretty beat," said the portly one to Connelly.

"The man was attacked," said the leader. "While he slept. Two men trying to roll a drunk, only he didn't turn out to be drunk. Is that so?"

Connelly shrugged, nodded. "What's going to happen?"

"Happen?" asked the leader.

"Yeah," he said, and jerked his head in the direction of the town. "About that?"

"To you, you mean? Probably nothing. I doubt if that's the first mugging those folks witnessed. Though maybe the first that wasn't successful. Hungry times breed discontent. Here, I have yet to learn your name, sir," said the leader, grinning again. "What would you go by?"

Connelly didn't think to answer. The slender one was still watching him calmly and Connelly did not take his sights off of him.

"Fair enough," said the leader. "I am Pike. They call me Reverend Pike, for I was once a man of God. I still am a man of God, in my own way, but with no flock. It's better this way. I was never much of a shepherd. I always preferred the sword to the crook." Pike swatted at the slender one with his cap. "Introduce yourself."

"What?" he said.

"Introduce yourself," said Pike.

"Why should I? I don't know him at all."

"He can fight, that's why. And he's here looking for the same man we are. And he wants what we want."

"And what's that?"

"Blood," said Pike simply, and produced two dead rabbits from his sack.

The slender one observed Connelly for a while longer and shrugged. "I'm Hammond."

"Jakob Hammond," said Pike, and grinned. "With a 'k.'"

"Yes," said Hammond tersely.

"But Lord only knows what your family's surname was back in Europe."

"Something different, to be sure," said Hammond.

Pike looked at Connelly. "Mr. Hammond here is a Jew," he said.

They seemed to expect something from him, having said that. "Oh?" Connelly said.

"Yes."

"Never seen a Jew before."

Hammond laughed. "Well, I can't say you were missing out on much. I'll do my best to make a good impression. Where do you come from to never meet a Jew?"

"Tennessee."

"You'll find that Jews are a rarity in most of this nation, Hammond," said Pike.

"So I'm learning."

"And that over there is Mr. Roosevelt," said Pike. "Like the leader of our great nation. Though he says he's of no relation, unless he's been drinking."

Roosevelt tipped his hat. "Nice to meet you," he said.

"As are we all," said Pike. "Now. What would your name be?"

"Connelly."

"Connelly," repeated Pike. "Good name. And good that a man worries about giving his name, Mr. Connelly. Names are important things. They're a part of you. A name can get a man into trouble. Seems like not long ago openness was a virtue. In days like these, it's a risk. Get rid of it while you can."

"They're just words," said Hammond. "Nothing more, nothing less."

"Maybe so," said Pike, and took out a small, well-cared-for knife and began skinning and gutting the rabbits, cutting off their feet and taking handfuls of their innards and flinging them away into the night. He wiped his hands on his pants as he began upon the second.

As he worked Connelly glanced sideways at the other two men, watching them in the closer light. Roosevelt was strangely dressed in some semblance of dignity, sporting a natty waist-coat with only two remaining buttons, both barely holding on under the pressure of his girth. On his head he wore an old bowler that had lost its fabric long ago. Hammond was far younger than any of them, several years from thirty at least. He wore a simple coat and pants with suspenders, but his hair was carefully slicked back. It smelled of camphor and oil, even in the smoke of the fire. He had a rushed look about him, as though he had run out of town in the middle of the night and had been running ever since.

"Why did you bring him here, Pike?" asked Hammond.

Pike turned the second rabbit over in his bloody hands on his bloody trousers, his entire being occupied in his work as he guided the edge of the blade through the gristle and meat of the carcass. Soon it no longer resembled a rabbit, no longer resembled anything at all. He took the feet and the head, then cupped the entrails in his hands and tossed them down the hill.

"I should burn them, maybe," said Pike. "Make a stink, sure, but that's better than bringing wolves or coyotes. But I doubt if wolves or coyotes roam a place such as this."

He sat back down and spitted the rabbits and strung them up on two stakes. All three of them stopped to look at the rabbits and they listened to the fat begin to bubble and pop and hiss. Then their eyes moved to Connelly.

"To break bread is a holy thing," said Pike. "What can you share?"

Connelly reached into his satchel and took out a single can of beans. Hammond laughed. "Beans! A can of beans. The bread and butter of a knight of the road. Here, I have an opener. Let me open it and toss her on."

"Been living off of them for a while," said Connelly. "Cheap."

"That's true," said Roosevelt. "My brother lived on nothing but beans for years. Said it did his stomach good. But good God, it sure didn't do any good for his house. Every single room smelled like something had *died* in it. I kept telling him to keep his windows open, he kept saying he didn't smell anything."

"Well," said Hammond, "we'll make sure to sleep upwind of you, then."

They smiled and laughed, and Connelly relaxed a little more.

The beans cooked just off the fire underneath the rabbits, catching stray drippings, which Hammond said would add to their flavor. They watched the meal cook with a deep gravity.

"It'll be ready soon," said Hammond.

"And then we'll talk," said Pike.

Pike lifted the spits off of the fire when the hares began to crackle. They took out knives and peeled off ribs and legs and ate, fingers and lips shining with grease. Connelly ate with them. They had not cooked long so the meat was gamy and full of fat. After the can of beans cooled they passed it around, their knives dipping down to the lip of the can and then up to their open mouths, gray and yellow teeth shining in the fire. They gnawed at the bones and pulled off gristle, then placed the bones in a pot and poured in water and began a stew. They watched it heat up without speaking. Against the backdrop of the stars their glistening, mournful faces resembled men burning alive.

Connelly looked upon these strangers sitting underneath the broken-dish moon, watching meat sing and hiss on a paltry fire with quiet, lost eyes. Somewhere a train wailed and the earth shook, but they did not move. And then he recognized in these men something that was also in himself, for they were men who had been struck deaf and dumb by a terrible grief. Men who had been robbed not only of contentment and joy but the capacity to have such things. They slept in the hills not because they wished to but because they could not sleep in the camp. Such a place was forbidden to them.

"God is great," said Pike finally. "The Lord is good to us. He guided these rabbits to our traps and so gave us this bounty today. And He has also guided this man to us, I shall say, and so I also say He has a purpose to us as we do to Him, and when the Lord speaks we should listen."

Across the fire Hammond and Roosevelt glanced at each other. Hammond rolled his eyes slightly.

"How far have you come, Mr. Connelly?" asked Pike.

"Far. Memphis. It was my home."

"And that was where you met him? The scarred man?"

"Never met him," said Connelly softly.

"But encountered him? Was that the city that started you here?"

Connelly nodded.

"How long ago was that?"

"Three weeks. Maybe more. Been coming by foot and train. I hitched a ride where I could. It was tough going. No one's heading west now. Not from the east, at least."

"We ran into that," said Hammond. "Boy, did we."

"*He* is, though," said Pike.

They shifted uncomfortably, unsure if they wanted to broach the topic.

"Who is he?" said Connelly. "The man with the scars? What's he done to you?"

"Why?" said Roosevelt. "What's he done to *you*?"

Connelly said nothing.

"You shouldn't worry so," said Pike softly. "You and we are much alike. All of us here, we are alike."

"What do you mean by that?"

Pike frowned at him sadly. "I mean that we have all lost someone to this man."

Connelly stared at them. The men looked back, grim-faced and silent.

"No," whispered Connelly. "I don't believe it. No."

"Mr. Connelly, I wonder if you'd be willing to let me guess at your past," said Pike. "I feel I may know it pretty well. Is that all right?" He considered it and said, "You are a quiet man, sir, if I may say so. You speak when spoken to and at all other times would prefer to attract little attention. I could see you living a peaceful life, not a life of means, per se, but one of quiet dignity, a...a modest but satisfying job working with your hands and a small family whom you held dearly. And at some point, not too long ago, a scarred man came into your life. It seemed a chance meeting, one of no importance, and yet later...Later, you found this man to have taken everything you cherished, all at once. I cannot and will not guess at what he took from you, Mr. Connelly, that is a private matter to you and should not be given to conjecture. But whatever it was, you cannot go home. You cannot. And neither can we."

Connelly stared into his lap, listening but refusing to believe.

"We all run into him," said Roosevelt. "All of us. We all come to find him. By road and rail, we come."

"Yes," said Pike.

"And we'll go further," said Hammond. "All the way across the country, if need be. Which we nearly already have done."

Pike said, "Hammond?"

"Yes?" said Hammond.

"Tell him how you came here. Tell him what started you here."

Hammond looked at him. Pike nodded. "Go on," he said.

There was a moment of silence and Hammond said, "It was in Massachusetts. That was my home. My town, Winthrop. I was born there. I still remember it, like it was yesterday. I-I saw him outside my home, a man in a coat that may have been black but had been worn and patched so many times it was gray. His face was scarred, here and here," he said, indicating the cheeks, "and here around the temple, mottling his eyes. He was watching my home. I didn't know why. He was watching when I left for work one day. When I came home the front door had been broken in and I...I went to the kitchen and found my parents there."

Hammond anxiously toyed with a little knife and pursed his lips. "They were old. Couldn't fight back. Not much, at least. I don't know why. I don't. I don't know why. He was just there, then...then he broke in, robbed them, and...and then he was gone. The police couldn't find anything, and then we heard a rumor that he had gotten a ride south, down to Pennsylvania. The police followed and they tried to find something but couldn't, so I did. I went out looking. I don't know why I did that, either. It didn't make sense to try and do anything else. That house and that town and that whole life was something gone to me. But I tracked him there, then heard whispers, rumors of a man like that headed further south, so I came south. That was nearly six months ago. He has taken me across the nation. I've seen more than I have in my life before and more than I ever wanted to see, but I've never seen him. I've just been hearing things. The man with the scarred face. Mr. Shivers, as the hobos call him."

Connelly snapped his head up.

"You recognize the name?" said Hammond.

"Yes."

"I can't say I'm surprised."

"They talk about him like he's not real," said Connelly. "Like he's a myth. Or the devil."

"I think they're getting him mixed up," said Pike. "There may have once been a story of a Mr. Shivers, of the midnight man, but there's this man out there and they've heard of him too and they get the two mixed up. They give him a name. It makes him easier for us to find, that's for sure."

"He's a man," said Hammond. "A man like you or I. He moves like one and he eats like one and he sleeps and shits like one. He's not a ghost story and he's not a ghost, no matter what the hobos say. We've all seen him. He looks man enough for me."

"He travels on the rails and hitches rides where he can, like you," said Roosevelt. "Like us. That's how he gets away, city to city and county to county. I was in Chicago when he found me. There were bad times and he came. Made them worse, I guess."

"How did it happen?" asked Connelly.

Roosevelt shifted in his seat. "Quickly. Work had been getting scarce at a factory I was at, this bumshit canning factory, and there was talk of a riot or a union and the entire place was just waiting for something to happen. Something bad. There had been beatings, union busters coming in and finding who said what and just beating the hell out of those fellas. And then he came. A ragged man in a ragged coat, with a great, ruined mouth and black eyes, ugly eyes. Like puddles of oil sitting in the road." Roosevelt began to roll a cigarette. "Don't know what he did. Maybe he said something. Maybe he hit someone. He was hanging around for a while and then one day the brawl just broke out and every man who could get a weapon was running into it, and the cops got into it and it seemed like the whole precinct was up in arms, fighting in an alley behind the goddamn factory. I don't know what he did, but I know he done something.

"My friend Tommy died. Someone took a wrench and busted his head open. His eyes filled with blood and one came out and his jaw was like it had no bone. And my brother-in-law died there, too. Someone busted up his ribs and he bled to death, in his heart and lungs. My sister...My sister went...She wasn't right," Roosevelt said finally. "She never got over it. Cried all the time, always crying, and she never got out of bed. They put her in an institution. One day I come in to see her and she...she didn't know my name. She kept asking me if I had any gum, just a stick of gum, it'd taste so good.

"So I just ran. I ran south. I was in the back of some truck, full of illegals and migrants, and someone said they had heard about a barfight in a town outside of Cincinnati and some fella had been cut up good. And the man who done it, well, he was some man with a cut-up face, they thought. Scarred as hell, they said. So I came south. And I met Pike. And we met Hammond. As you've met us. That was long ago. Almost a year. Almost a year before I met Hammond."

"And I ran into him in Atlanta," said Pike. "Where he killed my friend. Cut his throat. But that was longer than any of you. For I tell you now that I have been looking for this man for *four years* of my life. And still he has eluded me. Not until just recently did I know that I was not alone. There are others. This man is far worse than even you can imagine, Mr. Connelly. If we are here, then there are many others."

"And what has he done to you?" asked Roosevelt.

Connelly just bowed his head.

"Sometimes there are no words," said Pike. "There are no words."

"What the hell is he?" Connelly said.

"We don't know," said Hammond. "We don't, for sure. He's motivated to kill and he's smart enough to keep moving, and it's getting a lot easier now because the whole goddamn country is moving with him. Migrant workers are everywhere. Everyone is looking for something better. And among them, there's him. Something drives him to do this, I don't know what."

"Some madness, maybe," said Pike. "Some disease of the brain that urges him to butchery. I've heard of such men, like Jack the Ripper in London, years and years ago. Perhaps he's one of them. He goes from town to town, stalks someone for a few days, then strikes and moves on."

"But now he's doing something strange," Roosevelt said. "He's not moving with people anymore, but against them. He's going west, into the plains, while everyone else is trying to leave them."

"Lot of people going west from them, though," said Connelly. "People from Oklahoma and Kansas and the Dakotas. They're going west."

"That is true," said Pike. "We've considered he's trying to join with them. It'd be far easier to hide there. A whole country has been unsettled. These are dark times, and they are getting darker, I think. But we're close. Closer than we've ever been before."

Connelly said, "And if you find him, you'll kill him."

They did not react at first. Then Pike said, "Yes. We will. Would we not be justified in doing so? Would not God and this nation look approvingly on us if we were to kill him, Mr. Connelly?"

"I don't know about God," said Connelly. "I know less about God than I do the nation. I don't think about that. I don't need to. Some things don't need to be thought about. You just do them. And I aim to."

"I can understand that," said Hammond.

Pike stirred the fire again. "Will you come with us, then? Will you join with us?"

"You know I will."

"I don't. What I want may be different from you. Because there's no going back, and no turning aside here. I said at the start of this that I would die finding him if it came to it and kill if I had to. Would you be willing to do that?"

Connelly shrugged.

"You can't say. But listen, friend. Listen to me, now, Mr. Connelly, you must listen—should a man raise his hand to us and come between us and our quarry, it is in our righteous duty under God to strike that man down if need be. Nothing matters but the road and the man, and where the two meet." His greasy fingers crisscrossed over the fire. "Nothing matters but where this ends. And it will end, regardless of the cost, and it will end in blood. For everyone he's taken from us and for those he's taken from others, it will end in blood. Will it not, Mr. Connelly? Will it not?"

Connelly stared into the fire, hunched over his lap, his eyes aglow and his hands clenched. He said, "I suppose so."

"Then that is settled," said Pike, and spat into the fire. They watched it sizzle among the embers.

"But he ain't here," said Connelly. "No one saw him."

"He's not here any longer, no," said Hammond.

"We heard from some people in the camp," said Roosevelt. "Some folk in there said they seen a man with a cut-up face in Oklahoma, just across the border. He's headed south. They saw him in Shireden, not much more of a town than Rennah. But that's where he's at. That's where he'll be. That's what's next."

"Amen," said Pike.

And to that they had nothing more to say, and turned to sleep.

CHAPTER FOUR

Connelly listened to the men sleep restlessly around him. Stones dug through his bedding and the whisky did not sit right with him and so he chose to watch the clouds roll in above and think.

The hobos said that when Father Time woke up Mr. Shivers was there waiting, just sitting on the ground beside him and smiling. They said he took his blade and cut Father Time across the hand and ran away laughing, and from then on Father Time was bitter and cruel and gave every man hardship and ate every dream.

They said Mr. Shivers had been in every jail in the country. The bulls would lock him up and he would sit there waiting for nightfall and when the moon shone through the bars he'd climb up the beam like a man on a staircase and be out just as fast as you could think. The next day the cops would come on by and just sit scratching their heads at the empty jail cell.

They said that when bums and all the runaway boys and girls die they get their last chance to ride freight with Mr. Shivers, that he has a train made of night that rides straight to hell and the furnace don't run on coal or wood, the furnace runs on *you*. Mr. Shivers comes back and takes a foot or a hand or an eye or an ear and feeds it to his train, spurring it on, sending it down to the depths of the earth and to eternity as it eats you alive.

Mr. Shivers, the moonlight man, the black rider. Mr. Shivers, the bum's devil. The vagrant's boogey man.

There were a lot of stories about Mr. Shivers. Connelly had heard most of them. In the dark when he could not sleep they often came back.

It had been a hard time getting here. In the days in Memphis when it had just been him and his grief and his empty home he had not known what to do. But he remembered. He remembered that ruined face.

How could he not.

Months ago. Years ago. Lives ago. When he had still been himself and was not this wreck, this empty hulk that was half a man, functional only in terms of endurance and rage. Seas of time lay between himself and that man.

And Molly. Between him and Molly. His little girl.

"I'm close now," he mouthed silently. "I'm closer than ever before."

Someone has to put the world right, he said to himself. Someone has to make things right. And he shut his eyes.

Somewhere a train whistle moaned like a man dreaming under a fever. None of the other men stirred. Connelly rolled over and tried to sleep.

*   *   *

They spent the next three days waiting for a train that would take them into Oklahoma and close to Shireden. Roosevelt spoke to a man who was in at the freightyards and learned of the schedule and Pike told them to rest while they could, and so they caught small game and did their best not to drink or spend money. Each day they watched the camp outside of Rennah ebb and flow, grow and swell with the people who had abandoned their homes, and each of them would go among the people and ask if they had seen the scarred man. From two they heard the same — south, and to the west. If there's anything left of Shireden, they said, he'll be there.

"What do they mean, left of?" asked Connelly.

"Beats me," said Roosevelt. "But that's what they said."

And with each day the land to the west became a deeper red, like the horizon was a gash in the sky and it was bleeding out.

"Don't know what's coming," said Pike as they watched it at evening. "But it's not good."

On the third day Roosevelt came back from camp with a smile on his face and a small heavy bag in hand. He sat and produced a revolver and a box of bullets and began playing with the weapon.

"What in the hell is that?" said Hammond.

"It's a gun."

"What the hell are you going to do with a gun?"

"Shoot stuff."

"And what do you know about shooting?"

"I know where the bullets come out."

"Huh. Anything particular you going to shoot?"

"Whatever needs it, I suppose," he said, and he spun the cylinder and snapped it back.

"Damn, Rosie. Take care of that thing, will you?"

"I'll try," he said, and stowed it in his bag.

Finally their day came. They went down to the tracks and crouched in the soggy ditch next to the woods and waited for the train to pass. As it lumbered by they sprinted out and seized hold of the back railing. They lifted themselves aboard where they stowed away in a car carrying lumber. It was already occupied by two old men, both in denim and rawhide, and they watched the new arrivals with faint interest.

"Where you boys going?" asked one as Connelly and the others settled.

"South," said Hammond.

"To Shireden?"

"Yes," said Hammond, surprised.

They looked at each other and nodded. "You going to go see the gypsy girl?" one asked.

"The what?"

"The gypsy girl."

"No. What do you mean?"

"They got a gypsy girl down there, at this carnival. She's famous. She can tell fortunes, tell you your whole future. It's why we're going. I knew a fella who went and talked to her and she told him exactly where he'd be when fortune did him good, and the next week all she done said came true and he was in a gambling hall and he won close to a hundred dollars."

"And you're going to hear your fortunes?" said Pike.

"Sure are."

"Boy, I'd like to get a listen to what she had to say," said Roosevelt. "It'd be nice to know when the next windfall was coming my way."

"You don't really believe in that stuff, do you?" said Hammond.

"Sure I do. Why wouldn't I?"

"Because it's a bunch of baloney, of course. They're just scamming a bunch of yokels out there in the sticks. No offense to present company, of course," he said, and smiled at the two other hobos, who scowled.

"Come on, Pike," said Hammond. "Back me up on this."

Pike nodded thoughtfully. "I tend not to trust such things. Don't know much of devilry," he mused, "but if it can be used for our aim then I suppose in that sense it's all right."

"What? You aren't serious about going to see a goddamn gypsy, are you?" said Hammond.

"I am. And I'm also serious about the tongue in your head, Mr. Hammond."

"Seems like a waste of time."

"Why not? It won't be out of our way any. And as we grow close we need all the guidance we can get."

"Besides, it's a carnival, Hammond!" said Roosevelt. "A carnival! Maybe they got a Ferris wheel and...and beer!"

Hammond sighed. "Well, you can depend on beer to work," he said, "but I don't know about the gypsy girl."

They rode through Missouri and then Arkansas, sharing cigarettes and what meat they had, and so passed into Oklahoma. They jumped off at a set of fields close to Shireden and walked the next ten miles into town. When they arrived it was nearly midnight. They found a traveling carnival was arranged in one of the fields. The night was full of torches and reedy music and laughter and the scent of old ale. Aged booths and carts sat squatting in the grass, covered in peeling red and purple paint. Misshapen tents glowed beyond like jellyfish suspended in the ocean deeps. Men and women

smeared in paint juggled or sang or danced. Some ushered
the drunken townsfolk into games and shrugged indifferently
when they lost.

They asked for directions, then wound their way to a dilap-
idated cart in the far back. It smelled of horse and something
sickly sweet, like bile or rot. On the side was a sloppy painting
of a young girl's face with stars around her head, her lips thick
and her forehead large. As they approached a man in shirt-
sleeves came out and squinted at them.

"What you want? Game's over," he said sourly.

"We come to see the gypsy girl."

"The what? She ain't no gypsy. She's from Akron. Get out
of here, it's late as hell."

"We brought money."

"Lots of people bring money lots of places. It's a popular
thing to bring. Get lost."

"We come all the way from Missouri to see her."

"Really?" he said, thinking. "Well. We're getting popular. Huh. That's good news. You know what, sure, you can
see her. Let me see the money." They pulled it out and he
inspected the coins in their hands. "Fair enough. Hey, Sibyl!"
he shouted into the cart. He pounded on the side. "We ain't
done yet! Just few more!"

Nothing came. Then there was a voice but it could have
been just the breeze and Connelly did not hear a word in it.
But the carnie said in answer, "We got paying customers here.
Come on, get your stuff together."

"It's late," whined a girl's voice. "I don't want to see them."

"People don't want a lot of stuff. It happens." He turned to
the men and winked. "Takes a while, magicking and seering

the heavens. Takes some work." He took out a flask and took a belt from it, then shouted, "Come on, you're holding up the show!"

"I don't want to see him."

"See who?"

She didn't say anything.

"See who?"

"The big one," said the girl's voice, and it was quiet and shook with fear.

All of them looked at Connelly. He raised his hands and shrugged.

"Goddamn it, girl," said the carnie, and went into the cart. He was there for some time and when he came out he marched up to Connelly. "Let me see your money," he said.

"Why? You seen it."

"Let me see it again, then."

Connelly showed him. The carnie frowned, then returned to the cart and was there for a few minutes more. When he came back out he said, "Okay. We're good to go, folks. But you're last," he said, nodding at Connelly.

"Why?"

"You got a lot of damn questions. Why don't you ask the damn fortune-teller, huh?"

Connelly shrugged and sat down in the grass with the rest of them. They watched as the old men passed through the beaded curtain. It was too dark to see very far in and both were swallowed by the shadows.

Connelly listened to the drunken singing and atonal music from the carnival across the way. He turned to watch the stragglers go back and forth in the distant fairy lights, moonbeam-white and rose-pink. People staggered out and where they walked grasshoppers sprang from the turf under their feet and twirled away into the sky, faintly luminescent in the weak light.

"What do you think she's showing them in there?" asked Hammond.

"Not her titties," said the carnie. "Not for what they paid."

"Lechery sprawls across the face of creation," said Pike. "As it always does. One wonders what clay God made men from. Something weak and watery, I'd say."

"You a religious man?"

"I am."

"Funny thing, religious fella at a fortune-teller."

"When I was a boy there was a scrying woman on our street who could look in a teacup and see when the rains would come. She was never wrong. It's a foolish man who doesn't think God works in strange places."

"Or she could have just looked at the sky," said Hammond quietly, but Pike did not hear.

The two old men came out looking pleased and one said, "You boys are in for a treat!" They made their way into the night.

"I'll believe it when I see it," said Hammond. "You believe in fortune-tellers?" he asked Connelly as Roosevelt handed the man his money and went in.

"Don't know," said Connelly.

"Well, do you think it's likely?"

"How do you mean?"

"I mean, likely some girl knows what's going to happen to you?"

He thought about it. "No."

"Jesus. Me neither."

"What was it I said about blasphemy?" said Pike idly from where he lay in the grass.

"You said I was a Jew before you said anything about blasphemy. Jesus is your God, not mine."

"I think the whole northeast is lost to godlessness," said Pike. "All city folk and Yankees hold nothing sacred."

Time ticked by. The wind rose and fell. Then Roosevelt came out of the cart looking irritated.

"Damn it all!" he told the carnie leaning up against the cart. "That was just…just…Damn it, you just suckered me out of money!"

"Sucker hell," said the carnie. "I didn't sucker anything. You might've just not liked what she said."

"I didn't like any of it!" said Roosevelt. "Everything she said was just damn insulting! Come on, let's go, boys," he said to them, and began to stomp away.

"What did she say?" said Pike.

"What?" said Roosevelt, and he stopped.

"What did she say?"

Roosevelt looked at them a moment longer. Then he swore and strode away toward the carnival, shaking his head.

"Could be there's something here worth a listen," said Pike, and he stood and gave the man a few coins and went in.

After he was gone the carnie looked at Connelly and Hammond on the grass. He smiled at them. "Say, you boys want anything, uh…anything extra with this?" he asked.

"Extra?" said Hammond.

"Sure. You look like you boys been on the road a while. Probably been lonely." He took another belt from his flask and nodded at the cart.

"Probably costs a considerable amount more than a fortune-telling, huh?" said Hammond.

"Probably. But it improves your immediate future a hell of a lot, I'll tell you that."

Hammond eyed the people at the carnival and smiled. "I can probably improve my fortune for free."

"Jesus, you're not going to find anything under a hundred and fifty pounds over there. Any farmgirl still drinking beer at this time of night ain't nothing worth looking at."

"I don't know," said Hammond with a wry grin. "It's a pretty dark night."

"Goddamn. Suit yourself. What about you, big fella?" he said to Connelly.

Connelly shook his head.

"You don't say much, do you?"

Connelly shook his head again.

The carnie grunted, chuckled, then drank and spat.

Pike charged out of the cart looking downright furious. "A waste of time," he said angrily. "A *waste* of time and money."

"Told you so," said Hammond.

"Nothing but *lies* come out of her mouth. Nothing but lies. Just bitchery and foolishness is what it is." Pike spat at the carnie's shoes and strode off toward the carnival after Roosevelt.

"Well, hell," said Hammond, and got to his feet. "Now I'm curious."

"Ain't we all," said the carnie, who wiped his shoes in the grass. He seemed used to such treatment. He took Hammond's coins and he and Connelly watched as Hammond passed through the beaded curtain and vanished into the darkness of the cart.

"There he goes," said the carnie.

"Yeah," said Connelly.

"You know, it's funny. Most people don't like what Sibyl says."

"Is that so."

"It is. Most folk hate it. And I got to figure, that's odd. I mean, most fortune-telling acts around here now, they just say something nice and happy or something mysterious that don't mean anything at all. Bunch of fwoosh and bang and such. But Sibyl just makes them mad. Mad until one or two come true, then they just think she's heaven on earth."

Connelly grunted.

"I keep telling her that when she says something good, she got to stop right there. Don't go no further. But no. If she tells someone about marrying, well, then she'll tell them about how their woman will get fat after the first birth and go blind and then he'll be sick of her, or if they win money how they'll just blow it on some damn fool thing or just stupid idleness, and if they're going to have a lovely boy for a kid then she'll tell them when he's going to run away from home to go whoring around town. Shit. Girl just don't know when to stop."

They were quiet for a while.

"Then maybe what she's telling is true," said Connelly.

The carnie drank and nodded. "Maybe so."

Hammond came out, smirking to himself. "I never believed in any of this stuff anyways," he said. "Head on in, if you want. It's damned impressive, at least."

"Thanks," said the carnie. "You're up."

Connelly got to his feet and paid the man and then pierced the veil of beads with his hand. At once the heavy, sweet stink washed over him, like old perfume or bad fruit, and he looked back at the carnie, who shrugged and nodded forward. Connelly walked in. The beads clicked behind him as the curtain fell.

Connelly carefully stepped through the darkness. The cart was bigger than he thought. It was barely lit by a few slats of starlight that came filtering through the curtains. It seemed to go farther back than any cart should.

"Hello?" he said.

There was nothing.

"Anyone here?"

Then a voice murmured, "Connelly."

A match flared a few feet in front of him, dazzlingly bright. He squinted at it and saw pink-white fingers holding its end as its flame licked at a misshapen candle. His eyes followed the hand and the white arm until he found the pale, sad moonface hovering in the dark with doe eyes like toffee and a small, timid mouth. One eye's whites was a pus-colored yellow like curdled milk, and somehow he felt that this eye was the one truly looking at him, looking at and looking beyond all at once.

She was younger than he thought she'd be. She could not have been more than sixteen. His heart went out to her for one moment before he snatched it back and recovered himself.

"Marcus Sullivan Connelly," said the girl. The stench of bad fruit was overwhelming.

"That's an impressive trick," said Connelly. "You ask them my name?"

"Not in the business of asking. Business of telling." Then she shut her eyes like she was fighting tears and shook her head.

Connelly studied her. Her wrists were bone-thin and her

neck was barely able to support her head. A thin, wispy dress of powder blue hung about her shoulders like a ragged tapestry. It was meant to be mysterious but it was tattered and had not seen soap in months at least.

"Sit," she said quietly.

He did so.

"I didn't want to see you," she said.

"I heard."

"Didn't want to tell you anything."

"That's a pity."

"Dangerous."

"What?"

"You're dangerous, I believe," she said.

"This part of the act?"

"No."

"I was about to say. It can't lend itself well to commerce."

"I don't have an act."

"Then what do you have?"

"Whatever I can give you. People come and they ask me for the things they wish. And I give them, if I can. What do you want, Connelly?"

"You can't give me what I want."

She nodded solemnly. "No. I can't."

"You must be wore out. I can go if you want."

"You can go right now. Go all the way back home. But you won't. Will you?"

Connelly watched her carefully.

She sighed again. "You've come. You've already left. You're still coming. Still turning down the offer to bed me like a whore and still calling me a liar."

"I never wanted to do that."

"I know."

"I never called you a liar, neither."

"I know that, too. Don't let it trouble you." She blinked and brushed her hair back. "You want a reading."

"I do?"

"Yes."

"What from?"

"From everything," she said, and dumped a stack of cards on the table. They had unearthly paintings of kings and dogs and naked women on them.

"What are those?"

"Your future," she said. She shuffled them in her hands, her fingers oddly graceful while the rest of her body was limp.

"Mine or everyone's?" he asked.

She stopped and looked at him, her septic eye burning in her face. "Ask me not to do this."

"Do what?"

"Ask me not to. Tell me to stop. Don't tell me anything. You can move away. You have that option and you should choose it soon."

"What are you saying I should do?"

"Anything but this. Just go and leave what is dead dead and look at what is alive."

"What's dead?"

Sibyl did not answer. Connelly looked at her, thinking. He said, "How do you know?"

"I just have to look at you. Anyone can. Simply by looking you over I can see."

Connelly bowed his head. "I can't. I can't stop."

"I know," she said. Then she shuffled the cards and took one out and tossed it on the table.

He looked at it. It was a small painting of a crude-looking man with a wide, frowning mouth. He was riding in a chariot being pulled by two horses wearing blinders. On his head he wore a crown of pearl and in his hand he held a plain scepter, varnished with age. His free hand was lifted as though he was trying to both balance himself and acknowledge those he passed by, much as a king would.

"The chariot," said Sibyl.

"What's that?"

"The chariot," she said again. "He rides out, eager to conquer, willing to ride down what obstacles come before him. To conquer and kill and reach down into the earth and pick up what meets his disfavor and rearrange it in the way that he deems fit. But he forgets that he is being pulled not by his own strength but instead is at the mercy of beasts that he himself has chosen to blind. So you must remember that even though you burn bright and hard with belief, you believe more in your goal than the manner of arriving there."

"So?" said Connelly.

"What do you mean, so?"

"I mean, what does that matter?"

She held the card up to her face, then shut her eyes and took a deep breath through her nose, drawing in its scent. Then she opened her eyes, the fouled one first, then the clean one. "It means there will be a long road. Long and winding. Most will not wish to travel it. You will prevail upon it, and force your journey. But you may not like what you find upon it, or perhaps in yourself."

The cards shuffled in the darkness. Another one fell to the table. On it was the night sky and at the top was the moon, great and sick and pregnant. In its center was a formless face, its eyes and lips runny and its nose askew. Below it two dogs raised their heads and howled, their bodies long and slender with starvation, and they thrashed in the moon's hollow glow as it stared dumbly down.

"The moon," said Sibyl. "We are drawn to the moon. Aren't you?"

"I don't know. I guess."

"Yes. At night it occupies the mind, for we are drawn to the moon in dark times. It's said that when dogs howl at the moon they believe it to be a way out from this earth, that it is some exit set in the sky by an entity that even their minds recognize but cannot acknowledge. You seek an exit, Connelly. You seek a way out. Deliverance and purpose and meaning. It will find you, Connelly, and you will find it. But it will be a thing dark and forgotten and it will not be set in the sky. And I dread to think of the face you will find there." She leaned forward. "You will be offered the way three times. Beyond that I cannot see, nor do I wish to."

"No?"

"No."

Again the shuffling. The candle flame fluttered and as Sibyl breathed out the third card fell. On it was a woman dressed in ornate robes so thick they hid every inch of her frame. In her hand she held a scepter and on her head was a shining crown, set with either pearls or stars. Grass reached up and coiled about her feet and far behind were trees stretching to the dusky sky. A stream curled through the trees and gently fell into a cliffside pool. Connelly felt he could almost smell the fresh sting of fir-green air and the rich promise of dark earth.

"The empress," said Sibyl.

"The empress," repeated Connelly.

"Yes. The queen of rebirth. Quietly she slumbers in the forest heart, and when she wakes all that has passed from this earth comes again. Black and red succumbs to a cover of green. You can bring this, Connelly."

"I can?"

"Yes. Your heart has died within you, and you are not alone. Were you to step outside you would see that perhaps the heart of this place has died as well. A directionless land with no center. A people wandering and hollow. Can you not see that some great wound has pierced the very heart of all these lives? Yet that can be changed. You can change this, Connelly. You do not know how and you may not know until the very end. But you can bring rebirth."

"Can..."

"Can what?"

"Will I ever go home? Do you see that?"

"You can go home now."

"No. There's no home there now. Not yet. Not really."

"Do you mean peace?"

"I don't know what I mean."

She looked at him, the foul eye burning fiercely. "You may find peace, one day. You will have a great choice, Connelly. You carry rebirth in the palm of your hand, and it is your decisions that govern it, though you do not know it. Few are given such a choice. Between justice and contentment. Between home and the road. Neither will be easy, nor will either one fully satisfy you. It will depend on what you find in the west, and what you choose to do with it."

Connelly thought hard about this and nodded.

"But remember," she said, "birth and death have more in

common than you think. Neither is dignified. We enter this world violently and we leave it the same way. Each is marked by terrible suffering. You will bring this as well, or you will allow it to continue."

"I don't want to hurt anyone."

"You might. You might not. The shape of your life speaks of violence, though you may change its nature."

She took a breath in, shut her eyes, and shuffled once more. She drew the card and somehow Connelly knew it was the last one. His eyes found it in the dark, yet as it fell a wind blew through the cart and the light in the room died. He heard the card clatter to the tabletop but saw nothing but stars where the light had been.

"Where is it?" he said. "What happened?"

Sibyl said nothing. Then another match flared before him. Again he was stunned by the change and he blinked to get his eyes to function.

He looked at the card on the table. There on the small, weathered scrap of cardboard an ancient corpse danced and sang, grinning up eyelessly. In its ruined hands it held a scythe that it twirled overhead as though to rend the sky itself. Half-fleshed limbs and heads littered the ground at its feet like windfallen fruit and browning vines rose from the baking earth to claim these gifts as their own. Connelly stared at the grin, its mouth and teeth enormous in his mind, the black eyes looking at him but not looking at once.

"Death?" said Connelly.

She didn't answer.

"I'm going to die? Is that what you're saying? Is that it?"

Sibyl had not moved. The match was still in her hand and her eyes were still on the card.

"You're a damn liar," said Connelly. "A goddamn liar. To hell with you." He stood to leave.

"You won't die, Connelly," she whispered. "You won't."

"I won't?"

She shut her eyes and shook her head. Twin tears ran down her cheeks in smooth arcs.

"No. You will encounter it upon the road, that is certain. What you do after is a choice that belongs only to you." She opened her eyes. "Do you know what I found for the others?" she asked.

He shook his head.

The cards shuffled again. Her rose-pink fingers sped through the deck and lifted one out. On it was a capped man wearing a colorful, festive gown and carrying a rucksack over his shoulder. In his other hand he had a walking stick and dogs nipped at his heels.

"The fool," she said. "All of them, fools. Their way is easier than yours. But perhaps you were made for hard ways and hard worlds. For this one and the one that lies far to the west. Where things still remember younger years of joyful savagery."

Sibyl looked at the cards in her hands and then angrily threw them over her shoulder. They fluttered to the ground behind her like moths upset from old clothing. She shook her head and in her tantrum Connelly was again reminded of her age. She was no more than a girl.

Feeling his gaze, she lifted her eyes and said, "There's nothing you can do for me."

"Why not?"

"I can no more stop what I am doing here than you can stop yourself now." She toyed with her hair and sullenly watched him. "Did you get your money's worth?"

Connelly said nothing.

"I'm tired. Let me rest, Connelly. Go if you want, but let me rest."

He turned and walked out.

Outside the carnie was sitting on the stoop.

"Have fun?" he asked.

Connelly walked down to him. He gestured to the flask. "Give me a sip of that."

"What, this? Sure."

Connelly took it and drank. It was either vodka or half-decent moonshine, he couldn't tell. He breathed in. The air was still sickly sweet and the ghostly image of the match flame was burned into the bluegreen night.

"What'd she tell you?"

"A lot of things," he said, then handed it back and walked away over the fields. The music had died and the people had stopped singing. Somewhere a horn honked and a child began crying and would not quiet.

CHAPTER FIVE

He found the others seated outside of a tent watching the carnival workers break the show down. Tents deflated gracefully around them to lie on the ground like the skins of some unworldly animal.

"What'd she say?" asked Pike.

"Nothing much," said Connelly.

"It was a foolish thing. We shouldn't have let her delay us. Still, we have something useful now."

"Doesn't seem to be money or brains at the moment. What is it?"

"That boy over there," said Roosevelt, nodding at a young man helping the workers. "He seen him."

"How'd you find that out?"

"Asked a few folks. They knew of him, said one person had talked to him. That boy right over there."

"I guess they were right," said Hammond. "The man did come here."

Connelly could feel the anxiety washing off of them like smoke.

"You may not understand," said Pike, his voice quiet. "This is the closest we've come in months and years."

"I understand plenty," said Connelly.

They sat in the road and watched the tents topple and flounder and waited on the boy. He was a skinny thing, no older than thirteen, overalled and sandy blond and barefoot. When the carnival workers had given him his pay he came over and said, "You boys the ones looking for the ugly fella?"

"That would be right," said Pike.

"Why you looking for him?"

"He stole something from me," said Hammond smoothly.

"Huh. I'd believe it."

"Why do you say that?"

The boy didn't answer. Instead he said, "My brother owes me fifteen cents, still hasn't repaid it."

"Bastards the world over," said Hammond.

"Watch your language in front of the boy," said Pike, but the boy seemed pleased to have men casually swear in front of him.

"Come and sit with us, if you will," Roosevelt said.

"I will, thanks."

"What's someone your age doing out so late?"

"Working. Getting what I can. My folks is going to head west. We're going to pick fruit out there. They need what they can get. Maybe I can get me something, too."

"They going to California?" said Pike.

"Or New Mexico for cotton, they haven't made up their minds yet. They argue a lot about it."

"Times are tough," said Hammond.

"They are. Everything in the whole state just dried up. Like the dirt just decided it didn't care for plants no more and just cut them loose."

"Where did you see the scarred man?" asked Pike, impatient.

"Why?"

Hammond said, "I already told you, he's stolen something from me and—"

"Ain't what I was talking about. I meant why would I tell you?"

"Tell us?" said Pike, frowning.

"I ain't telling you what I know for free. Why would I do that?"

"Why you little scum!" snarled Pike. "How dare you talk to your elders this way? If I was your pa I'd whale you raw."

"But you ain't. You're just some hobos off the road, like the ugly fella was."

Pike started to stand to his feet. The boy sprang up and began dancing away, wild-eyed and frightened.

"Here," said Roosevelt. "Here. I got a nickel. Let's all sit down now, I got a nickel."

Pike glowered but sat. The boy looked at Roosevelt and the nickel in his hand. He came over and tried to take it but Roosevelt's hand snapped shut.

"You get it after you talk to me," said Roosevelt.

"You'll just keep it."

"I won't."

"You will."

"I may be a hobo, but I ain't a bastard," said Roosevelt.

Hammond smiled. "Bastards the world over, like I said."

The boy sat down, keeping his distance from Pike.

"Now," said Roosevelt. "Where'd you meet him? Where'd you meet this scarred man?"

"Over at my pa's."

"First of all, what did he look like?" asked Connelly.

"Fair question," said Pike.

"He was a tall man," said the boy. "Tall with tired eyes and he didn't blink much. And he had big scars all over his face and around his mouth that made it look like his mouth was three times as big as a normal man's. Here and here," he said, and drew the lines on his cheeks that they all knew so well.

"How'd you meet him?"

The boy hesitated, like he was about to impart a terrible secret about himself. "You won't tell no one, will you?"

"Why? What's he done?"

"I just don't want anyone to know. I just don't want anyone else to know what I saw him do."

"What did he do?"

"You promise you won't tell no one? I don't like them even knowing I talked to him."

"Tell us," said Hammond. "We're only interested in the man."

The boy shuddered in the wind and said, "We was slaughtering a pig."

And he told them.

The boy has been to slaughters before but he has never gotten used to the screams.

It is impossible to say exactly why the sow screams. They have done nothing to harm it or scare it, not yet, and yet somehow when the animal turns and sees the men in the doorway bearing a rope in hand it understands. There is something wrong. It looks at the men and even with its primitive mind it recognizes murder in their movements.

The men subdue it and the boy helps, trying to keep it in the corner, and they tie its neck and lead it out and bind its legs. It is a dangerous task. Its hooves are sharp and hard as stone and its teeth can crush and tear through fingers. But the men have done this before. They know the animal better than it knows itself. When it bites at their hand they snap back and when it lashes out or thrashes they are already there to restrain it. The men complete their lethal dance with a lover's care and the boy's father turns to him and says, "Watch."

The boy watches.

The creature trumpets and screams, its chest heaving and strings of snot and spittle running from its snout. The men loop a cord around its front two legs and pull the legs away to expose the throat and the boy's father steps forward, knife shining in his hand and his eyes shining in that strange dull way, and he looks at the animal for a moment and the arm stabs down, quick and sure, and punctures the animal's throat. The movement has no doubt, no question. It knows where it is going.

The spray of blood is terrific, as is its hue. Never would a man think that so much blood could come from an animal, and so red. It is a geyser bursting forth, a stronger and more violent flow than urination, more sporadic than any assault or sex. It pumps with the beast's heart, whipping out, and still the creature screams. The blood mixes with the clay dust, red on red, and it is hard to tell where the earth starts and gore begins.

Still it screams, bellowing in its death throes, an ancient sound. The men keep the animal subdued but now they all watch, letting the seconds tick by. Its cries weaken. Soon it is wheezing, breath whistling through its slackening chest. The pool of blood spreads, and still the tiny aperture in its throat dribbles blood, gentle spurts becoming arrhythmic.

The flow ceases to a seep. When the animal dies is difficult to say. The men do not consider it. They gather hay and pile it over the creature and set fire to it to remove the hair.

The boy watches the fire and wonders if the animal is dead. After all that screaming it may still be screaming on the inside.

"It won't take much," says a voice at his side.

The boy leaps and turns and looks. A man is standing beside him. He is tall and lank and the skin hangs loosely from his neck and chin. Wild tufts of white-gold hair form messy peaks on his scalp. A dusty black coat hangs from his shoulders, gray in some places and leathery in others, and his mouth has the curious feature of seeming almost distended, like melting rivers pouring out its corners and across his face. He watches the fire with distant eyes.

"What?" says the boy.

"It's not a particularly hairy animal," said the man. "I doubt if it will take many burnings."

The boy wonders where he came from. The man seems to have come from nowhere. Then he looks at the man's feet and sees his tracks leading away to the road. He came, thinks the boy, but came silently.

"Can I help you, sir?" says the boy's father, suddenly aware of the man on his property.

"I heard the screams," says the man. "I came to see. I'm sorry, I thought there may have been trouble."

The man speaks like he has only recently learned that words exist. Not English, but all words. The nature of speaking is foreign to him.

"Oh," says his father, disturbed. "Well, there's no trouble here, sir."

"No. I can see that."

The men and the boy look at him awkwardly, waiting for him to leave. He does not. He stares at the form of the animal slumped in the bloodclay, flames licking its sides.

The man becomes aware of them again. "I can help," he says.

"Eh?"

"I can help. I've been in slaughterhouses before. Many times. I can help."

"We don't need no help."

"No, I suppose not. But many of you have more work to do, I would think."

This is true. Today is the beginning of a busy day. They must salt the meat and then prepare the rest of the farm for their departure. The man has arrived at a difficult time.

"We don't have much to pay you," says his father.

"I didn't expect much. Nor do I want it."

"Fair enough," says his father, and hands the man the scraper. "Help him," he says to the boy, and most depart to other work.

Once the fire dies the boy helps the man hold the carcass down and the stranger straddles it, flipping the scraper over and over again in his hand with an easy grace. He looks at the body with a doctor's care, then takes the scraper with both hands and begins to scour the body, making piles of burnt hair and scooping them off with the curved blade and flinging them away. The other men watch him, impressed by the surety of his movements. When he calls to them to flip the body over they and the boy react quickly. But again the boy notices his unfamiliarity with words. At first the call was not even a word, just a bleating noise that called for aid. Then the stranger seemed to remember and changed it as it tapered, adding in some vague command. Yet still they obeyed.

They flip the body over and the man takes handfuls of hay and sprinkles it on the other side. The boy looks down and sees rust and crimson streaks on the man's coat.

"You're getting blood on your coattails, mister," he says.

"It's of no matter," says the man, and lights a match and begins the next fire. They stand back and watch it burn once more.

"You have seen a slaughter before," says the man to the boy.

The boy nods.

"That is good."

"Why?"

"Some places don't know of such things. They don't want to, either. They pretend they do not exist. But it is good to remember what we come from and what we go to," says the man, watching the body burn.

"I killed a pig once," says the boy.

"Did you?"

"Yes. It was a wild boar. I shot it."

"Hunting?"

"No. It come into our barn. Started eating the piglets."

The man nods, still watching the fire. He may not be listening.

"It was night and my pa was away," says the boy. "I heard screaming. I thought it was people, just as you did. I came out and it was eating them and I shot it in the head with the shotgun."

"You did well," says the man. "Most would have run, or missed."

"I know," says the boy quietly, but he does not feel like he has done well. He does not feel proud of that night in the barn with the screams and the musk and the breathing of the thing in the darkness, or the lightning flash and thunder of the shotgun. And the way the floor was soaked, soaked in blood.

They both look at the dead thing on fire and watch the hay blacken and curl. It burns out. The boy steadies the carcass once again and the man cleans it of all hair, and they flip it and burn again and flip it and burn again until it is smoked and smooth. Its ears are crunchy and they break them off and toss them away and peel the hooves off like old fruit. They brush it down to remove the rest of the hair and soon it is hairless and raw and pink, just as it would hang in the butcher's shop.

The man stoops now and removes the eyes and they begin to flush out the blood, again and again. They set up the butchering plank, an old, thick door that once hung in the front of the house. The stranger and the boy and some of the other men strain to lift the animal and set it up on the door, and still they flush out more of the blood. They step back to catch their breath.

"How'd you get those scars, mister?" asks the boy.

"I have always had them," he says.

"Since you were born?"

A queer look comes into his eyes. "Since I was born, yes." He looks back at the animal hanging on the door. "I cannot even remember the first slaughter I attended."

"Been doing this for a while?"

"Oh, yes. But then, everyone has, in a way."

"Huh? What do you mean?"

"Everything needs to feed. And, in doing so, it must kill. Perhaps not with a knife or with a gun, but all things strive to learn of more ways to eat, and consume, and live another day, and so they learn of killing. Even those with no mind such as corn in the field and trees in the forest rejoice and grow stronger with more to consume. And always in sating hunger, in some form or another, one can find death."

"Huh? Like, killing something?"

"Yes."

"Trees don't kill nobody. Unless they fall on someone."

"No. But if a man buys a steak, did he kill the cow? He did not kill it himself, certainly, but it died for him and so he eats it and is satisfied for a day or more. Just as a tree's roots eat the decaying bodies of animals and other trees, even if it did not choke out their life. And we eat the fruit of these trees, or the corn or the wheat or the animals we have raised from these fruits." He begins to approach the animal's body, hatchet now in hand. "All that lives kills. All that breathes murders. Prays for it, even. It is simplistic, yes, but so is life and death. All living things are friends of death, whether they know it or not."

And the man steps forward and stops as though struck by a

sudden thought, and he turns and looks at the boy. His cheeks twitch strangely, pinching around the eyes, and the boy realizes he is trying to smile.

"My friends," says the man to the boy. He walks to the dead beast without another word, flipping the hatchet in his hand as though it were no more than a toy.

The stranger takes the hatchet and prunes the legs off of the animal, cracking and tearing, and sets them aside like kindling. Then he splits the head of the animal with terrible ease and he wriggles the blade of the hatchet in the gash and then pulls it apart, one half in each hand, and the men say they have never seen someone do that so effortlessly. The stranger chokes his grip up on the hatchet and then removes the jaw until the animal is headless and legless. He swaps the hatchet for a knife and makes a cut in the animal from its groin to its neck and his eyes narrow in concentration as he makes sure not to puncture the intestines. The men all nod, seeing how familiar he is with this task. Then he takes a metal pail and removes the intestines, the stomach, the heart and the bladder, making sure not to rupture any and release their foulness.

It is practically done. Almost ready to roast or salt. The man steps back and nods at his work. He is not even sweating.

"That was the quickest I ever seen a man do that, mister," says the boy's father. "What's your name?"

His mouth twitches again as though to smile, but he cannot. "I have been in a slaughterhouse. It is an easy thing."

"We don't have much to pay you with."

"I wouldn't ask it of you. A bit of food would do me well, though."

The boy's father tells him to go into the house and fill a sack with rolls and jerky. The boy does so, and as he stands in the kitchen he watches the men working through the window. One man takes the pail with the animal's organs and sets it down by the back door. The boy continues his work, but then he hears something. It is the wind, or so he thinks, yet he hears it again. He goes back to the window. There is nothing there except the pail and the late setting sun, stretching out the shadows.

But then the boy sees him. It is the stranger, casually walking to the pail, yet he turns to see if he is being watched. Satisfied that he is not, he takes a small handkerchief from his pocket and walks to the pail, looking in. The boy withdraws, stooping to watch and not be seen. The man's eyes dart through the bucket, and the boy sees they are alight with wild delight, even hunger. The man looks about once more. His chest is heaving and he is sweating slightly and as he reaches down into the bucket his hand shivers. He picks something up, something hard and gray and red, and the boy sees it is the pig's heart. The stranger gazes at it, treasuring it, and swallows nervously. His head darts around, checking behind him, and then his mouth opens, opens more than any mouth should, revealing newspaper-gray teeth and a dull, sandy tongue, and he bites into the heart, ripping and tearing with his neck, and his head snaps back with his mouth full and his lips watery-red.

The boy ducks down, panting. He calms himself and listens. The man is still outside. The boy hears rustling, then footsteps trailing away, but the boy is unable to move from fear. He wants to run to his father but he does not. He does not want that man nearby any longer than he needs to be. And he does not want his father to know what he has seen. The image of the man's face still lingers in his mind, the way his face became distended and unearthly in his ecstasy.

The boy steels himself. He walks out front. The stranger is there, speaking amiably with the men. His hands are not red, nor is his mouth, and he is not quivering anymore. He looks nothing like the man in the window. Instead he looks stronger, more alive and alert, like he has been rejuvenated by what he has done here. He glances at the boy approaching, his eyes still dead and distant, and reaches out to take the sack from him.

"I thank you kindly," he says. "It is good to work with one's hands. Sometimes you forget what you excel at, or what you are here for."

"That may be so," says the boy's father. He does not notice the way the boy pales when he draws close to the stranger.

The stranger waves to them, tosses the sack over his shoulder, and walks back toward the road, heading southwest. He kicks up a trail of dust as he walks, red clouds going waist high and swallowing him. The trail hangs in the air as he walks away and the boy watches it disappear.

Connelly and the others listened as he finished his story.

"He ate the heart?" asked Pike.

"Yes sir," said the boy softly. "Just as sure as I'm alive and breathing, he took that heart and bit out of it like it was a great big apple. And he stowed it away in his kerchief and took it with him. I checked. It wasn't in the bucket."

They were silent as they thought about this.

"Any of you ever hear of him doing that?" said Connelly.

They shook their heads.

"I heard of injuns doing that," said Roosevelt. "With buffalo. They eat them 'cause they think it's holy. They think they're eating its spirit."

"Maybe the man is deluded," said Pike. "Maybe he believes that stuff."

"If he's a cannibal I never heard of it," Hammond said.

"No," said Pike. "No, I expect we wouldn't."

The boy looked at him. "He didn't steal nothing from you all, did he?" he said quietly.

"He did, in a way," said Hammond.

"You did right," said Roosevelt to the boy. "You did exactly what I would have done. You had to get him out of there so he wouldn't harm any of yours."

The boy whispered, "Will he... Will he come back?"

"No," said Roosevelt gently. "No. Once he's gone, he's gone. He doesn't come back. He never has."

"I just never seen a man's face look like that. He was so happy and so crazy. All over a heart."

"You say he went to the southwest from your farm?" said Connelly.

"Yes."

"Where's that at?"

The boy told them.

"And he's going by foot?"

"Yes. He may hitch a ride, I don't know. Ain't a real popular road, but you never know."

"What's southwest of your farm?" said Pike.

"Farmland, mostly. Odd town or two. Cutston is down that way, I think. Drought's hit them pretty bad, though. Just like the rest of this place."

"I see."

"Can I get my nickel now, mister?"

"Sure, sure," said Roosevelt, and he flipped him the coin.

"Thanks much," the boy said.

"Take care, now."

He stood and walked away across the fields and into the night.

"He ate a heart," said Hammond quietly.

"I think he would have eaten the damn thing alive if he could've," said Roosevelt. "Jesus. This guy's crazier than a rat in a tin shithouse."

"Watch the language," said Pike absently.

"So he's mad?" said Connelly.

"It would seem so," Pike said. "You heard the boy. He was overcome. He had to take a bite, like a naughty boy stealing goodies. He has no control over himself. Whatever drives him does so whether he wants it to or not."

"And he's worked in a slaughterhouse before," said Roosevelt.

"The world is his fucking slaughterhouse," snarled Connelly.

The men stopped, unsettled by his fury. They watched his rage mount and then dissipate.

Hammond said, "Why did he come to the slaughter in the first place?"

"He's attracted by things like that, I'd guess," said Pike. "I expect he enjoys the experience. After all, they say porkflesh is the closest to a human being's."

Hammond shivered. "Jesus."

They didn't speak for a while, thinking to themselves.

"Let's make camp while we can and get some sleep," said Pike. "We've got a long walk in the morning."

They withdrew into the fields, away from what was left of the carnival, and began to bed down without a fire. Roosevelt walked off into the brush and came back with a handful of sticks and reeds. Connelly watched as he sat down and began to weave something, setting the twigs together and then wrapping the reeds around the joints. He worked quickly, and soon Connelly saw that he was constructing a little man-shape, a small idol with spindly legs and a fat grass body and a small, blank thumb of wood for its head. He took a handful of earth in his palm and spat in it and smeared it about until it was a black paste. He rubbed some of the paste into the little idol's head and then blew on it until it was firm and then he scraped out two eyes. He nodded and pressed the little figure into the earth next to where he lay so it stood upright.

"What is that?" asked Connelly.

"It's my watcher," said Rosie.

"Your what?"

"My watcher. It watches over me in the night. Then if anything bad's going to happen it'll happen to him instead of me."

"What?"

"It'll take my suffering for me. In my place."

Rosie rolled over and soon was asleep. Connelly stayed up, looking at the little idol. It seemed strange, but the idol appeared different now that the mud had dried. Its face had more detail and its limbs were not as spindly. It looked more solid. More alive.

Connelly lay back and slept. In the morning when they awoke the idol was in ruins, limbs broken and its body frayed and the mud that made its face scratched and patched. Connelly thought about asking Roosevelt about it but did not.

CHAPTER SIX

They made their way southwest along the road. Trucks and jalopies drove by but none offered rides and soon they stopped hailing them. Each time they passed Connelly saw the dirty faces of young children staring out at them before they disappeared in a cloud of dust and exhaust.

The dust was getting worse, as was the drought. It was like they had landed on the moon. Everything was red and brown and the dust got finer. Simply walking kicked up dust that went up to their shoulders, and it stained everything the color of clay.

One night they walked off the road and camped in a field next to an old tank. They ate chicken and beans they had traded for along the road and Roosevelt produced a harmonica and proved himself to be an enthralling player. They listened as they warmed themselves by the fire.

"How'd you learn to do that?" said Connelly.

"In the stir," said Roosevelt. "They tossed me in for a nickel spot back in Chicago for assault. Just a barfight, some guy's leg got broke. Got out in a year, things were too crowded and I was on good behavior. But then, everyone's spent at least a little time in the clink."

"No," said Connelly.

"I haven't," Hammond said.

"Or I," said Pike.

"Oh," Roosevelt said, frowning. "Well, I guess, um, in certain circles in certain cities it's just common." And he went back to playing softly.

"I had a neighbor who could play like that," said Connelly. "Maybe he learnt it in jail. We'd hear him playing at night through an open window, and we'd sit and just listen. I like to think he knew we were there. Like he waited for us to get ready for dinner and chose that time to play."

"Do you miss it?" asked Pike.

"Miss it?" said Connelly.

"The stationary life. Home. Do you miss it?"

"Yes. Yes. Of course I do, yes."

"I can't remember mine, sometimes. It was so long ago. I was just a boy, fresh out of the army and hopping around to revivals. I remember girls with pigtails and eyes like honey. I remember the smell of bread baking. But everything else is lost to me. What else do you remember, Connelly?"

He thought. "Laughter."

"Laughter?"

"Just laughter. And my daughter's eyes. They were green."

"What happened to your wife?"

"Nothing. I still have her. She's waiting on me. I'm going to go back to her, if she'll take me back. Once this is done I'll go back. And everything'll be all right. Just like it was before."

Pike and Roosevelt glanced at each other. Then Hammond got up and strode away from the campfire. Connelly watched him go and looked at the others, surprised.

"He gets that way," explained Roosevelt. "He's younger than he looks. I don't think he's yet twenty-five."

"He'll come back," said Pike. "He'll be here in the morning. It must be a strange thing to be so young and know that you cannot have much of a normal life. In ways he has maybe lost more than the rest of us."

"No," said Connelly. "He hasn't."

Pike nodded. "I suppose not."

Eventually they lay down to sleep once more. And as Connelly's eyes shut he saw the desert.

White sands stretched to piercing blue horizons. Overhead the sun beat down, white-hot and unyielding, and as its rays fell upon the sand flats it made them glitter like snow. Harsh mountains lined the distance, muddy-brown and mutinous, and the wind barreled across the desert strong enough to knock a man over.

Connelly blinked, astounded at where he was. Yet somehow he knew he was waiting for something. Something was coming.

He saw it far away. Movement. Something small. He squinted at it but could not see it for the sun. It came closer, and soon he realized it was a man. A young man coming his way, directly toward him, and as he neared Connelly saw he was tall and pale and naked, and streaked with blood. He half strode, half staggered across the sands to Connelly, his arms dangling by his side, his crop of blond hair shining in the sunlight, his blue eyes agonizingly sad. The trail of his footprints wound away through the desert. They were red.

He walked up to Connelly and looked into his face.

"The world is changing," he whispered.

Then there was a clap of thunder like the sky was breaking. Connelly awoke and nearly screamed. He looked about. The fire had died down. Roosevelt and Pike were asleep, but Hammond was sitting cross-legged across from him, watching.

"Bad dream?" he asked.

Connelly nodded.

"What happened?"

He did not answer, just shook his head.

"What happened?" asked Hammond again.

"There was a desert. A young man, covered in blood. And he...he told me the world was changing, and I woke up."

"Well, it sure is, isn't it."

Connelly looked down at Hammond's hands. Roosevelt's gun was in his lap.

"What you doing with that?" he asked.

"Holding it. Getting the feel of it."

"Why?"

"We didn't come all the way out here to yell at him, did we?"

"I guess not."

"You ever kill a man before?"

"No."

"Me neither. I wish I had, though. Just so I could know. But I guess he'll be a good start."

"You going to practice on us?"

"No. I just like holding it. Just to know that I can. I can't say why, but it makes a man feel good to know that he can kill another. Not that he will. But that he has the capacity. You know?"

"I guess."

"You know, the hobos said you can get safe passage from Mr. Shivers, but you got to be careful."

"Yeah?"

"Yeah. You got to walk out to the crossroads on a moon-filled night with no clouds in the sky, and you go out and find a stone and write your name on the bottom of it and bury it in the road. He comes in the morning, leading his line of men he's taking off to hell, and he'll read your name and then you can pass through that town easy and you won't get harried by him or whoever he's running."

"Go to sleep, Hammond."

He turned the gun over in his hands. "I can't."

"Try."

"All right. I'll try."

"Well. Good night, then."

"Yeah," he said. "Good night."

CHAPTER SEVEN

They kept going southwest and managed to get a ride from a truck driver who had already delivered his payload of chickenfeed. They went some twenty miles crouched in the back. They climbed down where he turned off the road and headed to the highway and he shook his head as he drove away.

As they walked a car coming from the opposite direction pulled over. "I'd head back if I was you boys," a man shouted at them from the window. His family was in the back and all his belongings were strapped to the roof.

"Why's that?" said Roosevelt.

"Storm's coming. A duster."

"A what?"

"A duster. Dust storm. You won't be able to see three feet in front of your face tomorrow if you keep going."

"Thank you," said Pike.

"You boys not going to stop?"

"We don't have a choice."

"You all are nuts," said the man as he rolled up his window. "Bugshit. Just nuts." The wheels spun and he careened down the road.

"Bastard doesn't even know how to drive," said Hammond. "And he's calling us nuts."

They kept going. As midafternoon came they passed over an old road and a crumbling gully. There they heard a muffled shouting from far to their left. Pike motioned off the road and they stepped quietly into the cover of the weeds as Pike looked over the top.

"What was that?" said Hammond.

"Some people are camped along the road, I'd say," said Roosevelt. "Just off to the south of us."

"So?" said Connelly.

"I don't like this," said Pike. "This whole area's deserted, especially after that fella who told us about the... the..."

"The duster."

"Right. Could be cops, could be bandits."

"Bandits?" said Hammond, and laughed.

"I've seen them before. Hell, I've been robbed by them before. And if there's as many migrants all over the place as it seems then the cops are sure to be frothing at the mouth."

"Pretty sorry bandits or cops, talking so loud," said Roosevelt. "We could hear them from miles away."

"Maybe so. But I still don't like it."

"I could go take a look," said Connelly.

"What?" said Pike. "Take a look? What do you mean?"

"I mean I walk up to them and look at them and if I don't get shot then I guess things are okay."

"That sounds like a terrible plan to me," said Roosevelt.

"I don't see what's wrong with it. I don't think it's cops or outlaws. If it's cops I'm going to see my sister in town and if it's robbers I don't have much to rob, now do I? Just look at me. And it'd be a lot of work to rob me for a whole lot of nothing."

"He's got a point," said Hammond.

"You serious about going?" said Roosevelt.

"Yeah. Suppose so."

"Well, here," said Roosevelt, and he took out his gun and held it out to Connelly.

"Jesus!" Connelly said. "Get that goddamn thing away from me!"

"What? Why, what's wrong with it?"

"It's a gun, that's what's wrong with it. I don't know nothing about no guns."

"It's for protection. Just carry it and flash it so they know what's up."

"If they see me walking toward them with a gun in my hand they're likely to shoot me dead. I like having my head on my shoulders and I like the teeth I got. I'm not waving a gun at anyone."

"Well, damn," Roosevelt said.

"If that's settled," said Pike, "we'll stay here and watch you go. You get into any trouble, Mr. Connelly, you holler like you've been struck by lightning and we'll come running."

"If you say so," said Connelly, and began down the ravine.

He walked along the remains of the gully a ways before spotting them up ahead. They were squatting along the edge of the ditch where the side had fallen in, brown figures among the dry clay rubble. There were five of them, four men and a woman. He saw one man's bright bald head gleaming with his considerable backside turned to him. The three other men scrabbled with tinder in the ditch. Two seemed to be twins, with blond-red beards and moth-eaten porkpie hats, and the last was a scraggly, ratty thing who seemed more beard than man. Far to the outskirts sat the woman. She was thin and wore a leather jacket with jeans and boots and she had a hand-kerchief wrapped around her head, pulling her light brown hair back into a bun. She drew lines in the sand and watched the men with a face torn between irritation and exasperation.

As Connelly came up the large man turned to look, saw him, and said without surprise, "You wouldn't happen to have any matches, would you, mister? We've been trying to figure this out by hand and the only thing we've gotten is splinters and swears."

"Got a few," said Connelly. He took out a box of matches, shook it, and handed it to him.

"God bless," said the scraggly one, and took it from the large one. He began striking them in clumsy blows, snapping each one.

"Damn, Roonie," said the woman, "you didn't ruin your fingers trying this, did you?"

"Sorry, Lottie," said the man softly. "Didn't mean to waste your matches, mister."

"It's all right," he said.

The woman took the matches, then knelt and deftly struck one and held the flame down to the kindling. Soon the wood was crawling with flames. She sheltered it and blew at the base and soon the fire had grown through the wood like bright yellow vines filling a trellis. She took the matches, shook them again, and threw them to Connelly. He caught the box with one hand, and he and the woman looked at each other for a moment before the large man said, "Thanks a bunch. We been sitting here for hours trying to get this started."

"Never seen a man manage it by hand."

"I suppose you heard us fighting from off the road."

"I did. You folks robbers?" asked Connelly.

They looked at each other, confused. "No," said the fat man.

"Cops?"

"No. Why?"

Connelly leaned back and yelled, "It's all right. Just folks."

"What?" said the woman, but then saw Pike and the others come sheepishly crawling out of the roadside. "Oh," she said. "You boys really thought we was going to jump you?"

"These are strange times, ma'am," explained Pike.

"Then let's not make them any stranger," said the fat man, laughing. "Come down and sit with us a bit. Where you all headed?"

Hammond pointed down the road.

"Where we're heading, too," said the woman.

"They said there was a storm coming," said the scraggly one.

"We heard the same," Roosevelt said.

"Where in the hell are our manners," said the fat man. "My name is Monk, that there is Lottie — say hello, Lottie — and these boys are Jake and Ernie and the fella rubbing his knuckles is Roonie."

"Hello," said Roosevelt, and tipped his hat. They introduced themselves. Connelly noticed the woman watching him, sizing him up.

"We don't have much," said Roonie. "Just some rolls is all.

We'd be happy to share them in thanks for the matches. We'd be starved without them."

"And we'd be happy to share what we have with you, Mr. Roonie," said Pike, rummaging in his sack.

"How long have y'all been walking?" asked Lottie.

"A ways," said Hammond. "We took a truck down here, walked about six miles since. I'm hungry as hell and don't mind saying so."

They heated old rolls and tinned meat and some of them smoked cigarettes, the new friends eager as they had not had open flame in some time.

"Any idea what's down the road?" asked Hammond.

"Farmland, or what used to be farmland," said Lottie. "After that there's a meager little town that's not much more than a wide spot in the road."

"You wouldn't to have happened to been passed up by anyone, have you?" asked Pike.

They looked at one another, mouths full. "No," they said.

"No one?"

They shook their heads.

"Why?" asked Monk, suddenly suspicious. "Who you looking for?"

"Nothing. You would have remembered him."

"Would I?"

"I would expect so, yes."

"And why would I remember this strange person?"

"He'd be a scarred man. Scarred along the cheeks like—"

He stopped as the other five jumped to their feet and yelled. The woman and the twins tensed and moved away and Monk stared from face to face, bewildered. Everyone was on their feet except Connelly, who stayed seated at the edge of the ditch before the fire. He was unable to say why but he felt no threat, or not yet at least.

"What's going on?" said Roosevelt.

The other five looked at each other and Monk said, "You all are looking for the shiver-man?"

Everyone was silent for a great while.

"Yeah," said Connelly.

Lottie said, "So are we."

No one moved. Then Connelly reached forward and poked at the edge of the fire with his foot. "Well. That's something."

"Why you looking for him?" said Roonie. "What do you want with him?"

"Why? What about you?" Hammond said.

"We're no friends of his, if that's what you're asking," said Pike quickly. "I doubt if such a man has friends of any kind, Mr. Monk."

Monk mopped sweat from his brow with a soiled piece of fabric and thought. "Good God almighty," he said, "if this isn't crazy as all hell."

They looked at each other for a few minutes longer, sometimes making to whisper to one another before becoming embarrassed and giving up.

"Rolls are done," said Connelly, and reached forward and lifted the food off the flame. "You all going to eat or what?"

"What do you want from him?" Lottie asked them.

"Nothing good," said Connelly.

"Would nothing good be killing?"

He looked at her a long, long while. "It would," he said.

The other group considered this, then sat and began eating. Pike and the others followed, still watchful.

"I think it's sort of funny," said Connelly.

"What is?" said Lottie.

"How surprised we are. I mean, we met our own already. The folks we traveled with before this. So there's no reason to be upset if we meet more, is there. Makes sense that there's got to be more who's after him, and for the same reason."

"I don't think that's very funny," said Lottie. "That's not very funny at all."

"No," said Connelly. "I guess it isn't, is it."

The two groups looked at each other. Then they sat and began eating and did not speak for some time.

Once they were done eating they shared their stories. The other party spoke of lost kin, of dead friends, of loved ones slain. Lottie would not tell hers, merely shaking her head. All the stories were familiar, all the tellers quiet and broken-eyed. How far had they all tracked him? Were they to put their separate paths end to end Connelly would have guessed it would stretch across the country. A line of crimson footprints, twisting through the desert flats...

Connelly shook himself.

"And what's the most recent thing you heard of him?" said Pike softly.

The other party exchanged looks. "You haven't heard?" asked Lottie.

"No. Heard what?"

Monk leaned in. "You know that town up ahead? Wide spot in the road?"

They nodded.

"We hear there's an odd fella set up there for the night. Face all messed up. Heard it not more than four hours ago, from a man off the road."

A deafening silence fell over all of them. Hammond got to his feet and stood staring down at Monk.

"You mean it?" said Roosevelt.

"I surely do."

"Good God..." whispered Hammond. "He's here. He's here. He's right over that fucking field over there, is that what you're telling me?"

Roonie nodded. "Would be. We're going to wait 'til night-fall. Going to sneak up on him. Get him that way."

"What? You're *waiting*?" said Hammond.

"We are," said Monk.

"No! No, the hell with that!" he shouted. "Come on! He's right over there! We got one shot at this and we're going to sit around a damn fire eating fucking tinned *meat*, is that? Jesus!"

"Waiting's smart," said Roonie, but he looked ashamed.

"You're cowards," Hammond said. "Cowards is what you are. You've come all this way and now you're afraid."

Roonie got to his feet. "You say that again. You say that again to me."

"If you had an inch of spine," said Hammond softly, "you'd have done it already."

"What about you, boy?" asked Monk. "You killed a man? Are you a killer?"

Hammond faltered and made to turn away. He quivered and lashed out and kicked a nearby log, sending it flying.

"Hammond!" Pike said loudly. "Sit down! These folk talk sense."

"What's sense is going over there right now and putting a bullet in whatever brain he's got," said Hammond.

"That's not sense, that's idiocy. What we do is right, but no lawman knows that. You shoot that man in broad daylight and you're liable to get shot yourself."

"That doesn't matter and you know it," Hammond said, his voice smooth and quiet and deadly.

There was a moment of quiet.

"You don't think we want the same?" said Monk. "You don't think we said the very words you're saying now? Yes, we do have one shot. And I don't aim to mess it up." But Connelly noticed how he turned bright red as he spoke, and how he mopped sweat from his brow.

Hammond shook his head and did not respond.

"Come on," said Roosevelt. "Sit down, Hammond. Don't lose your head now. If you do you'll do it wrong and he'll just wind up laughing at you again. And you don't want that, do you?"

"No. No, I don't want that."

"Then sit."

He did. He wiped at his face, hiding his tears and smearing dust over his cheeks and eyes. In the fading light he looked like some child of war, face painted and awaiting battle.

"Make no mistake," said Monk. "We mean to kill him, yes. We need to see this thing dead. And we will. We'll come in at night. Find him. We'll all get him, make sure he can't escape. Then we move. And...and we take all the time we need." Again the chubby hand rubbed sweat away from his eyes.

"And we need a great deal of time," Hammond said.

"Yeah," said Lottie, her voice trembling. "Yeah, we do."

Connelly looked at her, then at the others. They did not look much like killers. They spoke the words but he saw desperation in them rather than resolve. These were not monsters or machines but anguished people clinging at a chance to put things right. But here at the penultimate moment a trickle of doubt worked into them, one by one. All except perhaps Pike... And then Connelly wondered about himself.

We'll figure it out, he reasoned. We got to.

Monk said to them, "We have just met, yet we know each other."

Pike said, "Are you inviting us to join you? For the moment?"

"Don't see why not. We get more folk we got a better chance of getting him."

"That's so," said Pike. And he spat in the fire and watched it sizzle and gripped his heavy walking stick and began to wait.

As evening fell their purpose weighed more heavily upon them. Their eyes grew flat and in that instance all of them were one person, one grieving heart and one vengeful hand. Yet each also felt they were alone in their suffering, for they had endured a loss that made the world a gray and silent place, barren and unpopulated.

"When should we go?" said Roonie softly. "When should we go?"

Monk looked at the sky overhead. "Don't know much about killing. It's almost night. I suppose now is as good a time as any."

"I would suppose," said Pike.

They did not move at first. They sat still until the sky was dark, like a dome had fallen across the country, trapping them and blocking out all light. Then they dumped dirt on the fire and stood without speaking and walked west, like ghosts passing through the empty fields, simply obeying the red song inside of them without thought.

CHAPTER EIGHT

It was less than two miles. Within minutes they saw a clutch of buildings silhouetted against the bleak light of the dying sunset. There was something wrong with the light in the distance, like it was shining through greased glass, but they paid it no mind.

"Where'll he be?" asked Hammond.

"Inn," said Monk. "I hope."

They spread out and approached the town in a tight half-circle. They saw no people, no animals, no sign of life save for a few lit windows among the buildings. At the outskirts they moved among the structures like hunters in a forest, seeking cover and shadow and lines of sight. Still nothing stirred.

"Whole damn place is dead," said Roosevelt.

"Seems to be," said Pike.

"What the hell's going on?"

"I can't say."

There was a crash from a general store and a man came running out from the back with arms full of food and bottles of alcohol. He wore overalls and a straw hat barely kept together and he had no shoes. He stopped when he saw them watching, then turned to run before one of the twins stepped out and stopped him, grabbing his arm.

"Let me go!" he cried. "Let me go!"

"What's this nonsense?" said Pike as he strode up.

"Let me go! You bastards let me go!"

As they struggled one of the bottles fell from the man's arms and shattered on the ground. He shrieked like a child and kneeled over it, crying, "You broked it! You done broked it! Why'd you have to do that?"

"Be quiet," said Pike.

"You done broked it! I had to go to all that trouble and everything and you all just ruined everything! Why, you—"

Pike slapped him hard, once, then twice. A trickle of blood began to form at the corner of the man's mouth and he whimpered.

"Will you be quiet?" asked Pike.

He nodded.

"What's happening here? Where're all the people?"

"They left," he said, and sobbed and rubbed at his mouth.

"Why? Where?"

"Don't know where. They left 'cause there was no reason to stay. Farms all dried up, got bought out, got dug up. There's only a few here now."

"And where are they?"

"Most left just now. A storm's coming. You can take what you want. The place is deserted. You can just go in and take whatever you want," he said, and smiled like this tip could fix everything.

"Get out of here," said Pike, and threw him aside. The man hurried to grab what he had dropped and ran down the street without looking back. Pike turned to the others. "This doesn't change anything."

"No," said Connelly.

They found the inn, a long, low-slung building that could have been built with the same primitive tools and designs of fifty years ago, even a hundred years ago. An oil lamp fluttered and swung in the window as the wind picked up. Connelly, Pike, and Monk entered while the others kept watch outside. The inn seemed abandoned as well until a short, fat man with a droopy mustache poked his head out of the back.

"What the hell?" he said. "Are you folks crazy or something?"

"No," said Pike.

"There's a goddamn storm coming in, don't you know to get cover?"

"We know. We're looking for someone."

"Oh?"

"Yes. Someone who may be staying here."

"Only got one man who's staying here."

"Does he have a scarred face, by any chance?"

The innkeeper looked at them, suspicious. "He might. What do you want with him?"

"Where is he?" asked Monk.

"I don't like this," said the innkeeper.

"Where?" repeated Pike.

"You boys get out of here. I don't want you here. Get out."

Pike walked around the countertop and the innkeeper opened his mouth to shout when Pike's fist slammed into the wall above the man's head. The innkeeper cowered before Pike, shielding his face with his arms. Connelly started forward but Monk put his arm in front of him, though he was trembling. Pike grabbed the innkeeper and thrust him back on the counter and clapped his hand over the man's mouth before he could yell.

"You stay quiet," said Pike to the innkeeper. "You scream and I will make sure you never walk or write again, do you hear me? I have walked miles and miles to find this man and I will have no issue walking over you, sir. Now where is he? Is he here?"

The innkeeper shook his head, terrified.

"Then where is he?" said Pike, and took his hand away.

"He left," whispered the innkeeper.

"Left? Where'd he go?"

"He said he was going for a walk. He does it every night but he said he was doing it again this time. I said he was crazy, just like you all are, you bastards. He said he was going for a walk and I said the sky was about to come down on him but he paid it no mind."

"Which way did he go?"

"Up the street," said the innkeeper, and pointed. "That a-way."

Pike left him where he was and they walked out. The others crept out of the shadows and joined them in the road.

"Well?" said Roosevelt.

"He isn't here, Mr. Roosevelt," said Pike. "He went for a walk. The man said he does it every night."

"So where'd he walk?" asked Roonie.

Pike nodded up the road. "So I suppose now it's hide and seek," he said, and spat.

They organized a search party as quickly as they could, each taking pairs. Connelly was paired with Roosevelt and they would travel with the twins. They each took a street and, if needed, decided they would search what few houses there were.

"No one's here anyways," said Lottie. "The damn place is a ghost town. Ghosts won't care if we bust in."

"Amen," Roonie said.

Connelly and his group moved north and wandered among the alleys and the stores. A handful of slums squatted toward the edge of town, along the ditches and the bridge and a scattered half dozen trees. They walked along fences and looked into yards and began to search the homes.

"You ever broke into a house before?" said Roosevelt.

"No," Connelly said.

He chuckled. "It's easy. Sort of fun. Can't see it being fun with no one around, though. Sort of spoils it."

The twins picked a ruined shack with no door, but for some reason Connelly was compelled otherwise. He would not want that, he realized. The scarred man would not want something so poor and already hopeless. He would want something comfortable. Something homey. Something warm. It would be of no worth to violate something already destitute.

"Where you going, Connelly?" asked Roosevelt as Connelly walked away from the twins, but he made a motion with his hand and Roosevelt was quiet.

He found a house trying its best to look nice. It was shabby and old but it had a fresh coat of white paint and its yard had once been clean and organized. Rows of flowers in the front.

A doormat. A knocker and a mailbox. It was a home more than simply a house.

This would be the place, he knew. Connelly's instincts said so in a way that had no words.

"Stay out here," he said. "Stay here and watch. Watch if he comes out. If he does, yell."

"You think he's in there?" Roosevelt said.

"We're about to find out."

Connelly surveyed the house once more in the pallid light. There was no noise but the wind. He pushed the fence out of the way and came up the front walk. Windows dead. Door slightly ajar. Something had come here and disturbed this dead place, like an animal whose path had stirred up fallen leaves.

He stood on the porch, minding the creaking boards, and pushed the door open a bit. Its hinges squawked and he winced, then squatted and spat on them and tried once more. Now it was barely a whisper. He moved to look about in the doorway but saw nothing, then he took off his shoes and padded inside.

Everything was dark and cramped. A hallway led away before him and there were stairs up to his left. Pictures hung from the walls and sat on shelves, their glass catching the light from the street and shining slick. The wind picked up, battering the windows, the panes rattling in their frames. Besides that there was no noise at all. The sense of abandonment was overpowering, and Connelly felt like he was not in a home but some stone chamber far below the earth, with narrow atriums splintering off into the dark.

He moved down the hallway and came to the kitchen. Cupboards all closed. Dishes on the countertop. A child's drawing on the far wall.

On the table was a light. A single candle, its flame inno-
cently dancing on the tabletop. Next to it was a placemat and
a dish, a nice one, white with flowers on the edge. Probably the
nicest dish in the house. But in its center was a muddy brown
stain, almost a smear. It was copper or red at the edges. A
knife and fork sat directly to the sides of the plate, also stained.
Connelly paused, then reached out to touch the smear. It was
still wet. He lifted his fingers to his nose and sniffed. Its scent
was thick and coppery and he knew without doubt it was
blood of some kind.

A black fly alighted on the fork. It twitched and flew to the
plate, then back to the fork. It was joined by another fly, then
another, their reedy whine near impossible to hear over the
wind. Connelly looked around, then glanced into the living
room. There he saw the blue light filtering through the window outside, yet it was strange. The light or the room itself
seemed almost alive. Everything moved and pulsated, everything shuddered.

Then he noticed a low, wet buzzing coming from in the living room. He thinned his eyes and walked in.

The air was thick with flies, dozens of them at least, swarm-
ing through the air. They filled the room and seemed to make
the shadows twitch. As he stood in the darkness he felt them
invade his arms, his neck, his legs. He suppressed a shiver and
tried to see where they were coming from. They seemed to be
pouring out of one of the walls.

He approached and saw he was at the top of the stairs to the
basement. They led straight down, ending at a small brown
door with cracked paint. Connelly reached forward and
pawed at the air and felt a string hanging from the ceiling. He
pulled and nicotine-yellow light filled the stairs from the bulb

above. The door seemed to change, to move in the light like it was awoken or disturbed. It was slightly ajar and Connelly could see the oily-black forms of the flies flowing out its crack, as though the basement was bleeding or leaking.

Suddenly a wave of stench washed over him, thick and heady, like the door before him had exhaled a putrid sigh. He almost staggered back, unable to bear it. His eyes watered and he turned his head to the side and the flies seemed to increase, like they were fleeing something from the basement, something that was waking up and stirring to greet him and pushing out that horrible stink.

How long has he been here, thought Connelly. Days? Weeks? It couldn't have been more than a few days.

He took a step down toward the basement, hesitated, then took another. He could be down there, he thought. The scarred man could be down there. But Connelly did not know if he could bear to see what the man had been doing for so long. What foulness had been gestating here in this deserted town, what prey had he been feeding on? And feeding was what he had been doing, after all.

Connelly rubbed his mouth and wondered what had been on that plate.

He stopped halfway there, the door staring up at him like some brown, blind eye. He held his hand to his mouth yet again and fought back retching.

No. He could not do this.

He walked back up the stairs and took a breath. As he did there came a tapping noise from upstairs, quiet and brittle. He froze and listened. It did not stop.

Connelly sped up the stairs and through the kitchen and

came to the stairs leading to the second floor. He put his foot on the first step and the tapping halted.

He waited. No other sound came. He treaded up the stairs on the balls of his feet, gazing into the darkness. He could see nothing, no movement, no light. He was nearly to the top when the sound of the wind rose and he felt air in his face. He thought for a moment and leapt forward and rushed around the right doorway at the top of the stairs.

Some room, a child's room, but on the west wall was an open window with the wind blasting through.

He raced to the window and looked out. There was no pole or fence or tree to climb down near the window, yet he had felt it open and the pressure change. Someone had been in here and opened the window, opened it to escape, he felt sure of it. He looked again. The yard was below him and beyond that the trees and the creek, but after that there was nothing. The trees raged and shook in the wind. Besides them and the swirls of dust he saw nothing move.

He heard something. There was a sound in the wind. A howling, like an animal. Something screaming in the violent night.

Connelly sprinted back downstairs and out the front door and saw Roosevelt standing in the street, shielding himself from the wind. "What the hell is that?" he shouted, but Connelly was already following his ears and running for the creek.

The howls grew louder. As he dodged through the trees Connelly saw him ahead. A man kneeling over a crumpled form on the bridge, shaking the thing before him and screaming wildly. Connelly slowed and walked forward. It was Jake. Snot and spit ran down his face as he shrieked yet again. Connelly looked at the thing at Jake's knees and could only tell it was Ernie by the clothes he was wearing. Blood shone black in the quivering starlight and the night seemed to go mad.

The others ran up behind him. They looked at the slain man and began screaming and swearing. Some went to try and pry Jake from his brother but he snapped and struck at them and clung ever tighter. Pike and Hammond began running through the streets and the nearby fields, crying that the scarred man could not be far, not far. Lottie struggled to hold Jake back and called to Connelly to help her, but he turned and followed Hammond and Pike.

He tried not to think about how the man had gotten out of the house and how he had gotten to Ernie so fast. How he had done what he did and moved on. Connelly couldn't think of such things because then he might be something more than a man and then Connelly might not be able to do anything at all.

He wouldn't like open spaces, thought Connelly as he ran through the streets. He likes small things. Alleys and boxcars and basements. He likes being contained. He likes little roads...

There was nothing. The town was deserted as before, nothing but coils of dust and blank windows, some broken, and here and there a dog or cat cowering at the onset of the storm.

Connelly ran until his legs burned and his throat hurt. The town turned into a blur as the wind picked up and his search became more desperate. He ran down a large street and then an alley and stumbled as he came out. He lifted his face from the gravel. The countryside unfolded before him, the dry creek running across the face of the hills like a scar and trees thrashing along it. And there crossing the creek at a quick but steady pace was a figure in a ragged gray cloak streaked with ashes, striding over the fields as though he had business on his mind.

Connelly stood and stared, unable to believe. It was impossible that this man was real. Then his body took over and he began running, trying to close the gap, but the man seemed to melt through the night, like he was being dragged forward by invisible strings. Connelly realized he was screaming, bellowing at the top of his lungs. He wanted some name to call, some name to curse, but the man had none and so Connelly did no more than scream.

The gray man halted and cocked his head, hearing him. He turned, his long, weathered face, swiveling to see him. Even at that distance Connelly heard the word the man said.

"*Connelly,*" whispered the scarred man.

Connelly stopped, stunned to hear his name. Then the man in gray looked at the night sky and the hills beyond, and there was a dreadful lull in the wind. The others were far behind Connelly, following his screams, and he heard one of them shout, "My God, look! Look! The stars!"

Connelly's eyes trailed up to the sky.

The stars. They were dying. It started in the distance, the farthest star they could see winking out, then the next, then the next. A black wave thundering across the sky, drowning out the stars and the moon. It was as though some unseen godly hand was reaching into the heavens and pinching them out like candles.

Something was coming. Something behind the hills, but he could not see.

The scarred man turned once more to look at him. His eyes stayed on Connelly alone. Behind the man the black wave crested the hill and Connelly heard the others begin yelling in panic at the sight of it.

It was a massive gray-red cloud, crawling up the tops of the hills and charging forward like a vast, blank army. It swallowed up the trees and the hills and the creek, consuming everything in its path. The others shouted for him to run, run, for God's sake, run, but he and the scarred man stood watching one another. They seemed to share some strange moment, caught between men screaming on one side and the sky raging down upon them on the other.

Then the gray man put his arms about his breast and bowed his head. The cloud approached and Connelly began shouting, "No! No!" but it was too late. The storm swallowed the man whole and he was lost.

CHAPTER NINE

The dust storm lasted for nearly three days. Connelly would have been marooned if the others hadn't shouted for him. It was impossible to see anything. They broke into one of the homes and used it for shelter, piling mattresses and blankets up against the windows and the doors to try and keep the dust out. It still seeped in, a fine mist that filled each room. Soon they learned if they did not frequently brush themselves off they would gather a coating of crimson-red, like they had just crawled out of the earth's bowels.

Jake would not leave his brother in the storm. He dragged the corpse through the dust and into the house and sat over it in the corner sobbing and praying and promising the dead thing he would make sure it was buried right. The others kept their distance. Though unnerved by its presence they did not have the gall to ask him to toss it out. Lottie convinced him to lay a sheet over it but before the first day was out it began to smell. Its intestines had been punctured and shit was leaking into its abdomen.

They did not know it, but this was one of the smallest storms of the time. Others filled the sky with red almost past the heavens. When winter came to New England, far away, it brought red snow with it.

Food quickly became a concern as they huddled in the center of the cloud. Neither party had packed much beyond a day's rationing. Eventually Connelly and Hammond bound their heads up in scarves and ventured out into the storm to the general store. They found the place ransacked and when they returned they looked like tribal clay puppets brought to life.

They tried to ignore their hunger and the stink of the dead man and the chalky taste that filled their mouths. Each night Roosevelt made a new little idol out of things he found around the house, and each morning they were all whole. Roosevelt seemed to believe from this that there was no real danger but no one took his word.

"I think it's dusk," said Pike one day as he stared out the window. "I can't be sure, though."

"All this dirt in the air?" said Roonie. "That's the livelihood of every fella in this state. Every man who grew cotton or corn, his future's in the air right now. We're breathing it in and brushing it off."

"God has forsaken this place," Pike said.

"That's awful harsh," said Monk.

"Certainly. It may be. But I find it hard to say otherwise. Look around. The land is a desert, cracked and empty. Hell's storms stride across the earth. I can't say what these people have done to incur His wrath, but His wrath is what they have and it is here now."

Connelly withdrew to a small bedroom and found Hammond on the mattress frame, cross-legged, a blanket around his shoulders.

"Don't know how much longer this'll last," said Connelly as he sat across from him.

"Wouldn't expect you to." Hammond sniffed and sneezed. "How are the others bearing it?"

"Not happily, that's for sure."

"I bet I know. They're all saying this is something new. Something about a curse for something we did. Aren't they?"

"Yeah."

Hammond laughed.

"What's so funny?" asked Connelly.

"It's not new. Things like this have happened before."

"I've never seen it."

"Doesn't mean it hasn't happened before. Just means you weren't around to see it." Hammond paused. His eyes grew wide and hollow and Connelly had never seen him look so fearful. "I think it's more than just the storm."

"What is?"

"I think it goes further. They say the storm is a curse and they say these hungry times are a curse. Like they expect things to always be safe and this hunger is new and strange. That there'll always be plenty. But *that's* the strange thing. *That's* the new thing. Living comfortably. That's strange."

"Think so?"

"I do."

"Well. That's an idea."

Hammond sniffed again, then said, "Hey, Connelly?"

"Yeah?"

"You hear about how the last thing a guy does is shit himself?"

"Yeah?"

He paused. "Think Jesus did that when He died on the cross?"

Connelly started up, then sat back down uncomfortably. "Goddamn. That's a crazy thing to say."

"Isn't it? But you have to wonder, don't you. He was definitely human. And He definitely died. It would stand to reason, wouldn't it?"

"I thought you didn't believe in Jesus."

"I'm just wondering, is all. We all want dignity. We all want plenty. But we're probably not going to get it, are we."

Lottie walked in, looked at the two of them, then sat next to Connelly. She undid her kerchief and her hair spilled down around her neck and she shook it out. Red clouds formed around her head like a halo.

"Look at me. I'm Irish," she said, and tried to smile.

"What's going on in there, Lottie?" asked Hammond. "Still a lot of moaning and groaning?"

"I'd be shocked if there wasn't." She chewed her lip. "He's long gone, isn't he."

"Yeah," said Connelly.

"I guess a man could run through that if he didn't care where he was going," she said. She chewed her lip more, then began to bite her nails. "Go over what happened in the house one more time," she said.

"I been over it enough," said Connelly. "Everyone's been asking me about it ever since we calmed down."

"We haven't calmed down. I can't imagine someone being calm in these circumstances."

"Well, since things got less goddamn crazy, then."

"It doesn't make sense, is all. How'd he get out of the house? Through the window? What the hell was he doing there? I won't ask Jake to talk about it, but how did he . . . How did he do what he did to Ernie so fast?"

"Jake won't know," said Hammond. "He wasn't there."

"You saw?"

"No. Stands to reason if Jake had been there to see he'd be cut up just as much as his brother."

She shook her head, eyes wide. "And the storm . . ."

"I don't want to hear any more ghost story talk," said Connelly. "He's a man. I know more than anyone. I saw him scared not more than a day or two ago when I almost caught him and pulled the guts out of him. Ghosts aren't scared."

"I hope you're right," she said, and patted his arm. Connelly looked at it. She took it away but did not seem to have noticed that he had looked.

Hammond coughed and said, "I don't know. I heard the craziest shit about him. One old woman told me he could make the night sing."

"Sing?"

"Yeah. I asked her what it sang about, and if it was a waltz or a march or anything you could dance to, and she got mad as hell. Thought I was making fun of her. Which I was. Then she said he could make all kinds of things sing, if he wanted. He could take a bone and write on it and make it sing. Make it sing you nightmares which would make you sicker than a dog. Said it tainted the land, sort of like poisoning it."

"Did you believe it?" asked Lottie.

Hammond snorted and laughed. "Hell no. Old lady was drunker than a boiled owl and had the French disease something fierce."

"Oh."

"Say, why are you after him?" asked Hammond. "You never told us."

"I didn't want to," Lottie said.

"We told you why we were."

"I never asked you to. I never heard Connelly tell his, either."

"That's right," said Hammond, looking at him. "I don't know why you're doing this, either."

"I'm doing this," Connelly said. "All you need to know."

"You two are terrible conversationalists," said Hammond. "Here, let's try again. Where are you from, Lottie?"

"Galveston. In Texas."

"Huh. What's that like?"

"Big. And pissed. Port cities usually are. Especially Texan port cities."

"I wouldn't know."

"No, I guess you wouldn't. Jews are a rarity in Texas."

"Christ," said Hammond. "How come everyone has to know I'm a Jew?"

"Because they're a rarity."

"Thanks," said Hammond sarcastically. He stood and grabbed a blanket off the floor. "I'm going to get some damn sleep. I'm in favor of pulling the mattresses off the windows. They're not doing any good."

"Suit yourself," said Lottie. "Make sure to put a blanket over your head as you sleep. I bet you could suffocate in this."

Hammond sighed, nodded, and walked into the living room.

"How's Jake?" Connelly asked her.

"Bad."

"I never heard anyone scream like that. I hope I never do again."

"How old are you, Connelly?"

"Why?"

"Because I want to know."

"I don't know."

"You don't know how old you are?"

"No."

"Why?"

"I never kept track."

"How can you not keep track of something like that?"

"It never occurred to me to try."

"Hammond's just a boy."

"He is."

"And Pike's an old man."

"Yeah. He don't act like one, though."

"I wonder now," said Lottie. "There's got to be more than us. If there's us there's got to be more. How many? Dozens? Hundreds? How long has he been doing this?"

Connelly was silent for a while. Then he said, "It was your child, wasn't it?"

Lottie flinched. She blinked, made as though to move away, then stopped. "Yes," she said.

"I can tell."

"How?"

"Don't know. Just do. These folks, they lost a lot. They each lost their own. But parents grieve for their children in a special way. It's a special kind of hurt. I don't know if it has a name but you can see it in a face. It's in yours. Suppose it's in mine too."

Lottie did not say anything. The wind clawed at the windows. She said, "It was my boy."

Connelly sat and waited.

"I wasn't a very good momma, I think," she said softly. "He ran away when he was fourteen. I can't blame him. I didn't miss him at first but then I did. That was years ago." She shut her eyes, breathed out. "Then I hear from a guy that heard from a guy that heard from a guy that he ran into trouble in Kentucky and he's not alive anymore. Killed. Some damn fight. Some damn thing. A scarred fella who just had it in for him, they said. It's a bad thing to lose a child but it's worse if you never got to know them and you don't even know where they're buried or how. Hell, I've . . . I've never even been to Kentucky. I don't know where he's lying now or if there's any peace in it. It isn't right that a man can take that away from you, can do that to you. It isn't right."

"No," said Connelly. "It isn't. But it happened."

"I heard something from a man south of here, down in Killeen. He said that when a woman's heavy with child and she feels the first hurts from labor she's got to take her first baby tooth and put it in a pot of dirt and put it on her windowsill. That way Mr. Shivers will pass that house over and leave that baby be."

"I heard something similar," said Connelly. "Coroners have to leave the teeth of men they find dead in alleys or ditches on their doorsteps or windowsills. As a signal. For him. People that die in the between places, in roads and switchyards. Those belong to Mr. Shivers."

"You believe it?"

"No." Then he considered it. "Though by now I'm willing to believe a lot of crazy shit I wouldn't have thought twice about before."

They sat together, not saying anything.

"Sometimes I wonder," said Connelly. "I wonder what he sees when he opens his eyes in the morning. If he's looking at the same place I'm looking at. Or if he sees something else."

"He's not a ghost," Lottie said. "You said so yourself."

"I did. I still believe it. When I first saw him, he was scared. Did I tell you that?"

"No."

"He was. When he...When he first saw my daughter. He was scared. I was with her. Just walking her to school as any father would, but she was at that age where, you know, she wanted to show she was on her own, so I let her walk ahead of me. And as she did I saw him on the other side of the street. Pale fella who looked at the world like it didn't matter an inch to him, like he owned it, with a scarred face and a mouth that stretched back to his jaw. He looked at her and I saw his face go all hungry and then he looked all scared."

"Scared of what?"

Connelly thought about it. "Scared of me, I think," he said.

"Why would he be scared of you?"

"I don't know. He looked at me and just was."

"He looked scared of you just the other day, too."

"I know. Don't know why, though."

"What was she like? Your daughter?"

"Like her mother. Which was good. She had blonde hair and she was smart. Smart as hell. When she was five she could name every bird in our garden. Said they danced for her, danced when I wasn't looking. Maybe they did. I don't know."

"Where's her mother?"

"Back home in Tennessee."

"She let you go?"

"Yeah. I wasn't even sure if we were married anymore. Not really. One day it was like two strangers stole our lives and we didn't do anything more than walk through the house. I said I was going to put things right. I was going to go out and find that man and make things right."

"Did she understand?"

"I don't know. I don't think so."

They sat in silence for a while.

Lottie said, "What time do you think it is?"

Connelly shrugged.

"I think I'll follow Hammond's idea. I'm tired. You should think about it, too. You look dog-tired."

"It's the dust. That's all."

"If you say so." And she left.

Connelly waited for her to be far away. He reached into his pocket and took out his wallet. He opened it and eased his fingers in and took out a tiny folded-up piece of paper, shiny with age and wear. He unfolded it. In some places it was worn until it was like cloth. On it was a charcoal drawing, done with some skill but not much. A picture of a girl's face, smiling and laughing.

He had paid a man at the fair to do her portrait. Hung it up in the living room later. Then when that life was over and he left, it had been the only thing he had taken. It was the only valuable possession he owned and the only thing that brought him to his feet in the morning and kept him walking in the day.

He tried to imbue it with color. Tried to use his imagination to project the things the drawing missed. Her crooked smile. Kitten's teeth. Her hate of the rain and love of the wind. And her eyes were green. He remembered that.

"Your eyes were green," he told the picture. "Green. They were green."

He looked at it, letting time pass in silence, then folded it up and put it back in his wallet. Then he just sat.

CHAPTER TEN

The next morning the wind died and though the dust still hung in the air they ventured out. They walked about through the town but they could not see anyone through the clay haze. None of them went to the house the scarred man had stayed in, nor did anyone suggest doing so.

They buried Ernie twenty paces from the dried river beneath the oak. They wrapped him in one of the blankets and covered him with layers of stone and earth and Jake tried to say something but could not. Pike stood at the head of the grave and said, "Lord, we lay this man to rest, fallen in the road that You have set for him that leads to glory. And in his trials and efforts to follow this road surely he has moved on to better worlds than these. His death was cruel but his life was righteous and we shall remember him as one of Your warriors. His memory shall stir us forward on the path and so he shall live forever as we try to achieve Your works. Amen."

"Amen," said Roonie.

The others muttered their own thanks. Jake stared at the rocks and did not move for the better part of an hour, even when called.

They walked farther into the hills in the direction the scarred man had gone. They were starving for meat as they had eaten nothing but a shared handful of beans and corn-meal in the past days. Roosevelt took his gun and found a nest of rabbits and tried to shoot some. He missed several times, stirring them up.

Lottie said, "Here. Let me see it."

He looked at her doubtfully.

"Let me see it. I've shot before," she said.

"So have I."

"Let me see it, Roosevelt."

He gave it to her. She took it and they sat for a while, watching, and then she picked up the gun and aimed carefully. They could not see what she was pointing it at. Without warning she fired, surprising everyone but Lottie, and she got to her feet and walked into the brush. There they found a mewling coney, bullet drilled into its side. She approached it, uncertain, and Pike strode forward and took it and broke its neck.

"That was well done," he said.

"I should have killed it in one shot."

"It's killed, either way," he said.

They cooked it and one other she managed to get and ate them with wild spring onions. They camped underneath the runny red sky and when they woke Pike said, "We have a decision to make. We've lost him. We've lost the scarred man. But we know the direction he was going and we know he could not be going far. Who knows this area?"

"I know a little," said Roonie.

"What would you say?"

"About what."

"About where he's gone, of course."

"Oh, I don't know. Could be a ways, could be a lot of places. Nearest town is some fourteen miles, I'd say."

"He'd want to move fast," said Connelly.

"And why's that?" Pike asked.

"He knows we're on to him now. He knows how close we are."

"So?"

"He likes to ride the rails. Where's the nearest freightyard, Roonie?"

"Ferguson," he said. "Straight north of here. Lots of cattle cars through there."

"Then that's where he'll be," said Connelly. "Dollars to pesos."

They nodded. "I see sense in that," Hammond said.

"We're agreed?" said Pike. "We keep together and keep moving, make for Ferguson?"

"It's our best shot," said Monk.

Jake frowned and rubbed his hair. "I don't like it."

"Why not?" said Lottie.

"Just don't. I don't... I don't..." He sniffed and looked over his shoulder to where his brother's grave was.

"We have to move," said Pike.

Jake shook his head.

"We've eaten," said Pike. "We'll search the town for what we can carry and what we need. Probably not going to be much, it was stripped clean. At first light we'll try and close some of this distance."

"Fair enough," Roosevelt said.

*   *   *

Connelly awoke to the pale dawn the next day. Just barely morning. Somewhere birds wheeled through the cold skies, whistling mournfully to one another. He sat up and looked and saw Jake's bedding deserted. He reached out and prodded Hammond.

Hammond rubbed at his eyes. "What?" he asked.

Connelly nodded at Jake's empty place. Hammond sat up. The two of them stood, looked at each other, then began searching the nearby area.

Somehow Connelly knew where he would be. He went down to where the dry creek ran and began walking along its side. He spotted him sitting on a large red rock, his form hunched and drunkenly leaning. Connelly approached slowly.

It had not been done neatly. The thin slice of obsidian had been a good tool but Jake had not known where the arteries would be and so had ravaged his upper arms and wrists. His lap was red and a pool spread from his crotch and ran down the face of the rock like he had shat or urinated blood. He was cross-legged and his arms were up against his belly like he was carrying some tiny precious package, like a child.

He was facing east. He had wanted to see the dawn. Perhaps he had.

They stood looking at Jake. No one spoke. Roonie began sobbing, small, weak animal noises. Lottie took him and held him and he buried his face in her neck.

"Despair is the greatest sin," said Pike.

"Go to hell," said Monk. "He had just lost his brother."

"All the more reason not to give up."

"What do we do?" said Roosevelt.

"Burial will have to be quick," said Pike. "If we give him one."

"We will," Lottie said savagely.

"Then we will."

"We should bury him with his brother."

"If you want to carry him the mile back to that place then by all means, do so," said Pike. "But we're limited by time and by distance. If we're going to do this it'll have to be quick and close."

It was a shoddy job. Not much more than a shallow hole in the ground. They piled stones upon it until it was a malformed cairn and made a cross out of timber and hammered it into the ground.

"Do we say anything?" said Roonie.

"What is there to say?" asked Hammond.

They did not answer. They took off their caps and held them before them and bowed their heads. Then they shouldered their grips and began their way to the freightyard.

CHAPTER ELEVEN

They came upon the trains nearly a day later. The filthy metal webbing spread out before them on the plain, smoke and ash rising in columns, gray trains milling and laboring forward like a nest full of snakes.

It did not take long to find someone. Find water, Roosevelt told them, and you will find other hobos. He was right. Near a small pond to the west they found a ragtag shack and a handful of men wallowing in soiled beddings. The smell of drink poured off them in cascades. Pike strode up to them and they scattered at first but then relaxed. When he asked of the scarred man they said, "Sure, sure. We know him. Came through here about three days ago."

"Three? You're sure?"

"Yep," said one man who seemed half-sensible. His face was long and he wore a cheap cap and a long overcoat. "He come through, asked when the next train into New Mexico would be running."

"Christ," said Roosevelt. "New Mexico? You're sure?"

"Yes. I sure am. You fellas got any money?"

"Not much," said Hammond. "You're sure it was him? Scarred on the cheeks?"

"I said it was, didn't I?"

"Did he say anything?"

"You got any money?" he said.

"We don't have much money."

He spat. "Then maybe you dumbasses should stop bothering a guy, huh? Get out of here. I'm sick of looking at you."

Pike grabbed him by the collar and shook him. "Shut your filthy mouth," he said to him, "unless I ask you to open it. Where in New Mexico? Where?"

"Jesus!" cried the man. "Some poor-ass town! Vuegas, I think! Let me go!"

"When did he leave?"

"The hell with you! I'll kill you, you old bastard!"

Pike struck him in the stomach. Hammond and Monk moved forward to face down the other hobos who were getting up.

"When did he leave?"

The man coughed and spittle hung from his mouth. "Yesterday," he gasped. "Just yesterday."

"Anyone know when the next train is running out?" shouted Monk to the other vagrants.

"Why you being so mean to old Bevis?" croaked one of the hobos. "He ain't done nothing to you."

"Because he has bad manners," said Hammond. "When's the next train out?"

"Two days. Just two days. You fellas don't got to be so mean about it," he mourned. Connelly saw he was weeping like an infant.

"Why couldn't you all just say so?" said Connelly as Pike dropped his man. "Why?"

"Because fuck you, that's why," the man gasped. He wiped his mouth and glowered at them. "I'll cut your throats. All of you dumb sons of bitches, I'll cut your throats."

Connelly looked at him and followed the others away.

That night Connelly could not sleep. Each time he shut his eyes he would see the shape of Ernie's shrouded body lying not far away from him, spots of red and brown seeping through and soaking into the patchwork of the sheet. Sometimes beyond it another person was sitting on the ground, leaning madly and painted red, arms clutched at their sides.

Finally Connelly gave in and sat up. He looked at the others lying around him, their chests gently rising and falling in sleep. Then he saw one figure standing far away, a small fire held in its fingers. It looked at him and held a finger to its lips and he blinked and realized it was Pike.

Connelly stood as quietly as he could and walked over to the old man. He was standing far out in the brush, watching the sleeping party, a glowing ember from the fire in his hand. He blew on it until it turned into a hellish spark and then he held it to the end of a damp cigarette and took a drag.

"Can't sleep?" Pike asked.

"No."

"Hm. I can't either." He sighed. "If there's one thing I can't abide, it's damp tobacco," he said out of the side of his mouth.

Each time he puffed his gray-black teeth would flash between his lips before being lost behind a fog of foul smoke.

"How'd it get wet?" asked Connelly.

"Roonie stored it next to his canteen. The man's an idiot."

"He's a bit off, yeah."

"He's an idiot," Pike said again. When he was satisfied with his dogend he lowered the ember and studied their party again. "Tell me, Mr. Connelly. What do you think of these new additions?"

"Think of them?"

"Yes."

"I think they're all right."

"Do you?"

"Well, yeah. I mean, they been roughed up a fair amount last few days. So have we, though. But then we never had anyone die on us."

"No," said Pike. "I suppose that's the true test of man, isn't it. If his beliefs quake in the face of death. If they do, does he really believe in them?"

"We've all seen killing," said Connelly. "Otherwise we wouldn't be here."

"Yes. But there's a difference between seeing killing and taking part in it." He shook his head, eyes not moving, face still faintly lit by the glow in his hand.

"You don't like them," said Connelly.

"I don't trust them."

"Why not?"

Pike turned the ember over in his hands thoughtfully, his skin never touching the glowing point. "Men," he said, disgusted. "They are such weak things. Do you know when I first saw death? Do you?"

"No."

"When I was nine. I saw my brother, kicked by a mule. He was two years older than me. Fooling about in the pen. My mother insisted on an open casket, saying we had to see his face. He had little of it left, though. I remember that." Pike turned to look at Connelly. "Do you know why he died?"

Connelly shrugged.

"Because he was weak," said Pike. "Because he was a fool. I know what you think now, though. I do. You think, surely the boy was twelve, and so cannot be blamed for his death? But I was twelve once as well. And I lived. What difference is there between me and him? Either a degree of stupidity, or perhaps those that live on are touched with the blessing of God. I think it may be both. We are all His soldiers, you see. I believe He can save us at any time. If we falter and fall it is of our own doing, none other's."

"You think so?"

"Yes." Pike shook his head again. "Mankind. Mankind is feeble. It is given to lust and hunger and greed. To cowardice. I have seen it in my years of traveling among them. Even when I preached to my flock, I hated them also. For they would weep or tremble, or most often simply forget my preachings mere moments later. Sometimes I sought them out, to see if they had listened. And I found them, then. In their moments of weakness. In their desires of flesh. Soft and senseless. When I found these things I did not let them forget me. No sir. No, I did not."

He spat on the ground. "I know now that my years of preaching were wasted on them. They were not worthy of the wisdom I had to give. But with the arrival of these new people . . . I worry. I worry that I have forgotten how weak men can be. That they may falter when we need them most. I say this to you, Mr. Connelly, because I know we are somewhat alike. You are strong. And I do not mean you are strong in arm, though I can clearly see you are. But in spirit. You are stronger than this new band. Stronger, perhaps, than Hammond or Roosevelt. Maybe stronger than me."

"I don't know that," said Connelly.

"No. But I worry for you. We are doing the Lord's work here. I know this. You and I are great tools in His plan. Do not weaken. We must stay forever sharp. Forever hard. Remember." Then Pike dropped the ember and crushed it into the dirt with the toe of his shoe. It smoked and sputtered and there was the scent of burning leather. Then he strode back to the fire and lay down.

Connelly watched him for a while longer. Within moments the old man was asleep and slumbering gently. Connelly waited and then returned to his bedding, but sleep still did not come.

They spent the next days in the hobo jungle outside the freightyard, waiting. They were joined by migrants from all over the country, men young and old, desperate and excited. Some were mere children, others young families. Some clung to the idea of travel as their only salvation. The young ones smiled through their hunger and dreamed only of biting the horizon, of the great iron machines eating up earth beneath their wheels, and of freedom.

Some in the camp said this was a tough yard, and Connelly listened. The line he and the rest were going to flip was rumored to be hot, hard bulls with no tolerance for hobos.

They spoke of men dragged off and beaten in the woods, whispered of being pushed beneath the cars and being bitten in half by the wheels. Others dismissed it as rumor. All agreed they would rob you, though. It was common for the bulls to herd men off and line them up and take every penny they had. Everyone who was a passenger on the line paid, the bulls would say. Sometimes they paid regular fare. Sometimes they paid more.

"I remember one time when a railroad man dragged us all off the train," said one old man. "Had a gun and a stick. Told us the fare to ride was half of whatever we had on us. Me, I didn't care, I barely had a buck, but this one poor bastard had been working day in and day out and had near to fifty. Damn railroad man was lucky that day. Took the money smiling, told us to clear out or he'd toss us in the clink. Laughed as we ran away. I wanted to kill him. Still do."

"One time there was too many," said a grinning man. "We was all over the train like crows on a telegraph line. The conductor took one look at us and sighed and waved the train on ahead. We cheered him as we sped by and I think he got a kick out of it."

Still, you gambled each time you stepped on the rail, they all knew. It was dangerous enough without railroad men kicking you off. The churning machinery would be happy enough to eat an arm or a leg or all of you, should you foul up your mount. Greasing the rails, they called it.

Connelly had been lucky and knew it. He had sewn a few dollars into the cuffs of his pants in case he ever needed to bribe his way out, but he had never been hurt and had been caught only once, when he was hiding in a car carrying piping. He had managed to stuff himself inside one and ride in something like peace, arms and legs crushed into the tube. Then everything had lit up and a man had been crouching at the front of the pipe, flashlight in hand. He had looked at Connelly for a great while, face invisible behind the light, and Connelly had frozen in fear. Then the light had clicked off and in the dark Connelly could make out a sad and sympathetic eye at the end of the tunnel. The man had thoughtfully tapped the flashlight against his leg, then stood and walked away. When the train had slowed, Connelly had crawled out and jumped off and had not looked back.

He never knew why the man had spared him, or even who he was. He told this story to Roosevelt.

"He was soft, that's what he was," said Roosevelt. "Men like that are few and far between, and getting fewer. You want to see something?"

"Sure."

Roosevelt led him out to the woods where the track was clear. A solid line of trees had been chopped down and uprooted, carving a path thirty yards across or so. It was clean and even like a man-made hallway and the rails slid through them like a ship through a canal.

"We're not going to hop one, are we?" asked Connelly.

Roosevelt laughed. "What are you, nuts? I just want you to come here and see." He knelt by the tracks and reached out and touched them. Parts of them were rusty red and other parts shone bright from where the train wheels had rubbed them clean.

"See this?" he asked.

Connelly nodded.

"You sure? I mean, you ever really looked?"

He shrugged.

"These here are the bones of this country. Know how many folks died doing this?"

"No."

"More than a hundred thousand. Maybe two hundred thousand. From when the first spike punctured the dirt to now, men died for this. To lay the bones of this country. Men are still dying. Right now. Did you know that?"

"No."

"They are. In the freightyards someone's had an accident. Someone's getting dragged, something's not loading right. A hobo like us is messing up his mount and getting chewed up like a doll in a cat's mouth. Greasing the rails. But, see, you got to sacrifice something. This is the first time in the history of anything that you been able to go from one ocean to another. One big...big architecture," finished Roosevelt. "And we're just a part, if that. You know, I had a bunch of different preacher-folk yell at me when I was a kid but I never had much of a head for religion or gods. But if it came right to it, why, I'd say train'd be something like a god. It's a god to plenty of us. Brings work, brings travel. Brings the future and it brings our loved ones. And it brings death. A lot of it, too. Maybe that's part of it. Maybe you got to feed it. Feed it a little more than coal."

Roosevelt stood up and brushed his hands off. His eyes followed the track, carving its wide alley through the woods. "That's how you know you believe something," he said. "If you wound up dying for it and thought, well, that's okay."

A thought wormed its way into Connelly's head. He tried to understand what it was asking but at first he didn't have the means. He hammered it out as best he could and said, "Roosevelt?"

"Yeah?"

"Would you kill for the trains?"

"What?"

"Let's say if a certain someone didn't die then one whole line would wind up breaking down or never getting built. So you had to be the guy to do him in. Would you do that?"

Roosevelt sucked his lip into his mouth and leaned on one foot. His brows drew close together and then he licked his teeth and blew a streamer of snot from one nostril. "God-damn, that's a crazy question," he said. "It's getting dark. Let's head back to the others."

Roosevelt led the way, following the path of the rails, but he did not look at them again.

CHAPTER TWELVE

On the night before their train left they resolved to get as much rest as they could. As sunset faded into evening the temperature began to drop. Fires were started here and there, people walking from campsite to campsite carrying envoys of burning brush. The air filled with the acidic haze of woodsmoke and people clapped rags and blankets around their shoulders until they resembled wandering mounds of offal, passing one another in the smoky night.

Connelly left Pike and the others and ventured out until the air was clear. He turned and looked back and saw the valley's face dotted with dancing sparks, a small sea of lonely light clutching the curve of the land. He listened to the coughs and the shouts, watched vague shadows toil around the shacks. It was a city of refuges, but refuge from what? He could think of no answer except the world itself.

He took his canteen from his pocket and sipped it to cool his burning throat. As he did a voice below croaked, "What you drinking?"

He started and looked around for the speaker. A man was lying on the ground not more than ten feet from him, hands behind his head.

"Just water," said Connelly.

The man scoffed. "Ain't worth it. I can't sleep a wink in a Hoover if I don't have some liquor in my guts. I need to marinade my head for a whiles before I can shut my eyes. You come to get away from the smoke?"

"Yeah."

"Cold nights does that. Nothing but green wood around." He sat up and grinned at Connelly. His eyes were red as plums and fine blossoms of burst veins circled his nose and cheeks. Connelly saw he had lost a hand and one of his feet was mangled beyond recognition. The cripple stuck out his good hand and said, "Name's Korsher. I'd shake with the other but I don't know where it is."

Connelly shook his hand.

"Where you headed?" the man asked.

"New Mexico," said Connelly.

"Hell. Who isn't? That or California, it seems."

"You going anywhere?"

"Son, I do my best to go nowhere at all at top speed. And that's what I'm doing right now."

Connelly took a step closer. "How did you . . ."

"Lose my hand?"

"Well. Yeah."

"Got et up by a train. Broked my foot too. It was something else."

"I bet."

"It was a long time ago."

"How do you get around?" Connelly asked.

"Slowly. But this helps," he said, and tapped a length of ash tree he had fashioned into a crutch. "I don't mind it so much. What's your name?"

"Connelly."

"Hm. Here. Sit you on down next to me."

Connelly did. Korsher absentmindedly reached into his pocket and took out a small ceramic flask, then offered it to Connelly.

"Take you a sip of that," he said.

Connelly opened it and smelled it first. It reeked enough to make his eyes water. Wood alcohol, perhaps. He pretended to take a sip and coughed.

"That'll put a lot more kick in you than water," said Korsher, and he laughed drunkenly. "Makes the ground a lot softer. Makes the night quieter and thinking easier."

"I'll say," Connelly said, and handed it back.

Korsher lay back down and looked at the sky. He unstoppered his flask, sipped and sighed, breath whistling between his teeth. "Oh, well. It's nice to get out from the Hoover. This is all right, ain't it?"

"I guess."

"You guess? That all?"

Connelly shrugged.

"No. No, I think I'm doing just fine now," said Korsher. "You got to say that every once in a while. I mean, sure, I'm hungry and I don't know where the hell I am, but I mean, just look," he said, and waved above.

Connelly looked. The moon sat high in the sky, a luminescent and muddy yellow. Webs of stars stretched out behind it, falling in a veil to the faint line of the earth.

"That's free right there," said Korsher. "I couldn't see any such thing in the city. Too much light."

"Yeah."

They sat in silence listening to the cicadas and crickets singing somewhere in the brush. Korsher smacked his lips and said, "My daddy once said the moon was a bone."

"Oh?"

"Yeah. Looks kind of like a bone, don't it?"

"I suppose. I don't know what kind of bone, though."

"Hell, I don't either, I'm no kind of doctor. My pa said it was the bone of whoever made this here earth. Said he chopped and beat stone all day, just working away, and when he was done he just plumb dropped dead."

"How'd it get out there, then?"

"Devil," said Korsher simply.

"The devil?"

"Yeah. Devil came on by, picked it up, all laughing, and gave it a toss. Now it's stuck out there for all to see." He took a drink from his flask again and made a face, then drank again. "Like a kid throwing rocks at an empty house, yes sir. You believe in the devil?"

"I don't know. Maybe."

"I do. I certainly do. My daddy talked about him all the time. You couldn't tangle with such a thing, not by a long shot. He said the world was littered with bones of men who'd try and get the devil. Try and sneak up on him and kill him, you know? But the devil was too smart for them. He'd act all innocent and lead them into a trap. Wind up getting them instead. Said it'd been going on since forever."

"Oh. That's something."

"He said when God was asleep the devil come down here and rearranged things," slurred Korsher. "Then God went on back and breathed a spirit into man and set us loose, not knowing any better. Meant to give us the world but gave us hardship instead, devil just cackling away. You believe that?"

"I could."

Korsher was quiet for a while. Then he said, "You know what?"

"No. What?"

"I believe I may have saw him the other night."

"Seen who?"

"The devil."

Connelly waited. Then he said, "You did?"

"Yeah," he said softly. "I think I did."

"What makes you say that?"

"'Cause he looked just like my daddy said he would."

"What did your daddy say?"

"Said he was a great, tall man in a great black cloak. So tall he could walk through a cornfield and his knuckles wouldn't scrape a single ear. Said he had eyes like stars, and that every inch of him was scarred from where the angels whipped him raw."

Connelly sat forward. "What?"

"Hm?"

"What did you say? Just now? About the scars?"

"Oh. I said the devil was scarred from where the angels had whupped him."

"Wh-what was he doing?"

"When? Last night?"

"Yeah."

"Just...I don't know, just walking by. I saw him pass through the town and go down into the yard. I thought I had gone nuts. Nearly...Well, I nearly pissed myself. People got out of his way like Moses and the sea. It was like just him being there made them want to run. I couldn't get away," he said softly. "Because of my leg. So I sat and he passed by just inches away and I looked into his face and I wished I never had. Not ever. I didn't want to sleep in the camp after that. He'd know where I was, see, and come and get me."

Connelly's mind reeled. He struggled to control it. "And before that? The part about...about all those men who'd chased him?"

"What about it?"

"What did you say happened to them?"

Korsher looked at him. "He killed every single one of them," he said. "Tricked them. My father said it'd been going on since before men could speak."

Connelly jumped to his feet. "You stay there," he said. "You just stay right there, you hear?"

"Well, sure, where the hell else am I gonna go?"

Connelly sprinted down to the camp, dodged between shanties and broken-down cars. He found Pike and the others crouched in the shadow of a tent. He grabbed Pike and said, "Come with me."

"What? Why?" said Pike.

"Just come on."

"Well, hell," said Monk, and stood.

"N-No," said Connelly. "Just Pike. I just want him to hear this. Just at first."

"Why?" said Monk, suspicious.

"I don't...I don't know. I just want to see what someone else thinks."

Connelly led Pike out to where Korsher lay. The cripple sat up again and said, "Who's that?"

"Tell him what you told me," said Connelly.

"Why should I?"

"Just shut up and tell him what you said."

Korsher frowned but went through it again, stumbling through his story. He was deep in a drunken stupor now and Connelly had to prod him along. Pike watched the cripple with flat eyes and did not speak. When Korsher finished Pike was quiet for a long time and said, "That's quite an interesting story, Mr. Korsher. I thank you for telling it to me."

"Why the hell are you folks so fired up over this anyway?" said Korsher. "It upsets a fella, you know." He lay back and drank more.

"My colleague here is somewhat...superstitious. I'm sorry if he upset you."

"Didn't upset shit. Just...just crazy is all."

"Yes, well. Good night, Mr. Korsher," said Pike, and tipped his hat. "Stay safe."

Korsher muttered something and Pike began to walk away. Connelly followed.

"Well?" Connelly said.

Pike kept moving and did not turn.

"Well?" said Connelly again, and he reached out and grabbed Pike's shoulder.

Pike spun around, angry. "Well, what?"

"Well, what do you make of that?"

"What do I make of it? What do I make of it? You mean, what do I make of a...a drunken cripple so besotted with moonshine he can barely sit up? What do I make of a bunch of silly ghost stories his *father* used to tell him to scare him? What do I make of that, is that what you're asking?"

"Yeah. Yeah, I'm asking you that."

"I think it's nothing. I think you dragged me out here to listen to idiocy." He began walking away.

"But what if it's real," said Connelly quietly.

Pike stopped. Then he turned and said, "Are you being serious with me, Mr. Connelly? You actually think this man may be the . . . what, the devil?"

Connelly shrugged.

"You know there's ghost stories about him. You know that and you didn't believe them. Just stories."

"Not like this. Not like what's going on now. He said other men had chased the scarred man. Said he'd trapped them. Killed them."

"And? Could it be that he spread those stories himself, fearing for his life? Could it be just mere chance? You caught the stink of that man, you know he could barely see you, let alone Shivers."

"This has happened before," said Connelly. "It's been going on since forever, he said."

"You don't know that."

"But what if it has?"

"But what? Would that change anything?"

Connelly hesitated. "It might."

"No. It wouldn't. We would still be doing the same. And besides . . . Even if it has, Lottie says the shiver-man is *afraid* of you," said Pike, his eyes shining. "Is that so?"

Connelly looked away.

"Yes," said Pike. "So if it's happened before then things

are different this time. Oh, yes. But I doubt the whole thing. I doubt it very much." He snorted and spat. "This is child's foolishness. We have business to do. Come back to the camp and rest."

Pike walked back toward the little sea of fires. Connelly watched him, then looked up at the moon. After a few minutes he left.

They awoke on the morning of their departure and traded for scraps among the other freight rats. They held stilted conversations over bogwater ditches and flaming oil cans and as the sun reached the top of the sky they moved out to where the train would pass through. They hid in the brush and readied their grips and watched for the numbers on the engines. Theirs was the second. They bolted out, sprinting through the grit and smoke, and managed to climb up onto one of the last few cars. They walked down its edge like tightrope walkers, jimmied open an empty grain car, then stowed themselves away in the musty dark.

They stayed as quiet as they could. Roonie said softly, "I once heard of a few 'bos that got caught in an empty grain car. The railroad man found out about it and filled it with grain anyways, laughing. They drowned in it."

"I heard the same damn thing, only it was a cattle car," said Hammond. "They loaded the cattle in and the hobos were crushed. It's crap. No one does that. Not really."

"No?" said Roonie.

"No. If they want anything they want your money. Not your blood."

"The train is still a dangerous mistress," said Pike.

Roosevelt grinned. "All mistresses is dangerous. 'Specially when they find out they're just mistresses and not the main event."

Pike shook his head, bemoaning the state of the world.

Monk took out a pack of cards. They took turns playing gin rummy and five-card draw for corn kernels they found. Connelly watched and began to nod in sleep in his corner, lulled by the throb of the wheels. As he drifted off he heard a distant thump and snapped awake.

He held a hand up for silence. Roonie began to speak, but Lottie grabbed him. Connelly pointed up above them, then cupped his ear. They listened carefully.

Footfalls. Someone was walking over the car before them. Several people, from the sound of it.

Then they heard voices, just barely audible over the sound of the wheels and the wind.

"...not seen anything yet," said one voice.

"We will."

"We been over most of this train careful as fuck all. How are you so sure?"

"He said they'd be here. I believe him."

"And how is *he* so sure?"

"What? Are you *doubting* him? Is that it?"

"N-No," said the voice, frightened. "I'm just wonderin'..."

"Well, wonderin' is a bad idea with him."

"I-I know. But still..."

"Listen, if they're following him there's only one engine they'd take, that's why, and it's *this* engine," said the other voice. "So shut up and do your job. Come on. Help me over this gap."

Scuffling sounds from the corner of the roof. The boards

above shuddered and seemed to bend, sending spirals of dust down among them. There were grunts, and then the weight increased.

"Here, is this one empty or full?" said the voice.

"Don't know. Probably empty. Check it to be sure."

They looked at one another. Pike leapt to his feet as silently as he could and grabbed the handle of the trapdoor in the roof and held on. There were more footfalls from above, and then grunts as someone pulled.

"It's locked."

"How do you know?"

"'Cause it ain't coming up. Must be full, then."

"That don't mean...Wait."

"What?"

"*Shh!*" said the other voice.

Drops of sweat ran down Pike's face as he hung from the ceiling. Connelly moved to look through the cracks in the ceiling and he saw something iron black and shining, something in a man's hand.

He waved frantically at Pike. Pike looked at him, confused, and Connelly made the motion of cocking a gun and waved again.

Pike's eyes shot wide and he dove away, crashing into the corner.

"Bastards!" shouted one of the voices. "They're in there!"

For a moment there was nothing. Then the boom of a shotgun crashed through the car and a shaft of sunlight ripped into the dark, a gaping hole right where Pike had been hanging. Splinters of wood flew like chaff and Connelly saw Monk roll away, his head dotted with blood. Roosevelt dove for cover as well, his pack falling to the ground.

"Jesus Christ!" shouted Monk.

Connelly staggered to the door and began trying to undo the wire they had used to shut it. Harsh pistol snaps rang out and more holes began appearing in the ceiling. Something cracked by Connelly's head. Roonie cried out, clutching his forearm.

"Out of the way!" Pike roared. "Out of the fucking way!"

"Shoot!" Connelly heard himself say. "For God's sake, someone shoot back!"

The shotgun roared again, this time clearly aimed at Connelly's voice. He felt splinters fly and a rush of air behind his back as slugs and buckshot bit through wood. It was like a hot tidal wave had passed him by.

"The gun!" shouted Hammond. "Rosie, your gun!"

Roosevelt came to life, crawling forward on the floor and grabbing his satchel, trembling hands digging through it. Someone laughed harshly above. There was a click as some deadly piece of machinery slid home, then a new wave of gunfire. Everyone sought cover again as the shots rent holes in the boxcar and the air. Roosevelt tumbled to the corner again and the gun slipped out and spun across the floor.

Connelly looked back up and saw the pistol beside Lottie. She gaped at it in terror, uncomprehending.

"Lottie!" he screamed. "For God's sake, Lottie, do something!"

She looked at him, then again at the pistol. She fumbled forward and grabbed it. Connelly's fingers sought the tangle of wire again.

"Mother*fuckers*," muttered one of the men above. There were so many holes in the roof Connelly could see them clearly now. Pistol round casings rained through the ceiling, twinkling and golden. Lottie stared at the pistol in her hands, then looked up uncertainly.

"Fuck's sake, Lottie, shoot! Shoot!" shouted Hammond.

She shuddered, then lifted the pistol and began firing through the roof, careful, measured shots in spite of her fear, one, two, three. Someone bellowed in pain up above and there was a crash as the men tried to move out of the way and still stay on top.

The last bit of wire came undone and the car door slid open. Connelly recoiled from the sting of the smoke, then braced himself and vaulted up and out, looking over the top of the car.

Two men were lying on the roof of the car, one injured and holding the inside of his leg, near the crotch. The injured one held a .38 in his free hand, the other clamped over the spreading stain on his leg. The other man had a shotgun and was trying to load another two shells. He looked up and saw Connelly and tried to snap the shotgun shut and butt him in the face. Connelly reacted faster, reaching forward and grabbing the man's ankle to throw him from the train. He pulled and felt the man slide forward, the man's face changing from snarling rage to shock. Connelly's shoulder strained to the point of popping and he felt Hammond grab his waist to brace him against the door. The corner of the boxcar dug into his belly as he dangled on the side of the car and someone somewhere screamed.

Connelly gritted his teeth and pulled again, harder. The gunman slid forward more and he shouted, "No! No!" as his fingers tried to find purchase somewhere, the nails digging into the splintered wood as the other hand stupidly held on to the shotgun. The corner of the boxcar bit into Connelly's ribs, creaking and cracking. The man with the .38 looked at Connelly, his eyes woozy. His hand shook but he lifted the big pistol and waved it at Connelly's face. Connelly kept pulling, not thinking, and when the gunshots cracked through the sound of the train he was sure he was dead.

He opened his eyes and saw the side of the man's belly erupt. Red shining ropes of blood leapt up in the air like fireworks and arced back down. More holes punched up through the roof and Connelly heard Lottie cry out from below. The wounded man shivered and rolled as though trying to hold his entrails in and when his weight changed he tumbled off the roof of the car and out of sight.

Connelly pulled the remaining gunman toward the edge of the train. His shoulder screamed in raw pain and his teeth hurt from gritting them so hard but still he pulled. The man shrieked, his free foot kicking out at Connelly's face and striking him once, twice about the ear, opening up the rim of his eye, but Connelly barely felt it and instead waited for the moment when the man's center of gravity would reach its tipping point and then, and then...

The man's mouth opened in dull surprise. The shotgun clattered from his grip and was devoured by the wheels below. Connelly's arm was made of broken glass and barbed wire but the man was slipping over, screaming madly and slapping at Connelly, but Hammond held fast. The man's body began to move, pulled by wind and momentum and gravity. Connelly let go and saw the man twist as he dropped. He was struck by the next car and he flipped and tumbled and then there was a hideous flash of bright red blood as the wheels found something finally worth eating.

Someone screamed. Connelly did not know if it was his own

voice or the train's. Hammond pulled him in and he saw Lottie kneeling on the floor of the car, face to the sky and hands together almost in prayer. The sinister black gun was clutched in her fingers. Drizzled blood ran across one of her cheeks and she was saying, "Blood... There's blood on me. I think I hit him, Roonie, I think I... I think I..."

Roonie did not answer. He was squealing and trying to stop the flow from his arm. Monk was holding his face, picking out splinters of shrapnel and wood, wiping away the blood that welled up in his forehead like water from underground springs. Pike stood to his feet and the overwhelming violence of the train car seemed to focus around him.

"We need to get off!" he shouted. "We have to get off! The train's already slowing. Whoever sent them knows something's wrong or is coming to check. We have to get off!"

Connelly was trying to listen but everything was still screaming. He was, his attacker was, the guns were still going off and the train was still screeching, fingers still clawing over gray wood and the wheels churning below...

Pain again. His cheek. He looked up and saw Pike had slapped him.

"We need to get *off*," shouted Pike again.

Connelly nodded. "We need to get off," he mumbled.

"Come on."

They got to their feet, Hammond and Pike rounding them up. When they judged the train was slow enough they leapt onto the dry ground below, their bags falling around them. It was dangerous, still too fast, but they were forced to risk it. Monk sprained his ankle and Connelly knew he hurt himself falling but he couldn't tell where because everything hurt, all of him, face and arm and waist and knees.

"This way," said Pike's voice. "This way."

The sun was fading. They sped into the forest, limping underneath the leafless trees. Behind them the train was slowing to a stop and men were shouting to one another. The musk of dead leaves and old earth filled Connelly's nostrils. He wiped at his nose and found half his face was slick with blood.

"Come on," murmured Hammond. "Come on, Con. Come on."

They ran as far in as they could. Soon the sky overhead was choked out by trees and they could see only by the blades of dusklight that rained through the branches. Hammond said something about hearing dogs and Pike rebuked him harshly and dragged Lottie forward.

"We need to go as far as we can," he said as they ran. "We have to get away from the rail. There's bodies back there and they cause a fuss, yes sir, they do. I don't like it but I like not being one of them even more, and I don't plan to join them, so come on."

Hours passed. Maybe days. Connelly lurched from tree to tree. Soon he saw the shattered moon glaring through the woven branches. Hidden watchers observed their ragtag procession from the dead canopy above and made comment or warning. Soon the forest was alive with hoots and calls, snaps and whistles. The song spread through the treetops like wildfire. The sounds mixed together in Connelly's head and he turned aside to vomit beside a tree. The others watched him retch with worried faces. He said nothing as he rejoined them.

"...concussion, probably," said Lottie. "The guy nearly kicked his head off."

"What?" said Connelly, slurred. "What was...What was that?"

"Hush," said Lottie. "Just hush."

They found an old stream in the woods, no more than a trickle, but it had eroded through enough soil that they could use it as shelter. They camped on its banks and drank their fill but they had no food to eat and Pike would not risk a fire.

"The woods may be crawling with men for all we know," he said. "I don't think I'll give them any signals we're over here, no thanks."

"What in the hell makes you say that?" said Monk.

"Because that, back there, was a trap. Pure and simple," said Pike, slapping his arms to stay warm.

They looked at each other.

"Set by who?" said Hammond.

Pike thought, then looked at Connelly, lying barely conscious on the riverbank.

"We'll discuss this when...Well. We'll discuss this when we can all discuss this," he said. "Get some rest."

Things swam together for Connelly and thankfully went black.

CHAPTER THIRTEEN

Connelly awoke to a sharp, stabbing pain in his forehead and a rumbling ache everywhere else. He opened his eyes and saw Lottie was daubing his forehead.

"Mmm? What?" he said, still slurred.

"Just trying to clean you up," she said. "You need stitches. Probably. Hell, I don't know. Your forehead is a mess. Half your face is unrecognizable."

He felt his cheek. It was stiff and swollen and felt like rubber. Speaking was difficult. He lay back down and saw Pike standing on the ridge of the stream, leaning into his staff and staring out at the woods.

"He hasn't slept yet," said Lottie. "It's been almost a day. Everyone's slept but him. He hasn't even moved. You saved his life, you know."

"No. I didn't."

"Didn't know or didn't save his life?"

Connelly waved his hand, sick of conversation that wasn't yes or no.

Lottie gave him a brittle smile. "Sleep more," she said. "You got to."

"Fine," said Connelly, and then again, a whisper: "Fine."

They used cool mud and dry moss to stop their bleeding. In the wan starlight they looked medieval, wandering partisans wearing some diseased warpaint. Lottie bound Roonie's arm in a piece of Hammond's coat lining and he whimpered as she drew it tight. Connelly allowed her to do the same to him, bandaging the gash on his face. His arm was still useless and they made a sling of his coat but it pained him when they walked.

When they came under the cover of a passing cloud Pike judged they were ready and they ventured downstream in the inky night with hands held out like blind men. They stopped to rest in a nest formed of fallen trees and Pike and Hammond peered out through the cage of boughs around them. They saw nothing and went from one person to the next, silently touching them to tell them they were ready to continue on.

In this fashion they walked for nearly three miles, injured and starving in the blind night. Connelly wondered if it was possible to fall asleep in one world and wake up in another. He had slept on the train so perhaps this was some feverish nightmare, a dream-place where men killed and died for no reason he could see and each minute was spent in a starved, sightless silence, like animals far under the earth. Perhaps the moment of change had happened before then. Some other occasion when he fell asleep. Waking to the crimson sky of the drought.

Waking to his new, hellish Memphis, ruined and gutted by a grief caused in the space of a day, an hour, a second. It seemed then that the world was a terrible, wounded place whose revolutions were driven by panic and madness more than love or reason. A directionless freefall toward something, maybe toward nothing. He no longer knew.

That night as Connelly lay on the damp ground he wondered for the first time if there could ever be any return from this. He had considered the futility of it. Had considered wandering out and searching and never finding. And he had considered the law, the chance that his future might be confined to cement walls and damp stone floors and colorless monotony, should his quest succeed. Neither of those seemed very different than any alternative. To live with such a violation was the same in many ways.

But there was always a chance he could succeed, and go back. That things might return to what they were before, at least a little. Before his daughter was taken. He could go home, and though it would be a home without Molly it would be one he could live with. One that made sense.

Now a sliver of doubt worked its way into his mind. That life seemed very far away now. The farther he traveled the less he could recall what he hoped to return to.

He remembered what his wife had said before he left. Remembered sitting on the front porch, looking through the fog of the screen windows and watching tree limbs dance in the night wind, the streetlamps turning them into wicked fingers on the grass below. The warmth of a cup of coffee clutched to his belly. The gentle sigh of a placid evening in a city that was content. His mind was already slowed with whisky, his thoughts turgid and wordless. He did not know how long he had been sitting there.

He heard her walk down behind him but did not turn. Neither of them did anything for a long while.

Then, "I'm going to my mother's."

He turned to her. She was dressed nice. A yellow dress with white trim, full of springtime. Hair brushed and neat. But in her eyes there was a place where a fire had long gone out, and when she looked at him he felt the emptiness behind them. The empty place where yesterday had been.

"All right," he said.

"I'll be staying for a while."

"How long?"

"I don't know. Long enough. Maybe longer."

He nodded and turned back to the street.

"Don't you want to know why?" she asked

"Why what?"

"Why I'm leaving."

"All right. Why are you leaving?"

"Jesus, Marcus," she said, and leaned her head up against the glass of the front door.

"What?"

She shook her head. Grinding the veins of her forehead up against the door. "Do you know this is the first time we've talked in four days?"

"Four days?"

"Yes."

"That can't be right."

"It is."

"I've said things. I've said good night."

"No. You're always asleep before me. You've slept in the chair downstairs. Or out here. After drinking. I've slept in our bed, sometimes. But not usually. I sleep in the tub mostly."

"Why?"

"The smell. Of the bed. I can't stand it. I don't know why." She turned to face him, her back now up against the jamb. Her eyes trailed up to look into the ceiling. "It's all right."

"What is?"

"This. Mrs. Echols said they usually don't last."

"What don't last?"

"Marriages that lose a child."

Connelly stood up. He put down the coffee and walked to the screen door and crossed his arms and stood there.

"She didn't say it to me," she said. "I overheard. Overheard her at church."

"She's full of shit."

"Marcus."

"We'll be all right."

"Marcus. Marcus, we're not all right now. I don't see why we would get better anytime soon."

They were both quiet then. A truck came up the road and puttered by, its one-eyed headlight roving through the brush. They watched it leave and as the mutter of its tires died away the silence became more unbearable.

"You're leaving, aren't you?" she asked. "I can tell. You want to go out. To go after that man."

Connelly nodded.

"I know. I can see it. I can see it in you. It's eating you alive. That part. That part he took away from you, that part that was her. That empty part is just getting bigger. Eating you up."

"It isn't right," he said.

She shook her head. She moved to wipe away her tears but there were none.

"I can make it right," he said.

"How? By going out and killing him?"

"Yes."

"How will that make it right?"

"It'll make things make sense. I have to make them make sense. That shouldn't happen. If I fix that then I can come home again."

"You're home right now."

"No. I'm not. You know that." He turned to look at her. "Would you take me back?"

"What?"

"If I went out there and killed that man and came back, would you take me back?"

"Marcus..."

"I have to do it. I have to. I just want to know if there'll be anything left for me once it's done. If it ever gets done."

"I don't know. You can't make things right. This will never be right. Not really."

"It'll make things quiet. Make them bearable, then. Would you take me back then?"

"I don't know. I might. But, Marcus, if you go out there, if you leave your home and this place and me and take to the road like God knows many others have done now, I don't know who'll come back."

"I will."

"No. The man who goes out there and the man who comes back won't be the same. I don't think so. It depends on who comes back, Marcus."

"I will. The way I was before."

"You won't ever be the man from before. And I won't ever be the same, either. But I do know that there isn't anything here for us anymore, either. Every day we're here we bleed a little more. On the inside, in places we can't see. If you think that will stop that for you, stop whatever it is from dying inside you, then...then I can't hold it against you. I don't know if I can take you back after, but I can't hold it against you."

He bowed his head. "But there is a chance."

"Yes. There's a chance. There's always a chance."

"I hope things will be better," he said softly. "I hope I can love you again."

She looked away. "I hope so, too."

He shut his eyes. He heard her walking away and he began to say something after her but could not think of anything. Then he sat and thought.

Hours later he realized she was gone. He had not even seen her head toward the street. Had not even heard the car start. He imagined her fading into the night like some ghost, her dress a warm honey flame swallowed by the dusky shadows, traveling forward into the darkness with a hat on her head and her suitcase in her hand. Movements slow and dignified and normal. Like she was expecting something. Waiting for something to appear before her on the road.

Then he had walked back into the house. Every inch of it had been soaked in silence. He had stood there in the living room and known he stood in the belly of something once pregnant and full of promise. A future and a life violently aborted without even a cry to mark its passing from the world.

*   *   *

Dawn climbed in the distance and gave the gray land texture. They stopped again to scout. Hammond saw no pursuers but then he did not see much of anything; whatever forest they were in was a deep one. Roosevelt and Lottie foraged for food but Pike whispered an order not to use the gun. He would also not bother to set traps for they would not be staying long.

They returned later with mushrooms and roots they figured were good enough to eat. Pike inspected them, having some rudimentary knowledge of this, and they muddled a thin, watery broth of the ones he approved and sipped it gratefully, trying to ignore its gritty texture. They continued on until the trees came to an end and the stream turned into a river. They bathed and washed their wounds and their clothing, Lottie going downstream for decency's sake but not all that far as decency didn't have much to do with anything right now, she said. Connelly and Hammond watched her walk away, undoing her shawl and letting her hair spill out. They shared a look but said nothing.

Roosevelt had woven fishhooks into his coat lapel, each sharp prong carefully wrapped in paper to protect him. They made makeshift poles out of string and reeds and Monk managed to catch three of some kind of small trout. They gutted them and cooked them over an open fire and they had stew once more, but this time their bellies awoke to the fat and meat and for a while they were sated.

Lottie undid Roonie's bandage. It was ugly but she said it was healthy enough. Pike agreed. They both undid Connelly's and winced at the gash running down his eyebrow and temple.

"It'll scar," said Lottie.

"He still has the eye," said Pike. "You do, don't you?"

Connelly turned to look at the glimmering surface of the

river, and though the specks of light came through somewhat smeary he said he could still see fine.

"Good," said Pike. "Now we'll risk a fire. A real one, for warmth. And we'll talk."

"Back there," said Monk softly, "back there in the woods... You said that was a trap."

Pike nodded. "I did indeed."

"What'd you mean by that?"

He hesitated, idly drawing in the mud with a finger. "Well, you heard them back there, didn't you? Just a snatch of conversation, but it was enough. They had been sent. Sent by someone who we were following and didn't want us following anymore. Someone who knew we had to be on that train and that we'd be traveling illegally."

There was no sound but the running water. No one looked at one another.

"He's covering his trail," said Pike finally.

"Who?" asked Roonie.

"The shiver-man. The gray man, of course. They were helping him."

"Why would anyone agree to that?" asked Monk. "I-I can't imagine him... imagine him..."

"What?" Pike said. "Buying thugs?"

"No. I can't."

"It's a challenging thought, that I admit. We think of him as a monster. But others may just see a scarred man. We know what he is, they do not. They would just listen to the money in his pocket."

"Could be more to him," said Connelly, looking keenly at

Pike. "Could be he's used to being chased. Used to tricking the folks who chase him."

Pike returned his gaze, his face fierce and furious. "Yes. It *could* be. But there also *could* be countless stories he's told himself. It'd be wise to think before giving them credence. I hardly think clumsy men with shotguns are in league with all the terrors of the supernatural."

"So what does this mean?" said Lottie. "What does this have to do with us?"

"It means we can no longer use the rails," he said.

"That will cripple us," said Monk.

"Yes. Yes, it will," said Pike. "But it's better to be crippled than dead. We've killed two men on the railroad—"

"But they were trying to kill *us*!" Lottie said.

"That's true. We know that. We know that well and good. But will a lawman? Will the railroad man? For all we know the railroad man was in on it. And besides, who are we to trust? Who are we to be believed?"

"Americans," said Roonie defiantly. "American citizens."

"We are hobos," Pike said harshly. "Beggars. Vagrants. We have no town or state and we barely have a country. We operate outside of the law and the law knows that."

"I don't," said Hammond.

"Yes you do," Pike said. "You travel illegally on trains. You have intimidated men for help. And don't forget why all of us started this journey in the first place. Murder is usually illegal no matter where you go." He surveyed their faces in the firelight. "That's what we wish to do, isn't it? To murder?"

There was no sound but the crackling of flames. Connelly said, "Yes."

"Yes. You all've just tasted violence. You'll taste more, certainly. If you continue, that is."

Lottie covered her mouth with one hand.

"So what do we do?" said Roonie quietly.

"We keep going. We can find out where that train stopped and search for the gray man there."

"But he'll be miles away by then!" said Hammond.

"I've never let distance deter me," said Pike, and his voice was like ice. "It didn't at the start. It won't now. I'll walk until my legs are stiff and broken, that I'll do, amen."

He fixed his gaze on them, and, feeling its force, they nodded, one by one.

Connelly's thoughts strayed back to the few words they'd heard their attackers share. He couldn't help think that they were somehow familiar with the scarred man, which made him wonder if more than miles lay between them and their quarry.

"How many more rounds do you have, Roosevelt?" asked Connelly.

"Dozen or so," he said softly.

"I hope that'll be enough, if we need them," said Hammond.

"I hope so, too," said Pike. "Buying bullets gets a lot of attention. Attention we don't need."

Lottie shivered and wiped at her eyes. Roonie was rocking back and forth like a clockwork toy. The only ones who did not move were Pike, Hammond, and Connelly, who sat like they were made of stone.

"Well, then," said Hammond. "Well, then."

They then turned in for sleep, and, exhausted, slept soundly.

CHAPTER FOURTEEN

They awoke in the morning cold and hungry. They walked north and west, roughly in the direction they thought the train was headed. Roosevelt said the track curved west after a ways, but he did not know when. They trekked across dry brown fields and far, far to the west they saw the hint of mountains, mere bumps underneath the wide sky. Clouds seemed farther away than normal and sunlight fell in streaks and shafts, like rain.

"Big country," said Monk, and they agreed.

They came to a fence and realized they were on someone's land but saw no sign of livestock or owner. They climbed it and headed north and came to a road headed west and took up upon it. They saw no other travelers, no cars nor trucks. This path appeared to be one unused by the flood of migrants searching for better lives. It was an empty place and they passed through it silently, as its greatness seemed to eat words before they were even spoken.

Toward midday they saw cars pulled off the side of the road, big heaps of jalopies parked in a circle in a field. Pike slowed to a stop and Connelly and the others followed suit. Pike looked the cars over slowly, his bright, cold eyes watching each flicker of movement. Then he made a motion and they continued forward.

As they neared the vehicles they were spotted by a small dirty child sitting by the road. He got to his feet and stared at them. Then he ran back to the trucks. Four men came out and behind them five women. They watched Connelly and the others approach, their faces blank, their eyes thin.

Hammond came forward, smiling. "Good day!" he said.

One of the men nodded. " 'Day," he said.

"Sorry to be so forward, but you folks wouldn't have any food you'd be willing to trade, would you?"

The man examined them. "You boys 'bos?"

"I suppose you could say that, sir."

"Looks like you folks been on the losing side of a few beatings."

"That's so. We were trying to get up into Colorado. Headed west, like everyone else. We got tossed and robbed something fierce. Beat the hell out of a few of us."

"What line was it?" said another man.

Hammond told him.

"All the lines have gotten tougher," said the man. "My nephew tried to ride down to the city. He got tossed and they whupped the tar out of him."

"Sounds familiar," said Hammond with a smile.

The first man sighed, pushed his hat back, and scratched

his rangy red hair. "You folks wouldn't happen to know much about cars, would you?"

They looked at one another. Connelly said, "I know a little."

"Do you?"

He nodded.

"Well...We got one of these cars broke down," said the man. "Damn bastard sold us a lemon—"

"*Clark*," hissed one of the women in reprimand.

"Sorry. My apologies," said the man, "but I just knew he was doing it by how he smiled at us. I knew this thing would break down soon enough on the road. But we did it anyways. If you could get us back on the road, sir, well, we'd help you folks in any way we can."

"I could take a look, I suppose," said Connelly. "Which one is it?"

"That one yonder," said the man. He and Connelly started walking over to it. The man stuck his hand out. "Clark. Clark Hopkins. My wife back there is Missy."

They shook.

"Connelly."

The truck was hardly a truck anymore. Its bedding was made of slats of wood, with everything hanging from it that could hang—mattresses, lanterns, bags of produce, bits of string and wire, rope, and jugs of water. As Connelly walked to it the rest of the family emerged from the back of the cars. Three boys and a girl, all barely past toddlers, a young man almost a teen, and a girl younger than Hammond, he supposed, about twenty. He felt nervy with them watching him.

"Damn, I hate cars," said Clark, and glanced around to make sure his profanity had gone unnoticed. "Never used one before. I didn't know what I was doing. The others, my brother and my brothers-in-law, they know how to drive, but how its guts work, that's beyond us. I prefer mules, I got to say. You know how a mule works, what goes in, what comes out. Cars, well. That's a different story."

"Mighty young family to be traveling with," said Connelly.

"Don't I know it."

Connelly took off his coat and hat and rolled up his sleeves. His arm still twinged but at least it worked. "What happened?" he asked.

"Thing was going fine before. We cut off the main road, thought we'd take a direct road into New Mexico. We pulled off for the night and in the morning we couldn't get her started again."

Connelly wiped at his forehead and squatted to look below. Clark joined him, then the children did, then Pike and the rest joined him as well.

Connelly glanced at them, uncomfortable. "I'm going to need a little light," he said.

"Oh," said Clark. "Oh, sure."

The family shuffled backwards. Pike motioned and led his followers away to the side of the road. Connelly looked at the car and thought.

"Can you start her up?" he asked.

Clark's brother climbed in the cab and tried. Connelly listened to it turn over but never catch, nodded to himself, and popped the hood and lifted it up. He looked in, then made a circle in the air with his finger, signaling to try again. The engine wheezed and clicked and clanked but never caught. He reached in and began sorting through it, not pulling but touching carefully, remembering which parts of the engine

did what, like greeting old friends at a party. He was examining the carburetor when he noticed a small mop of brown hair
peeking over the side, and below it two brown eyes looking
into the hood with him. The eyes moved down and darted
about the workings of the car like their owner was trying to
sort out enemies. The looker noticed Connelly watching him,
blinked, and stood up. It was a boy, small and gap-toothed,
but he had been fed better than most boys Connelly had seen.
They stared at each other and the boy said, "Is it sick?"

"It's a car. Cars don't get sick."

"What do they get?"

"They get broke."

"You going to fix it, then?"

"Going to try," said Connelly.

The boy nodded gravely, then pointed at part of the car.
"What's that?"

"That's the rotor," said Connelly calmly, not dismissive,
not irritated. Just treating the question like it had come from
anyone.

The boy nodded again. Connelly returned to the car.

"And that?" said the boy, pointing at another part.

"That's the spark plug," said Connelly.

"Is that the problem?"

"Oh, I don't think so."

"What is the problem?"

"I'm not sure yet." He glanced at the boy, then made another
circle with his finger. The engine groaned and grunted as it
tried to move and the boy jumped back, startled by the noise.
Connelly's hand shot out and grabbed on to the boy's arm to
stop him from falling. He was still breathing fast as Connelly
eased him back onto the bumper of the car.

"Watch out," said Connelly. "It won't bite, but don't hurt yourself."

"For Chrissakes, Frankie, get down from there and let the man work," said Clark from behind.

"It's all right," Connelly said. "I don't mind."

The boy nodded at him gratefully and Connelly went back to work as though nothing had happened.

Connelly reached in and touched two slender wires. He looked at them, then carefully brought them together. There was a spark. He nodded and placed them back together and then made the motion with his finger again.

Clark's brother hit the ignition. Again there were the clicks and grunts as the engine sought the connection, but then it caught, rolled over, and with an unhappy grumble began to run again.

There was an eruption of cheers from behind him so loud Connelly swung around in surprise.

"Hot damn, you did it!" shouted Clark. He ignored the slap his wife gave his shoulder. "How'd you do it?"

"It's the condenser," said Connelly quietly, and waved Clark up. He pointed at the wires he had connected. "The points had come loose. It happens all the time with these older models. Usually I'd say you just need to have the condenser replaced, but you should be good until you can get to the next auto shop. If it happens again, check there first."

"We're lucky it was nothing serious," said the little boy solemnly.

Connelly looked at him, amused. "Yeah. Yes, we are."

"Well, you just saved the day for us," said Clark.

"It was nothing. Just a few stray wires."

"Oh, be quiet," said Missy. "Come on down here. Lunchtime's coming on and you and your friends look hungry as wolves. When's the last time you ate?"

Connelly hesitated and glanced sideways at Pike and the others, who were getting to their feet. "A while," he admitted. "A long while."

"Well, we've got salted pork and nice rolls we can cook up for all of you."

"There's a lot of us," said Connelly.

"That don't mean nothing," she said, grabbing his arm and steering him toward their makeshift shelter. "There's a lot of us, too. There's a lot of everybody. If you hadn't come along at the right time we'd have been stuck here for... Oh, well, I shudder to think. I shudder, I really do."

"God looks after His own," said Pike as he approached.

She smiled at him. "If that's not the truth, I've never heard it. Are you a man of the cloth?"

"Once," said Pike. "Now I'm just a man."

"Well, anyone who's done the Lord's work is a welcome guest at our table." She frowned. "Even if we don't have a table."

"Ma'am, we haven't even seen a bed in weeks," said Roosevelt. "We'd be awful picky to turn you down just because there's no dinner table on one of your trucks."

"These times," said one of the other women, fussing over them. "Oh, these times. I seen little boys with arms like sticks. We're lucky to be doing as good as we are."

They sat them down among the entire family and began their preparations for cooking. Connelly and the others could tell the family didn't have much and so did their best to refuse what they could, but they were ravenous and soon accepted.

"Where you boys heading?" asked one of Clark's brothers.

"West," said Hammond. "South and west. To wherever we can find work."

They accepted that. It was a common story among everyone.

Connelly turned to survey Clark's cars again. "I could look those over for you," he said. "I don't mean to be rude, but I bet there's a few, well..."

"Problems," Clark finished. "Because the man who sold them to us was a snake."

"I guess you could say that."

"I would appreciate that. I really would. And we'd be happy to help you folks out."

Connelly smiled a little. "Getting tossed from a train isn't exactly fun."

"We'll do whatever you need in return," said Pike. "Any help you need, you let us know."

"Well, sir. I suppose all we want is just the chance to keep moving," said Clark. "That's enough for me."

The Hopkinses' convoy was in worse shape than they had imagined. Connelly spent the next day checking whatever came to his mind. He managed to scrounge up a crescent wrench and went to it before the sun came up. Cleaning fuel lines. Teasing radiator lines back into place. On one wheel the bearings were run down to the point of dissolving, mere days away from smoking and catching fire. Connelly used a jack and managed to remove the wheel and scrape away what was left of the bearing. He took a piece of rind from the pork barrel and cleaned it of salt. Then he wrapped it around the spindle and replaced the wheel. He told Clark this would not last for more than a hundred miles or so. Clark and the other men listened. They listened to every quiet word Connelly said like it was the word of Christ himself. And Clark's son Frankie refused to leave, having assumed the role of Connelly's tagalong. He stood beside Connelly whenever he could, like a lieutenant standing beside his general, looking out on a battlefield.

It was not long before Lottie joined the women in looking after the children. They cleaned and cooked and spoke, made sure the loads in all the cars were even, and spent time mending clothing and tending to wounds. For every second they were awake there seemed to be four more things to fix.

Pike and Hammond did not fit in well. Sometimes they came forward to help Connelly and the others but mostly they stayed at the outskirts, conversing in tones too low to hear. Roonie stayed with them, as he proved too nervous and uncoordinated and his help was more of a hindrance. Connelly, for once, was the center of all the attention. Monk and Roosevelt joined the Hopkinses and Connelly quietly gave them all direction, taking apart this and putting together that. Rubbing bar soap over holes in the fuel tanks caused by gravel from the road. One car burned oil and if Connelly had not gotten to it the engine would have been lost. Whoever had pawned the heaving wrecks off on the Hopkinses had done so knowing he was sending a family out on the road to flounder.

And Connelly enjoyed himself. He liked working with his hands again and he liked helping. He enjoyed seeing something wrong and putting it right. As afternoon came on his muscles ached but it was a pleasing ache. His body was letting him know that he had done something worth doing.

He sat and leaned up against a car and surveyed his work. He sipped water in the noonday heat and felt more satisfied than he had in weeks, even months. Frankie came and sat next to him, looking sideways to take in Connelly's posture, then mimic it. Connelly offered him his canteen and the boy took it and sipped from it with a serious air.

"We're going to New Mexico," the boy said.

"You're in New Mexico now," Connelly told him.

He considered that. "New Mexico is where cotton is, though. And work. Money to make."

"It's out there somewhere," said Connelly. "But not here."

The boy struggled with something. "New Mexico is where we can build another house," he said, and he looked at Connelly earnestly. "New Mexico is where I told Jeff I'd be."

"Jeff?"

"Jeff's my dog," he said proudly.

"You named your dog Jeff?"

"'Course I did. Jeff's a good name. There was a man named Jeff who lived a county over who could toss a ten-pound stone farther than anyone."

"Was there?"

"Yes. So I named my dog Jeff because, well, that seemed like a pretty good thing to be named after. When we moved I told him we'd be in New Mexico. Pa says I should have said goodbye, but I know Jeff. Jeff'll know what to do. He's probably just a few turns of the road away." He contemplated something very seriously. "Jeff is my friend," he said. "I told him we'd have a house, a house just like the one we used to have. I'll see him again."

"I'm sure you will."

The boy looked into the sun and shaded his eyes. "I hope he's happy."

"I hope so, too," said Connelly.

Then the boy looked at Connelly, suddenly embarrassed, and he jumped to his feet and ran away. Connelly watched him go.

"He'll be back soon," said Missy.

"What did I do?" asked Connelly.

"You? Nothing. But you can't just up and move a boy away from his home and expect him to be all right."

"He's a good boy."

"He bears it better than most," she said. "Some of the others... Well, they ain't as hopeful as Frankie. You know, you're good with children."

"I'm not that good."

"Sure you are," she said. "You know how boys work. You know not to treat them like boys, for instance. Do you have any of your own?"

Connelly did not move. Then he said, "No."

"No? Never wanted to settle down or nothing?"

Connelly shook his head.

"Well, it's not for everyone, I suppose," she said, and smiled kindly. "Just seems like a waste, is all." Her smile faded from her face. "Have I said something wrong?"

"No," said Connelly, and he stood up.

"I... I didn't mean to overstep or anything..."

"It's nothing," he said. "I'm just going to get some more water from the creek."

He turned around and walked away, down toward the bend in the land where the silver string of water ran through the pasture. The wind picked up, sending fingers of dust twirling into the air. He heard shouting and saw the boy running out in the fields, a stick in hand, crying at some unknown attacker or maybe urging on invisible comrades. Thrust and parry, feint and dodge. Then a gruff battlecry, dust rising in clouds around his feet as he fought the very air.

Connelly walked down to the creek and filled his canteen. He dipped his hands in the water, felt the eddies form around his fingers and wrists. Then he took them out and went and sat on a stone by the creek and did his best not to cry.

CHAPTER FIFTEEN

They spent the next day working more on the cars and preparing to leave. They shifted loads and strapped down everything they could. As night fell they ate what was left of the salted pork and huddled around the fire. The day had been warm but the night was freezing out in those dry reaches.

"How many folks have you all seen so far?" asked Clark.

"Seen?" said Pike.

"Yeah. I just...I just want to know how many are headed where we're headed. I think a fella should know what he's up against."

"Clark," said Missy, "don't talk about such things in front of the children."

"They should know, too," said Clark. "I don't want anyone walking into this with just dreams in their heads. I want to know. How many?"

"I don't know," Pike said. "I don't know where you're headed."

"South and west. Away from all this dead land."

"People have moved in a great wave, Mr. Hopkins. Did you not know that?"

"I did," he said, "but... but I haven't done as much traveling as you all. How many?"

Pike shrugged. "Like the ocean."

Clark looked down at the fire and crossed his arms.

"Those who hold steadfast will always survive," Pike said. "You and your family are strong. Stronger than most. I'm not exactly a holy man anymore, if I ever was, but I do see a future for you, Mr. Hopkins. For people as strong as all of you, how could it be otherwise?"

"That's awful nice of you to say."

"It's not nice," said Pike. "It's the truth. No compliment, but fact."

"You people are all right. I was sort of scared of you at first, that I admit, but you're all right."

Roosevelt took out his harmonica and began to play. They listened as they lay around the fire. Connelly was rubbing his hands slowly when someone touched his arm. He looked up into the face of Clark's oldest daughter.

"Are you cold?" she asked.

"A little."

"There's a little whisky, if you want it."

"Thank you, uh..."

She smiled. "Deliah."

"Thank you, Deliah."

She brought him a tin cup full of bourbon and he sipped at it.

"Where are you from?" she asked.

"A ways back," he said.

"Yeah, but where?"

"Memphis."

"I never been outside of Oklahoma. I never been anywhere but my hometown."

"You should be thankful," said Connelly. "Country's a wide, mad place."

"I guess," she said. "I always wanted to travel. I never wanted to do it this way."

"I believe that."

"Deliah," said Missy. "You leave him alone. He's tired."

"I'm all right," said Connelly.

"Come over here," Missy scolded.

Deliah scowled and went over to her mother, but smiled at Connelly over her shoulder. He frowned and drank more. Clark took the bottle out and began passing it around. It lit little fires in their stomachs and made the night bearable and soon they were chattering and talking just as though they had been at home.

"These are nice people," said Lottie to Connelly.

"They are."

"It's a sad thing to see them out on the road. I'd like to see them right. It'd be nice to just stay with them and keep moving."

"It would be," said Connelly.

"Do you know what I think, sometimes?"

"What?"

"I think sometimes that...that every step I take I seem to lose a little bit more of myself. Every step I take chasing that man, I forget what I'm doing. No...That's not so. Not what I'm doing, but *why*. Do you know what I mean?"

Connelly shrugged.

"Like, back in the jungle," she said. "When Pike beat that man so he'd tell us where Shivers had gone, I just stood there like it was nothing. It seemed okay to me. And it had, after ... after what had happened to the twins. But that night I lay sleeping and I thought it wasn't more than a year ago that I hadn't never seen a man get beaten in my life. Not like that. Not like that."

Lottie bit her lip and toyed with her hair. She seemed eager to say something, but stopped, smiled, and said, "Pardon. I'll just be a bit," and she walked away.

She was gone a long time. Connelly drank more with the other men. It was the first time any of them had tasted liquor in a while. His head began to swim and the fire became a yellow smear in the night. He wondered where Lottie went, and as he wondered the voices of the other travelers mixed in his head and in the circle of cars he felt trapped, like he had fallen into a hole and was unable to crawl out. He tried to convince himself it was only the drink, but soon it was too much. He stood up and staggered off through the ring of cars and out of the light. Someone called to him but he paid it no mind.

Soon he was out among the scrub. At night the countryside had become a gray and violet inversion of itself, the pasture stubbled like man's cheek, the creek a narrow braid of shimmering light. Far up above the sky was filled with an impossible number of stars, some large and shining, some the barest suggestion of light at all. The moon seemed closer than it did in any other place Connelly had ever been. It was so close he felt he could almost touch it, its pockmarked skin the color of honey and wheat. He wanted to touch it and then smell his fingers and see what scent it carried across the sky.

He looked back. The campsite was more than a hundred yards away. He could not make out their faces. A strange fear came over him as he listened to them sing, their voices carried to him on the wind. He went and sat beneath a lone cedar, gnarled as an old man's hand, and he watched them. He remembered the gray man turning and speaking his name as the sky was eaten by shadow. Remembered the look of dull surprise on the face of the man he had dragged off the train car, how the man twisted when struck by the next car and the way he seemed to dissolve beneath the wheels. And he remembered Molly. How small and fragile his memory of her was now. It felt dangerous just to caress it in his mind.

He watched the distant fire and people laughing and sharing one another's company, and inside of him a voice quietly said: This is not for you. These things are not yours, will not be yours, could never be yours. Not now. Not ever. Not ever again.

And Connelly listened, and he agreed. The cars fenced him out. He could not go back.

He fumbled in his coat and took out a cigarette. He lit it and its coarse red ember burned bright in his hands. When he looked up a figure was walking to him across the field, white and fragile in the starlight. He thought it was Lottie but instead it was the girl, Deliah.

"What are you doing out here?" she asked, smiling. She was wearing a white dress that was so beaten by now it was almost sheer. She came close and he tried not to notice how it gripped her body in the wind. She was barefoot. Pale white feet smeared with dark earth. Each inch of her skin's texture visible to the naked eye.

"Having a smoke," he said.

"You could have smoked with us. We wouldn't have minded none."

"Just felt like quiet, I suppose," he said.

She laughed. "Would you like another drink?"

He shook his head.

"Anything?"

He shook his head again.

"Come on back by the fire," she said.

"No, that's...that's all right. I've got some thinking to do."

"You can think with us if you want."

He did not answer.

"Come on back," she said. "Please. For me."

He shook his head. "That's...that's kind of you, but..."

"But you just want to sit out in a field, huh?" she said, now pouting. She looked him over and sniffed. "Well, fine, then. Sit under this damn tree. I don't care. Sit here all you want."

She turned and strode across the fields. In the faint light she seemed a ghost, each line of her body an ivory curve, each motion agonizingly clear. Her hair glistened and bounced and toyed with the nape of her neck, her delicate hands bunched into fists at her sides. Connelly felt the urge to cry no, no, come back, come back and I will come with you. I will come wherever you ask.

But he did not. He was silent. He looked down between his feet and when he looked up again she was gone.

Connelly rubbed his arms, fighting the chilly night. An animal voice cried in the darkness. Somewhere in hills another cried back, answering.

He looked up at the stars again and considered this spot on the land, this tree he sat under. These empty square feet of land had always been here, would always be here. To this place he was no more than a dream. And he wondered about those who had come before, wandering over the plains, treading this spot. People that came before names. Animals that came before sunlight. Perhaps it had been so.

He touched the coarse earth. Once something had died here. It was a fact of chance. Some animal had dragged itself to this spot or maybe had fallen, limbs askew, its lifeblood leaking onto the earth. And then perhaps it had lifted its thoughtless eyes to the infinity above, looked at the endless, bejeweled dark, just as Connelly was now, and made some sound, some mewling cry. Asking a question. Begging for a few seconds more. And then expired, maybe leaving its question behind.

One death, at least. Perhaps hundreds of things had died here. Thousands. Millions. And maybe all had spent their last moments watching the stars swim by.

Connelly looked at the sky for a long time. He wondered if the stars knew what lived in their depths. If they knew anything at all.

CHAPTER SIXTEEN

In the morning they readied to leave. Pike accepted the food the Hopkinses could spare, though he denied it first out of politeness. Connelly was looking over the cars and their packs once more when Lottie came to him.

"We need to talk," she said.

They walked away from the ring of cars. She led him down to the creek and said, "I'm not going."

"I know," he said.

"You do?"

"Figured as much."

"Are...are you mad?"

He shook his head.

"I thought you would be," she said.

"No. I'm not."

She shut her eyes. "I thought you would be. I said I was in this, I said I wanted to see this man dead."

"I know," he said again.

"Yes, but do you know why?"

"No. I don't need to."

"But I want you to. Let me speak my peace." She rubbed her temple. "Back there on the train, did you see?" she said.

"See what?"

"When I... When I shot that man, you could see him... Did you see what I... What I..."

"I saw."

"Did I... Did I kill him?"

Connelly thought. He looked at the ground and said, "No."

She let out a breath. "No? I didn't?"

"No. You missed. It scared him. He moved away and while he was trying to reload he lost his balance and fell."

"I could have sworn I-I..."

"You didn't," said Connelly flatly.

She touched her cheek, fingers caressing where the drops of blood had fallen. She shook herself. "I'm sorry. I don't want to kill a man. I don't ever want to have that on me. If the man we're chasing was dead and gone it would be all right but I think there's more killing between all of you and him. Do you know that?"

Connelly nodded.

"I was thinking... Connelly," she said. "You... you shouldn't go, either. I don't think I can convince any of the others but, well... I don't think this is worth it anymore. I mean, you met this family. They'd let us come with them. They're nice and there's good things waiting for them. I know. I know it in my bones."

Connelly stood for a long time. Then he shook his head.

"For God's sake, Connelly, men are *dead*—"

"There were dead before this," said Connelly. "Long before."

"But—"

"We speak for them. We speak for the dead. To do right by them."

"And this is the way you'd do it?"

"Doesn't seem to be another."

"Connelly, nothing *good* will come of this. There are people looking for you. And if you all keep on like this, more people are going to be after you. More bloodshed. More tears. More dead to speak for. We got a chance at something good here. Don't pass it by. Don't." She smiled. "There are people who *like* you here, Connelly. That family. They like you. That girl, I think she likes you. And she...she isn't the only one," she said softly, and touched his arm.

Connelly breathed deep, then bowed and shook his head again. "It isn't good to me."

"You don't mean that."

"That's the way it is. I look at these people and I just know. I look at you and know these things aren't for me. Not yet. I-I can't go back. It'd be wrong to do that, to abandon this and let him go on. To let my little girl's death go unanswered. But...this family. You. Maybe one day I can have things like that. But it isn't for me. Not now." He took a breath. "This is all I got now. This is all I got. All I am. Just chasing him."

Lottie closed her eyes, wiped them. "You have a *choice*..."

"I know I do. I'm choosing to make this right. And I can."

"You don't want to come with me? At all?"

"I-I do. You know I have a wife?"

"I remember."

"I'd like to go back to that. One day, to the way things were in the beginning. But I can't yet. And, Lottie, once this was done, if it was so that I could never find her again or if she wouldn't welcome me home, then I would come to you. I would. But I have to do this. I have to."

She looked at him for a moment longer, then walked back to the camp without saying anything. He waited for a second and then followed.

It went much as Connelly had expected. Lottie spoke to them a few paces away from the camp so the Hopkinses would not hear. Connelly did not come close, so he could not hear everything that was said, nor did he want to.

Pike became angry right away. He shouted at her, pounding his fist into his hand, pointing off into the west and throwing biblical language at her alongside curses about the weaknesses of bitchery. This she took without the slightest reaction. Then Roonie wept and she comforted him, holding him in her arms, his crooked fingers playing with her hair. Monk tried to reason with her, blustering and confused, but she simply shook her head. And Roosevelt and Hammond stayed quiet, Roosevelt looking nervous and Hammond standing ramrod-straight, his narrow, handsome features pulled taut, his mouth in a hard grimace.

Then the words finished. Lottie nodded, then walked back to the Hopkinses with a queenly, steady stride, though as she walked by Connelly he could see her fingers trembling. She spoke to Missy and the other woman listened and embraced her hard, and Lottie hugged her back. The children came down and began bombarding her with questions, spinning around her feet. Connelly watched them. Watched their passion for one another. Their happiness in being one.

Clark came and spoke to him. "You sure you boys are going to be all right?"

"I suppose," said Connelly.

"We're happy to have her aboard, you know."

"I'm sure she's happy to be with you."

"We could use you, sir. We could use all of you. It's more mouths, sure, but it's more hands working."

"We have business in the west," said Connelly.

"Who doesn't," said Clark. He looked at Connelly sadly. "If times were different, I-I..."

Connelly nodded. "If things were different," he said.

"I hope you find what you're looking for. Whatever's in all of you is burning you up. I can see it."

"Maybe so. I think it's best we all get going. We're wasting daylight."

They shook hands.

"Maybe I'll see you again," said Clark.

"Sometimes I think I'll see everyone again," Connelly answered.

Clark walked back to the cars and they started up, a small armada of crumbling machinery shuddering in the field. One by one they lurched forward, gravel crunching under the tires, and they made their way to the road. Everyone waved, each car a heap of junk and waving white arms. The children cheered and the men called good luck and the women waved as well. With a great belch of dust the jalopies picked up speed and soon were moving down the road, speeding away, south and west.

Connelly and the others went north. It was not until night-fall that he realized Lottie had not looked at him once after their discussion, nor had she said goodbye.

CHAPTER SEVENTEEN

Near Privet they saw the dead man.

As night fell they came into the surrounding farmland to find it empty. No one stirred in the fields and they saw no one in the homes. The streets were empty save for a few stray dogs who fled yelping as they approached. They passed through wondering if perhaps some plague had come and taken all of them away when they heard the noise in the distance.

"Someone's yelling," said Roonie.

"A lot of someones," said Connelly.

They made their way around to a field on the windward side of the hills. There was a large crowd assembled and Connelly thought perhaps it was another traveling carnival until he saw the tree overhead and the strange mass dangling from its branches.

It was a man. A black man. He was hanging from one of the topmost branches by the neck. His face was swollen and his eyes were red and his tongue hung out of his mouth, lapis blue and glistening. His clothes were tattered, as was his skin, and blood stained his collar and back. A dark stain ran across the front and back of his pants and brown streaks ran down his ankles. His whole body weeping. Beneath him people milled about with torches, chatting and shouting and talking until finally a few of them noticed the strangers.

"What are you all doing here?" asked a woman.

"Just passing through," said Monk.

"You heard about this here nigger?" she asked.

"No."

"Goddamn," she said, and walked off.

"What the hell?" Roosevelt said. "What the hell was that? What happened here?"

"I don't know," said Pike. "How should I know?"

They found an old man who reeked of whisky who told them, "We caught this here nigger rutting about with a white lady. I never heard of such a thing before in my life, not ever. I figured it was rape, but that nigger'd have to be dumber than hell to think he'd get away with such a thing here. She must've gone in for it. You ever hear of that?"

"No," said Connelly.

"Damn it all, it's astounding. It's astounding what's happening to this nation, ain't it?"

"You can say that again," said Hammond.

"You being smart with me, young man?"

"No."

He eyed Hammond carefully. "I can't abide nigger-lovers. That wouldn't be you fellas, now would it?"

"Just passing through," said Pike evenly.

"Lord almighty," said the old man, and he shook his head.

"End of the world come, end of the world go. All souls did burn. No one noticed. Not a one. Not a one but me."

They stared at the thing hanging from the tree. The noose had pulled its head strangely, giving it the look not of a dead man but of a man poorly made from inanimate parts. Connelly gazed into its eyes and tried to see what spark was there, what motivation or animation had once dwelt there to give it life, or perhaps a vacancy where it had been. Just a sign that it had once been a man and had walked and talked and perhaps loved somewhere on this fading earth.

He found nothing. It was a dead thing. It had no history and it had no future. It was just a dead thing, murdered and hanging from a tree. He could no more find a man in it than he could find reason in its dying.

He wondered where Lottie was.

"Think...think he had something to do with it?" said Monk as they walked away.

"Who? The scarred man?" said Pike.

"Yeah, think...think he caused this?"

"I doubt it."

"Why?"

"It would be easy to blame all the evils of humanity on one madman, wouldn't it? It'd be simpler. And comforting. But that doesn't make it so."

"Let's go," said Hammond. "I don't want to talk to these people."

"We need to. We need to know if he's come by."

"He hasn't."

"But how do you know?"

"I'll do it," said Connelly. "I will." He left them to reenter the crowd.

None of them knew the scarred man. No one had heard of him. But Connelly noticed a strange excitement in them, a queer sort of awful joy that made them restless and jittery. It was in how they touched each other and looked at each other and in how they spoke. There was fury and self-satisfaction, a kind of relief. It was as though an enormous celebration was about to begin, but they did not know what they were celebrating nor when the celebration would take place.

Connelly returned to the others with no news. Pike looked back at the people in the field. The lights from the torches caught in his eyes, making them flicker in the depths of his sockets like lanterns in caves, burning low. "I have heard before that certain truths are written on men's bones," he said. "That may be so. If it is true then I believe they are written in a language not known to men, and even if they were translated I doubt they would be of much comfort." Then he snorted, spat, rubbed dirt over the spittle with his shoe, and walked down the hill to the road.

They walked all day, stopping only briefly for lunch at noon. There were no trees to shelter them from the sun so they sat on the edge of a ditch, sweat dripping down their necks as they tore at the salted pork the Hopkinses had given them. Then they rose and continued on.

Everything looked the same. They seemed not to travel at all. Always the thread of brown road stretched ahead, cutting through the fields. Always the same spindly fence, leaning awkwardly by the road. The same fragile yellow grass, so dry it seemed to crumble merely by breathing on it. And the sun never moved, content to sit upon their backs.

When they came to a small stream Pike decided they should stop, more to break the monotony than anything. Hammond and Connelly kept a lookout as the others lowered themselves down to the waters to fill their canteens. The two of them stayed by the road, then crossed and leaned on the fence, watching all the nothing.

"Sometimes I wonder if we're going anywhere," said Hammond.

"Think someone mentioned something like that a while back," Connelly said.

"Yeah. I hate that feeling, though. The feeling of not moving. I always have." He looked out at the fields, watched the wind tousle the brittle grass. "I remember this place back home," he said. "It was this bar. This underground bar that was below a fabric store. You know what I mean, a bar in the basement?"

"Yeah. I know."

"It was one of those. I loved that place when I was a kid. I thought it was like some kind of secret. I'd walk by it in the evening and see all these little windows just poking up above the sidewalk. All lit up. People talking and laughing and playing music. You'd feel the music in your feet when you'd walk by. I wanted to get in there so bad, to see what they were doing. To be part of the fun. But I was just a kid, so they wouldn't let me know.

"It was the girls that did it. Me and the other boys, we'd climb a fire escape and look down on them as they walked into the bar. We'd never seen girls dress like that. Not our moms, not our sisters. Wearing dresses that shone, shining in that nice light coming up from the ground from those little windows. And there were girls with blonde hair, real bright blonde hair, which I never seemed to see. What's the word? Tawny? Is it tawny?"

"I don't know," said Connelly.

"Well. I think it is," said Hammond. "Still. Those girls. They were the most beautiful things I'd ever seen. I couldn't wait to get older so I could get in there and see what they were doing.

"Then one day I dressed up real nice so I looked older and I put on a good suit so I'd blend in and I went down there and knocked on the door. A man looked out at me, from this little peephole. And he looked at me a while and then he let me in. And you know what?"

"What?"

"It was just a bar. Just a little room that stank of beer, full of drunks, with real loud music. Everyone was drunk out of their minds, sad and sloppy and ugly. And the women. They were tired old things. Tired old things wearing dresses they had no business wearing. Too much makeup, everywhere," he said, and gestured to his face. "They were different. Different from what I'd seen. Maybe it was the way I'd been looking at them." He shook his head. "There's never … There never is anything. You go somewhere so hard and so fast and then when you get there you're in the same place. Feels like there's no reward. Nothing to go for. I hate that feeling. That feeling that you're not getting anywhere. That you're not getting anywhere good. I wonder if it's that way for everyone."

"Not everyone. Some people are getting places."

"Well. I haven't met any of those people in the past few years."

"Someone has to be going somewhere good," said Connelly. "Someone has to be doing okay."

"Just not us right now."

"No. Just not us."

"Do you think we ever will?"

Connelly thought about it. "I don't know."

Hammond nodded. "I don't," he said.

Then Pike and the others climbed back up from the stream. They handed out the canteens and rubbed their feet and then continued on.

The better part of the day passed before their walking was compensated. They were carefully making their way down into a valley when they heard a train far to the west. They stopped and Roosevelt judged the sound.

"Two miles off," he said. "Maybe three."

"We'll come close enough to see it," Pike said. "Then we'll follow. But we'll keep a half a mile between us and it. I don't want anyone to notice us until we get to its next stop. Wherever that may be."

It was not long before they sighted not the track itself but the gray remains of smoke in the air, a dull haze where the train had just passed. They followed its curve up through the land. Signs of civilization began to appear. More roads, a ditch. The odd road sign. More fences. Then homes appeared, squatting far away, and then they saw the first person they'd seen in hours, a young man carrying a shovel. He took no notice of them but they did not relax.

"Be alert," said Pike under his breath.

The tracks led up to what had once been a jerkwater town, nothing more than a few buildings clinging to an intersection of tracks and roads. Roonie spied it from far off and Pike dropped to his knees and scoped it out as best he could.

"What do you think?" asked Hammond.

"I think that's where the train we were once on stopped," he said. "That's what I think."

"And?"

"And we're going to play this very, very carefully," he said.

They waited until almost nightfall. Hammond spotted a few people ambling up the road, a little less than a dozen. Pike said it would be best if they joined them and muddled their numbers. If there was a lookout at all, he reasoned, it'd be for six or seven men, not more.

"If that," he added. "Those boys on the train were probably going to kill anybody riding the rails. Seemed to be their orders."

They mixed with the other strays and moved in as the sun sank below the earth. The new people did not mind. They assumed Pike and the others had hopped some line a few miles back. When they made it into the town proper they split off. Pike turned and said quietly, "It'd be best if we split up. Two groups. Roonie, Hammond, Monk, you go around to the north end. Rosie, Connelly, you're coming with me. We stay low, we don't raise any attention. Don't ask any questions, none about the shiver-man, none about nothing. You just keep your ears open. You just listen, see?"

"We see," said Connelly.

They parted and Rosie and Connelly decided an inn or bar would be the likely place for talk to be heard where a hobo was acceptable. They dusted themselves off and wound through the side lanes and broken fences until they found a shanty inn, some dirt-cheap gin house with riotous clientele and no small measure of whoring. Men with skin like leather drank ale from metal tankards while women smeared in makeup swanned through their ranks. Someone somewhere pounded on a piano to the point of ruin. Everything stank of tobacco and moonshine.

"I like it," said Roosevelt with a smile.

"Keep control of yourself, boy," Pike muttered to him. "It'll be far easier to avoid attention with your eyes in your head and your prick in your pants."

"Oh, these ideals, Pikey," said Rosie. "These lofty ideals you have."

They sat at the bar and rustled up change and bought a few drinks. Connelly still had money sewed into the cuffs of his pants but he didn't think now was the time to mention it. They sipped at their drinks and tried to keep their heads.

There was no news of interest, almost no talk beyond bar banter. "I don't know why you were so worried," said Rosie to Pike. "These fellas is all just worried about the railroad lines. Who's signed up on what engine and who's shacked up with whose whore. This ain't enemy territory. This ain't even territory. Just a whole lot of nothing."

"Maybe so," said Pike reluctantly.

"Come on," said Roosevelt. "Let's rent a room."

"A room?" said Connelly.

"When's the last time you seen a bed, Con? It'll be worth it, I swear. Listen to your back, not your wallet, for once."

"What do you say?" asked Connelly, looking at Pike.

"Pike would say we're living our cover," said Rosie under his breath. "Three drunks fresh in town, getting a room? That's no news at all."

Maybe it was the liquor or maybe it was the days of walking, but Pike eventually gave in. The bartender called his boy up to lead them to their room. He groused and clambered to his feet, but then stood up straight as a pole when he saw Connelly. The boy's eyes grew wide with fear as they wandered up his towering frame.

"You going to lead us to our room or what?" said Rosie.

The boy blinked, then looked from Roosevelt to Pike. His glance stayed far too long for Connelly's comfort. The boy shook himself and led them up.

The room was no more than a closet with a bed that seemed hardly better than the ground. The three men climbed into it and shared the mattress along with a blanket. When Connelly was flat on his back he had to admit, it was slightly better sleeping arrangements than normal.

Sleep fell on him quickly, better sleep than he had had in weeks.

Connelly awoke in the middle of the night. Something troubled him. He could not place what it was until he realized that he could no longer hear the racket of drinking and piano from downstairs. It had halted sometime, sometime recent.

He stood and went to the window. The streets were empty, but he saw something far down at the end of one. Two little sparks, fluttering in the night.

Torches. Two, maybe even three.

He went to the door and opened it as quietly as he could. He walked out and peered around the staircase. He could see and hear no one, but the lights were on downstairs. Then he heard hushed voices, whispering to one another, and the fall of a boot. He snaked into an empty room across the hall and stood there, listening. More footfalls came until there were at least four men outside the room where Roosevelt and Pike still lay. Connelly ducked his head around the doorway, just far enough to see the shining cylinder of a rifle. He pulled back into the shadows, heart pounding.

The men kicked the door in and the inn filled with yelling. Some shouted for them to get up and some shouted for them to stay down, a confused and furious assault that soon degenerated into a flat-out beating. He heard Roosevelt and Pike crying out, their attackers shouting back to shut up, only to cause more noise. Finally one of them shouted, "Where is he? Where is that bastard?"

"Who?" said Roosevelt's voice. "Who the hell do you mean?"

Another blow. Roosevelt moaned.

"The big one! Where's the big bastard you came in with?"

"Who? I don't know!"

Someone shouted in rage. A crack, and this time it was Pike who howled and snarled.

"You stay back! You stay back and down, old man! Now where's the big damn bearded bastard you came in with or I swear to God, I'll shoot every one of you men right here and now!"

But now Roosevelt and Pike were beyond answering. "Christ," said their attacker. "Look at these fuckers. Blake, round them up and get them out on the damn street. Boss wants to look at them."

"I thought there'd be more," said a voice.

"So did I," answered the other.

Connelly stayed pinned to the wall as Hammond and Pike were dragged out of the room. The men spoke and laughed to one another as they tossed their prey down the stairs. Connelly did not move until he heard their voices move outside.

Then he dashed back into his room, put back on his boots and coat, and tried to find some section of the street outside that was empty.

He darted from room to room, peering through badly built windows to the streets below. Firelight flickered from the front. There was either a lot of fire out there or a lot of people carrying fire, but he could not see, nor would he risk a glance.

He wound his way through the second story of the inn until he found a small window that opened out onto the back. Behind the inn the land sunk down into a ditch filled with refuse and gravel. He pried the window open and shouldered his way through. Then he looked down at the ground below and thought. He turned, dug his fingers into the windowsill, and lowered himself down slowly. His right arm screamed, still tender from the train. He hung there and then dropped to the ground.

He collapsed in a heap and tried to suppress a cough but could not. Someone shouted, "What was that?" and Connelly got to his feet and began running.

Clouds strafed across the midnight sky but there was still light enough to see. He ducked between fences and tottering buildings that slouched on one another like ancient winesots. He checked around a corner, desperately searching for the dancing, roving torchlight that would be searching for him. He saw nothing and bolted forward and scrambled through a lumber yard, great logs leaning and seesawing against the violet sky. He vaulted himself up and over one and it was damp to the touch. As he crested shots rang out. Their hot riptide washed over him and he knew they had been close, buzzing by just over his shoulder. Splinters and chunks dotted his right side as he descended and more shots whined through the air like angry bees. He landed and checked but felt no blood on him, then lay there breathing.

There was no noise, no shouts or calls. He turned and peered through a small gap in the logs, eyes scanning the roads and streets. Still he saw nothing. He crouched, ready to spring, when he heard the vicious snap of a rifle cocking.

"Eh," warned a voice, high-pitched and friendly. "No. No, no. I wouldn't do that, I certainly think I wouldn't."

Connelly froze.

"Okay, boy. I think you're in one piece, and it's a big piece at that. I can see you well and good, and though it may be a tight shot I think I can wing you through them logs. You agree?"

He didn't answer.

"I said, you agree?"

"Yeah," said Connelly.

"Okay, then. And you also don't seem like the kind of fella to be running around with a gun. Otherwise, well, we'd have heard a shot already. So. So, how's about you put the backs of your hands on the top of that pile so I can see there's nothing in them? Does that sound agreeable? Does it?"

"Sure," said Connelly.

"Sure," purred the voice. "Sure it does. So do it."

Connelly lifted his hands, placed the backs on the top corner of wood, and slowly pushed them up.

"There we go," said the voice. "There it is. Okay now, son. You just pull the rest of yourself up. All the way up. Real slow."

Connelly stood.

"You're just as big as they said, ain't you? Well-fed boy. Now turn around, big boy, turn on around."

He did. His attacker was standing in the lumber yard, rifle gently resting at his shoulder, not hard and alert, but not afraid, either. Connelly squinted to see him in the night. He was a small man, late middle age, with white hair and a gentle baby face and a happy, knowing smile that never left his lips. Connelly could see the man's blue eyes even in this light, blue as chips of glacial ice, merry and gleeful as though all of this was just a small joke for everyone to enjoy.

"Come on over here, son," said the man chidingly. "Come on over here and say hey to me."

Connelly walked over with arms still in the air and stood before the small man.

The man nodded, satisfied. "You boys put on quite a show," he said.

Two others rounded the far corners of the yard at either end, torch in hand, and Connelly saw one of them was the boy from the inn. He trembled to see Connelly. As the Halloween-orange light washed over them Connelly saw the twinkle and shine of something at his attacker's breast, something polished silver-bright. A metal star.

Connelly looked at it. "Jesus Christ," he said.

The man nodded, still smiling. "Yeah," he said, almost wistfully, like he was reliving a fond memory. "Yeah."

Then his eyes hardened and the rifle butt flashed up and struck Connelly's temple. The ground spun around him and everything faded.

CHAPTER EIGHTEEN

Light lanced down at him through the pain. He cracked open an eye. A lone bulb hung from a dark wood ceiling. Someone was smoking a cigarette somewhere, acrid and tangy. His hands were bound behind his back and he was lying on a wood floor, wood shavings and sand worked into every crack. He tried to move his head and saw Roosevelt and Pike sitting on a bench across from him, hands cuffed and in their laps, heads bowed, their faces purple and misshapen.

Roosevelt saw him and tried to smile. "Hey, Connie," he said. "You got no luck with your head. Every time you turn around someone's busting it open again."

Pike shushed him, but it was too late.

"Boss," said a voice. "Boss."

"Yes?" came the answer. That high-pitched voice, mild and sweet.

"He's awake."

"Oh, that so?" it crooned. "Is he?"

Connelly rolled over. He saw the small man standing over him in jeans and a white shirt, the sleeves rolled up. The figure swam in and out of focus and as Connelly thinned his eyes he saw a nasty brand on the sheriff's inner arm, brown and pink, a circle with a lizard's head mounted in the middle of the edge, eating itself.

Connelly's skull pounded. "What's that on your arm?" he whispered stupidly.

"What's that?" said the sheriff. "What's that you say? What?"

"On your... On your..." mumbled Connelly.

"Speak up boy, speak up," said the sheriff. His mouth quivered and he began savagely kicking Connelly over and over again, in the side, then the arms, and then finally landing one blow on the head.

Things blurred. Darkness melted in from the corner of his vision. He heard someone laughing but was unable to see who before his mind failed once more.

Connelly's body clanked to life. Air forced its way through his shuddering lungs and when his consciousness rose he doubled up and retched in the corner. He lay there breathing and trying to still the nausea before flexing his fingers, then his arms and toes, then his knees. Nothing seemed broken. He pushed himself up to a sitting position and looked around.

He was in a small, damp cell, no doubt in the jail. Like the rest of the town it was poorly built. The floor was uneven and there seemed to be no straight lines, every board badly cut and every surface warped. Gray light streamed through a window at the top. It was day but he could not pull himself up to see. The door was heavy and there was a slot for food and water, but none had arrived yet.

He checked the money sewn into the cuffs of his pants. It was still there.

"Hey," said a voice. "Hey."

Connelly looked around. The cell was empty except for him.

"Over here," said a voice.

He looked down and saw there was a thin crack at the bottom of the wall that ran through to the other cell. He peered through and saw a sliver of a face, no more than a smiling eye.

"You alive in there?" said the voice.

"Yeah."

"You okay?" said the voice.

"I guess," said Connelly.

"I'm Peachy."

"You're what?"

"Peachy. That's me. That's my name."

"Oh."

Connelly held a hand to his head and rubbed at his temple. He wished he hadn't vomited in a closed room, especially since he wasn't going anywhere.

"What's your name?" said the voice.

"Connelly," he said.

"What'd you do, Connelly?"

"Puked."

"No, I mean to get in here."

"Oh. I don't know."

"You don't?"

"Not really."

Connelly looked around. He thought over the last few days. The boy had only noticed him out of all of them. And there was only one person who knew what Connelly looked like who wasn't in his group, and that happened to be the man he was hunting.

He stood up and went to the door. It was thick and heavy and the hinges seemed strong, as was the lock. There were two slots, one for food, one for the guards to observe him. He pushed on it. It did not even rattle.

"What you doing?" said Peachy.

"Nothing."

Connelly tested the door, the ceiling, the floor, the wall with the window. They were all heavy, not even flexing to his touch.

Peachy chuckled. "Ain't no popping out of these boxes. They might not look like much but they do their job."

Connelly grunted.

"What you think they're going to do to you?"

"I don't know. I hope not much. Doubt that, though."

"Maybe someone will bust you out."

"You ever hear of anyone doing that in here?"

"No."

Connelly shut his eyes. His legs trembled underneath him and his head throbbed. "Well," he said. "I'm going to sleep now."

"At least, no one's broked out while I been in here. I been in here three months," said Peachy. "I broke a man's hand in a fight."

"Okay."

"He was a son of a bitch."

"Okay. I'm going to sleep now."

There was a pause.

"They kill people in here," said Peachy softly. "Did you know that, Connelly?"

Connelly shook his head.

"I said, did you know that?" said Peachy again.

"No," said Connelly.

"I just . . . I just thought you would want to know that."

"Well. Thanks."

"Connelly?"

"Yeah?"

"Think they going to kill you?"

He paused. "Yeah."

"Why would they kill you?"

"Don't think they need a reason," said Connelly, and he lay down to sleep.

As he drifted off he heard Peachy's voice say, "Shit."

The door opened. Flat electric light bored into his darkened room. He lifted his hand to block it and someone said, "Up you get," and grabbed his arm and hoisted him to his feet.

He was dragged out and led down a long low hallway at the end of which was an iron door that opened on a room with walls of cinderblocks. Again, a lone bulb in the ceiling. Plain, boring desk at the end. A small drain in the center of the cement floor. It was the sort of room in which wars were planned.

The men pushed Connelly in and the door clanked shut behind them. Pike and Roosevelt were sitting on two stools set in the floor. A third was empty. At the far end of the room was the sheriff, leaning on the desk and smiling at them. His men forced Connelly onto the third stool. It was absurdly small for him. Pike and Roosevelt did not look at him or at each other, though it was hard to tell through their bruised faces. Connelly guessed that some of the marks were fresh.

"How was your night?" asked the sheriff.

Connelly shrugged. He kept his eyes on the floor, then found himself looking at the drain set in its middle. Faint rust-red stains ran around its rim. The floor itself was scrubbed clean.

"You thirsty?" said the sheriff. "You look thirsty."

"I'm pretty thirsty, yeah," said Connelly.

The sheriff nodded and took out a small tin cup and filled it with water from a basin. He brought it to Connelly and Connelly drank it quickly.

"Yeah," said the sheriff. "You were thirsty. Care for some more?"

Connelly shrugged, nodded. The sheriff filled the cup once more and brought it to him. Connelly drank just as fast, fearing some imminent violence would kick it from his hands.

"Rainwater," said the sheriff. "Rainwater's never been sweeter than it is in dry countries. Now. I'm going to ask you a question. Are you ready? I hope so." He sniffed and rubbed his nose. "Where's your friends?"

"Friends?"

"Yeah. Your friends. Where they at, big boy?"

Connelly gave him a puzzled look and pointed to Roosevelt and Pike sitting on their stools.

He almost didn't see the sheriff move. The only thing he sensed was the lightning bolt of pain that shot through his shoulder, from his wrist to the base of his brain, every ligament and nerve turned to razor wire. He looked up and the sheriff was gently patting a short, thick pipe in one hand.

"Like that?" he said cheerfully.

"No," said Connelly.

"That's okay. You weren't supposed to. Where are your friends at?" he said more clearly.

Connelly didn't say anything.

"Why don't you answer, boy?"

"Don't want to get hit again."

"You won't get hit again if you give me the right answer."

"But I don't know the right answer."

"Hmm," said the sheriff thoughtfully. "Hmm." He walked around like he was contemplating something and then he brought the pipe down on Pike's forehead, stabbing down with the short base. Pike roared and bent over, a stream of blood flowing from his hairline.

"Did all of you like that?" asked the sheriff. "Did you? You going to tell me where they're at now? Huh?"

None of them answered. Pike sat frozen, ignoring the flow of blood from his forehead. He could have been carved from wood.

The sheriff looked at them all, face fixed in disgust. "Reynolds?" he called.

"Yes, Sheriff Miles?" said a voice outside the door.

"Cuffs, please."

"Sure."

A young man brought in cuffs and they were handcuffed with their wrists behind their backs. The chain of the cuffs went down around one leg of their stools so they could not move forward or away.

"Now then," said the sheriff. He rolled his sleeves up, again revealing the raw brand on his arm, the snake eating itself. "Now then. I know that you boys aren't alone. No sir, not a chance. So there's some other boys out there running around and, well, I'd like to chat with them, too. Are they chatty folk? Are they personable?"

No one said anything. The sheriff paced around them, walked behind Pike, then Roosevelt, then Connelly. Connelly tried to turn to see the little man but he could not. Suddenly there was a fierce pain in his wrist and he groaned and slid forward and tried to twist it in his cuffs. He could not see what the man had done but he felt sure his wrist was broken.

"Oh, relax, son," said the sheriff. "It's barely a hairline. Barely a hairline, if that."

Roosevelt muttered something.

"What was that? What?"

"I said, you can't do this," said Roosevelt.

"Can't do what?"

"Can't just haul up some fellas and cuff them to the floor and beat the hell out of them and not have a reason for doing it."

"I do have a reason. You boys killed some men on a train. Some good men. Killed them dead, like they were animals."

"We didn't do any such thing."

The sheriff looked at them, eyes flat and dead and distant.

They looked alien on such a quaint little old man. "Yes you did."

"You can't do this," said Roosevelt. "Can't beat on prisoners. There are laws. This is America."

"What is?" said the sheriff.

"Huh? This is. All this is."

"This?" said the sheriff, and waved at the bland, gray room.

"No, this... this country. We're... we're in America, right now. There are laws."

"Show me," said the sheriff.

"What?"

The sheriff grinned. "Show me America."

"I don't... I..."

"If it's going to tell me what to do and what not to do, it better be on hand. You know?"

Roosevelt frowned.

"Show me a law," the sheriff demanded. "Pick it up and show it to me. Show me a part of America. What, is it this country? This is just dirt we're standing on, son. Dirt and stone. Ain't no lines in the earth, no directions saying what I can and can't do. Show me a right. Pick it up and hold it in your hands and put it beneath my ever-loving nose and show me a thing that says I cannot do what I am doing now. Show me that this is forbidden."

"This is America," insisted Roosevelt.

"America is back east," said the sheriff. "Rights are back east. You're out on your own out here. And no one gives a damn about any such thing. See?" He sidearmed Roosevelt across the neck with the pipe. Roosevelt gagged and cried out and spittle hung from his lips in streams.

The sheriff crouched and smiled into Roosevelt's face. "All this stuff you talking about," said the sheriff. "All this stuff. Well. You take it out here and you see it's just made up. Imaginary. Santy Claus. It's only real if you and everyone else shuts your eyes and pretends with every inch your pretty little hearts. And no one out here's willing to do that, son. Now," he whispered. "Now, now. You want to see what is real?"

The sheriff smiled, then reached behind him and held up the lead pipe, like a lawyer presenting evidence. He laid it on the cement floor in front of them. Then he took out his gun, the metal wicked black and lustrous, and laid it in front of Roosevelt. All of them watched it, their eyes following its movements.

"Argue with that as you would a law," he said. "Argue your rights with that. Go on. Do it."

None of them spoke.

The sheriff smiled. "With things like that a fella makes a place far more . . . I don't know, *real* than one of laws and rights. What about you, old man?" said the sheriff to Pike. "What do you have to say?"

Pike's cold stare moved to the sheriff. "Laws are made by men," said Pike. "I serve a higher power. A power higher than any butchery you have in your hands and heart."

The sheriff laughed. "If God wants to come on down and give me a yell about what I'm doing, I—"

"I bet if the scarred man came out here and said not to, you'd jump," interrupted Connelly.

The sheriff froze and turned to look at him, eyes thin with fury. "What?"

"You're his man, aren't you?" said Connelly. "He's put some cash in your pocket to scoop us up. Isn't that it?"

The sheriff stared at him a long while, then stooped and picked up the gun and held it to Connelly's head. Connelly felt the muzzle bite into the patch of scalp behind his ear, felt it grinding into his skull, felt the sheriff's hand quivering with rage and felt Pike's and Roosevelt's stares. He shut his eyes and waited for the mindless lump of metal to enter his head and push everything that made him what he was out the other side onto the cement floor to be washed down into the drain with God knows what else that had met its end in that room.

"Say that again, boy," said the sheriff softly. "You just say that again."

Connelly did nothing.

"You say it!"

He still did not move. The sheriff let the gun fall and he walked around and pressed the gun under Connelly's chin, forcing him to look up at the sheriff's face. "He says I can't kill you," said the sheriff. "You know that? I said, did you know that?"

"No," said Connelly.

"What do you think about that?"

"I-I guess I'd say that's mighty polite of him," he said, confused.

"No!" shouted the sheriff, and cracked Connelly with the handle, then placed the gun under his chin once more. "Not like that. The Mithras-man says . . . says you're unkillable, boy. Like even if I tried it wouldn't stick. You think that's true?"

"No," Connelly said honestly.

"No," echoed the sheriff. "No. Me neither. I don't believe that at all, boy." He took the gun away, inspected it. Wiped off the small flecks of blood. "Not at all. Reynolds?"

"Yes?" said the young man.

"Get these men out of here. Make sure to rig up the big fella's cell nice and good." He stayed focused on the gun, cleaning it over and over again. "Nice and good, you hear me? Nice and good."

"Yes, Sheriff," said the young man, and opened the door.

CHAPTER NINETEEN

They tossed Connelly back into his cell a little more than ten minutes later. He looked up and inspected the walls, the ceiling, the floor. He did not know what they had meant by rigging up his cell. It seemed just as damp and uncomfortable as before. His sick was still pooling in the corner.

Except it was a little different. The light felt different, like the source had changed, but he could see the sunlight still streaming through the window at the top. Yet it seemed greasier, oilier, like water tainted and fouled by some foreign contaminant. Connelly dismissed it. Surely a man who had taken as many beatings as he had over the past days was allowed some confusion. He felt ill as well. There was a constant ringing in his ears that would not go away. Perhaps he was permanently damaged.

"Connelly?" said Peachy's voice through the crack in the wall.

"Yeah?" he asked.

"They beat on you?"

"Yeah."

"Oh," said Peachy. "They beat on me sometimes, too. Not too often."

"When are they going to let you out?" asked Connelly.

"They never said. I-I don't think anyone knows I'm in here. Except maybe a few of the other deputies and I don't think they care."

"Christ," said Connelly. Never had he felt more alone and miserable. Before this he had trudged through whatever he needed to but at that moment all the lonely days and terrified nights collapsed on him at once. He curled up and shrank into the corner.

"What do you think of the sheriff?" asked Peachy.

"Don't care for him much."

"They had a man in the cell before you. Did you know that? It was him that pried open the little slivers of wood so he could talk to me. Do you see any carvings he left there? Anything at all?"

"No." For the first time Connelly wished Peachy would be quiet. The ringing in his ears had increased to a whine.

"He was old and crazy as hell. I don't know how long he'd been in here. I almost wished he never did carve that gap. At night he'd just sit there and lean against it and whisper to me. He'd say the most terrible things. About screamings coming from under the jailhouse and about the sheriff. He said the sheriff could make the cells sing to you at night, sing about all the bad things that had happened to you, and drown you in them. And he said he was old. You know how old he said the sheriff was? How old would you say he is by looking at him, Connelly?"

"Don't know. Fifty. Fifty-five."

"He said he thought the sheriff was nearly ninety years old."

"Bullshit."

"I know. That's what he said, though. But it makes sense, don't it? I mean, you've seen him. Have you... Have you seen his eyes?"

"Yeah."

"They ain't right, are they? Even though he's a little old man, his eyes is older. Like they seen too much. Or maybe they seen things most folks shouldn't see."

"What are you saying?"

"Oh, just something that crazy old man in your cell said once. Said the sheriff'd been working in this town for so long it was unreal. Said the sheriff'd made a deal with a god."

Connelly stopped. "What did you say?"

"Huh? I said the sheriff made a deal with a god."

"Which... which god?"

"Which god? I don't know, he was crazy. 'Sides, seems to be a lot of gods."

"What did he make the deal for?" whispered Connelly.

"What for? To live longer, that's what for. I don't know what the god got. Maybe just... just help. Maybe one hand washed the other, I don't know."

Connelly half listened to Peachy's words. He felt sick. He swallowed and said, "You... you think he can make people live longer?"

"Who? The god? Why, sure. He's a god. Old man said he'd come down out of the hills. Said sometimes there'd be scream-ing in the jailhouse, and those screams, they'd call to him. Wake him up. He'd come on down and see what was what.

Like the mountains opened up and bled and he rose up out of the ash, just tapping his foot."

"What did he look like?"

"What?"

"The god. What did the god look like?"

"He never said. Why? What's gotten into you?"

"Jesus," said Connelly. "Jesus Christ." His head began pounding again. There was a high, warbling whine in his ears, boring into all his thoughts. He grasped his skull and pushed his fingers into it as though to squeeze the pain out along with this new revelation.

What was this thing they hunted? How old was he, how long had this been going on for? Connelly remembered Korsher, drunkenly rambling in the grass. Remembered the look on the young boy's face as he recounted the scarred man's appearance. They had lived in his wake for so long, but what was he?

"What?" said Peachy's voice. "What'd you say? How long what? What you doing over there, Connelly?"

Connelly mumbled something in reply. He felt sick. Without thinking he began tearing strings off of the cuffs of his pants. Then he pulled splinters out of the wood around him and began trying to get his fingers to work. He was not as skilled as Roosevelt so the idol he made was crude but still good enough, he thought. He made its face out of dust and spit and though the eyes were lopsided they still were vaguely human.

"There," he wheezed, and lay back. "There." He placed it in the corner. Then he began coughing.

"Don't...don't you die on me, Connelly," said Peachy. "I ain't had no one to talk to in over a month. Please, don't you die on me, Connelly. Please don't..."

Connelly did not answer. The high-pitched squeal trapped in his head was drowning out all other thought. He curled up tighter on the floor and through watering eyes stared up at the ceiling. Above him he saw the shaft of sunlight flicker like a dying bulb, strobing the cell with shadows. But that was impossible. For if the sheriff had the power to kill the sun itself, even for a second, then Connelly and the others were surely in their graves already but did not know it yet.

Time became soft to him. Hours bled into weeks bled into months. Whatever part of Connelly's mind still worked believed he was sick, some infection, perhaps another concussion. He shivered all day and all night and when the deputies dropped off gruel and water he did not eat or drink. They laughed when they took away his full plate, their chuckles leaking through the slot in the door, and sometimes he believed they were staying on the other side of the door, watching and smiling.

The whine in his ears grew louder each day, his head filling up with pressure like a balloon. It made sleep difficult and thought almost impossible. Simply breathing was hard with that whine rattling in his head, turning his mind to jelly. He tried to feel his forehead to get a gauge of his temperature but his palms were clammy and wet with sweat. He shivered at all times and tried to tell his complexion by examining the backs of his hands but it was far too dark.

On the first morning the idol he had made was gone. There was no scrap of string or piece of twig left to show that it had ever been there. He suspected that something had come in the night, crawling out of the darkness and devouring it before retreating again. So he made a new idol. And when that one disappeared in the night, he made another, and another. And though he could not be sure he felt somehow that all these little souls he made and blessed in the dark cell were keeping him alive and staving off death. That each time they disappeared they had bought him another day.

He tried to count the days by the shaft of sunlight at the top of his cell but could not, as with each minute the light seemed darker and darker, like the very sun was fading or its radiance was being eaten by his cell. Peachy spoke all day and all night, telling him about the family he had, his mother and sisters, about frying fresh perch next to the river and drinking ale in the evening and kisses sweeter than any wine. Sometimes Peachy would sing and when he did Connelly's sickness seemed to fade a little. He knew Peachy was doing it to keep himself sane as much as anything, but Connelly did not care.

Then there came one night when Peachy slept and Connelly did not have voice enough to wake him. Connelly listened and believed himself deaf, he blinked at his cell and thought he was blind, and when he felt the boards beneath or beside them it was like touching air.

And Connelly said to himself, I am dying. And he believed it. Perhaps he was dead already.

Darkness swooped down on him, dripping out of the corners of the cell and swallowing him. He lay staring at the wall for what felt like ages. And when he shut his eyes he saw the desert.

White and brown and blue. The pale line of the desert burning against the chilly azure of the sky above. Dry air rushed over him and he blinked his eyes as their moisture evaporated. He focused and looked at what was before him.

He was sitting on a small hill, looking down on an immense basin. The sun beat down from the cloudless sky and to his left and right great arches of plateaus formed the edge of the bowl, their wrinkled, rusty skirts sloping down to the ivory floor of the desert. The air was so crisp and hot it felt electric. A land so striking and beautiful it pained the heart.

"Look," said a voice, and he turned to see the pale young man sitting beside him, still flecked with blood, his flaxen hair dancing in the wind. A wide smear of red still shone on his forehead, like the bill of a cap. The boy gestured into the desert before them.

Connelly turned to look. There was movement in the basin. On the far side he saw the edges of the plateaus almost quiver, like the sporadic rain of rocks that precedes a landslide, but as he watched he saw that the movements came not from rocks but from men, men with dark skin and long black hair. They poured from some unseen pass in the mountain face and even at this distance he saw they were sprinting at a great speed. Their teeth shone white and wild and in their hands they carried rude weapons hacked from wood and stone. They wore no clothing, and once they were close he realized some were women as well.

"Watch," said the young man to his left.

Connelly heard a cry from below. Another group of people came running from the near side, worming their way through a hidden crack in the slope. They were indistinguishable from the band of people in the distance save for streaks of mud across their faces and chest, like warpaint. The screams from the two groups intensified once they saw one another and their paths curved to meet, charging head-on, each party throwing themselves to greet the other's approach.

"What are they doing?" said Connelly.

"Watch," said the young man.

"What's going to happen?"

"You must watch."

As the two bands closed the distance they both let out shrieks of bright, glad rage. The heads of many weapons rose up into the sky like some feral salute, axe and spear and crude blade all hungry to crush and bite. All things seemed to stand still and tense, pausing to leap.

The two groups met. The spray was terrific on the white sands. Arcs of crimson spun out through the air and traced graceful circles on the desert floor. Axe and spear bobbed up and slashed down, bringing with them a rain of gore. Connelly watched as one man was spitted through the abdomen. He fell to his knees shrieking while a painted woman stooped and began sawing at his neck with a small black blade. Another painted soldier stood over a fallen foe, beating his opponent's head into pulp with a wide, flat stone. He screamed incoherently, unaware or perhaps not caring that the man was dead. Perhaps he could never be dead enough.

Connelly could not tell the screams of agony from those of triumph, the dances of victory from the death throes, the anguish from the joy. He watched as one woman picked up a severed head and held it above her and howled with pleasure, and was in turn attacked by a painted man who coveted her prize. He brought his mace down and her knee bent strangely and the head tumbled from her grasp. Two of his comrades crowded around to savage whatever part of her still lived.

"Why are they doing this?" Connelly asked.

"Why?" asked the young man. "They would not even know the word. If you were to ask they could not tell you."

"Who are they?"

"Killers. Killers of men. Killers of what can be killed. That is all they know or wish to know."

"So they kill for no reason? Not for land? For hate?"

"They do not know territory, nor do they know the past, and so they cannot hate. They may someday. In the future they may understand it and use it as their reason, as their means. But it is not their end."

"What is?"

The young man gestured before them. The desert floor was a deep red now. To Connelly it resembled a great red eye, a ring of white and a ring of red and then a circle of glistening brown, twitching and heaving. Almost none remained standing now.

"They're killing their friends," said Connelly.

"They have no friends. To them, friends are merely devices with which they may conquer their enemies. And when they cast down their foes, who remains? More enemies."

"They got to learn. They got to learn eventually."

"They have not yet."

"How long have they been here?"

"They have always been here. They change, some. The method of battle changes, the stakes grow, but the battle itself is always there."

"They could give up. They could go someplace else. Live peacefully."

"There are no peaceful lives," said the young man.

"What?" said Connelly. "No."

"Yes. All life is struggle. It is always battle. These people choose this way because it is simpler. It is easier for them."

"I knew peace once. I once lived a peaceful life."

"Then go back to it," said the young man.

To that Connelly had nothing to say. The young man nodded.

"It always finds you, in the end," he said. "It does not matter how you come to it. But you will. Struggling against someone, seeking to cast them down and make the final blow. One day each man and creature will find themselves doing the same."

"I don't know what to do," said Connelly. "How can I stop it?"

"Die," said the young man simply.

"I can't do that. I can't choose such a thing."

"Yes. And who can?"

Connelly looked at the carnage below. Vultures wheeled in the deep blue sky, mimicking the patterns below them, whether they knew it or not. "They could have never come in here," said Connelly. "They could have stayed out. Stayed away. Stayed far away and never come close."

"That would have meant denying the truth."

"The truth?"

"The truth of this place. If you were to halt the revolutions of creation, much like slowing a record with a single finger, and then find the center, that place where it is still and always had been still and always would be still, and then having found the center you opened up that tiny heart like a locket, why, inside you would see an arena like this one. Two people trapped within, each scrambling to kill the other."

"I don't care," Connelly said. "I don't give a damn. A lie

would be better. Any lie. I would rather live with a lie than this, and they could have chosen that."

"They could have. But they did not."

Almost nothing lived on the desert floor now. The vultures circled lower. The young man sighed and lifted his face to the sun. "You will see me soon," he said. "You will see me soon, Connelly."

"I will?" asked Connelly.

"Yes," said the young man. Then he lifted his hand and touched the red on his forehead, and with glistening fingertips he reached forward and touched Connelly's brow. "Wake," he said. "And see."

Connelly felt consciousness crystallize somewhere within him. He saw darkness. Then the walls of the jail cell formed in the shadows and he smelled vomit somewhere and knew he was still alive.

"Connelly?" said Peachy's voice. "Connelly, you there?"

Connelly touched the floor in response, scraping the wood.

"Connelly, I think they did something to your cell. I don't know what. I think they hid something in it. Something to make you sick. I-I think I figured out what it is just now."

He tried to pull himself awake. He knew these words were important but it was difficult to grasp them, like trying to catch greased snakes.

"Look for something wedged in the cracks," said Peachy. "Something little, no bigger than a finger. Maybe it's up in the roof."

He looked up at the roof. It might as well have been miles away. He could barely stay awake, let alone stand.

Peachy said, "It'll be making a noise. A funny...a funny kind of song, I think."

Connelly moved to the corner and pressed his back into it for support. Then with trembling legs he pushed himself up the scarred wood but fell once, then twice. On the third he was not standing but was on his feet, leaning into the corner of the cell. Once there he listened carefully, or at least as best he could.

The whine was louder here. It was not an infection. Something in the room was singing to him.

He wiped at his eyes and mouth and found his lips slick with drool. He spat on the floor and then rolled his head to one side. There the whine was fainter. He rolled his head back in the other direction, still listening. It was louder there, painfully loud. It made his teeth hurt just to hear it.

"You find it yet?" said Peachy.

Connelly leaned against the wall and stumbled along it, one ear turned toward its cracks. He passed one crack and the whine was so loud he almost fainted. The room shuddered around him, the light flickering and fading at the corners, like the sound was choking the very air.

He fumbled at the crack, forcing his fingers deep down into it. Finding nothing, he looked higher, fingers wriggling in the small space. He touched something, something rough and smooth at the same time, something knobby at one end. He pushed deeper, fingers toying with the thing's end, and it fell out and clattered to the floor, the wail intensifying as soon as it was dislodged.

He squatted and looked at it. It was a bone. A small bone, like the thighbone of a chicken or the bone of a man's foot. It was gray as ditchwater and on its surface were tiny, fine engravings, writing as thin and ghostly as a cobweb, running in rings and circles down its edge. He reached down and with shivering hands picked it up and looked at it and as he brought it close he could hear words in its shrill whine, quiet chanting in some tongue he had never heard before.

He said the sheriff could make the cells sing to you at night. Sing about all the bad things that had happened to you, and drown you in them.

"Oh my God," said Connelly.

"For God's sake, Connelly, do something," pleaded Peachy. "It sounds so awful. Break it or something, please."

Connelly looked at the little bone for a minute longer, then took it in both hands and tried to break it in half. He found he was too weak to do so and so he lodged part of it in a crack in the wall and leaned on the exposed end. The bone bent, then snapped in half and he swore he heard the little bone scream, a yelp like a dog being kicked, and from its broken end something foul and black and thick poured out, covering his hands and running in streaks down the wall. It reeked of chaw spit and spoiled beer and old leaves.

"It's alive," he heard himself say. "The goddamn thing is alive."

As soon as he spoke he felt the air around him clear and the light from above him strengthen, and while the cell was by no means clean or comfortable it felt like bliss after the past days. His head was clear and his heart strong and he felt alive enough to stand on his own feet without leaning.

"Good God," said Peachy. "Good God, that sounds so much better."

Connelly breathed deep, in and then out. "Yeah. Yeah, it does. What the hell was that?"

"I think it was a taint," said Peachy.

"A what?"

"A taint."

"Last I checked a taint was the part of you between your asshole and your pecker."

"Well, I don't know anything about that. I was just thinking about what that old man said and I...I just remembered something the other night. Maybe it was a dream, I don't know. I remembered something my momma told me once when I was a boy, something to scare us, but sort of a joke, you know? She said there used to be a witch in her neighborhood who could take a bone and put a little bit of her own black soul in it and then she'd hide it in your room and it'd tell you to do things as you slept. She'd write on the bone what you were supposed to do and the bone would whisper to you and in the morning you'd do it. I thought it was crazy."

"Yeah."

"But it wasn't."

"Think I heard this before," said Connelly. "From someone else. Said it tainted and poisoned the land." He shook his head. "Jesus. Jesus Christ. Jesus Christ almighty, things like this don't happen. Things like this aren't real."

"But it did happen," said Peachy. "It is real."

Connelly thought about it and said, "Yeah."

CHAPTER TWENTY

The next day when the deputies dropped off his gruel and water Connelly grabbed the tin plate and ate hungrily. They did not laugh and reacted with some surprise and he heard their footfalls quickly fall away.

"Going to be trouble," said Connelly.

"Yeah," said Peachy.

But there was not. The two of them waited in silence, letting the hours pass by, yet no one came. There was no sound at all. The entire jail was quiet.

As night fell a gray sheet of clouds crawled over the moon. The wind rose until it hammered the building and the temperature dropped until the two men shivered and they began to see their breath. Somewhere in Connelly's belly the animal thing yowled and cried, full of strange knowledge of being hunted, of something watching out in the night.

"What's going on?" asked Peachy through the crack in the wall.

"Something's coming," said Connelly.

Less than an hour later the sheriff came for him. Two deputies put him in handcuffs and marched him down to the cinderblock room where the sheriff had beaten them not more than a week ago, by Connelly's reckoning. He cuffed Connelly to the stool and looked at him without speaking, eyes heavy as though he was envious of him. Then he took his pistol and whipped Connelly across the side of the head. Connelly curled in his seat and the sheriff bent down and spat into his face. He looked at Connelly a moment longer and then left, shutting the door behind him.

Connelly sat and tried to recover. No one else entered. Minutes ticked by. He waited, trying to stay conscious.

Soon he was aware of a horrible stench in the room, a stink of putrefaction and lye. He coughed and tried to find some pocket of fresh air.

A quiet, cold voice said, "You're taller than I remember."

Connelly looked up and around for the source of the voice. At first he saw nothing. Then he spotted a pair of scuffed shoes in the shadows next to the desk, and above those a pair of patched trousers and a coat the color of trainsmoke with gray-white hands nestled in its folds like chunks of quartz in granite. And somewhere above that he could make out a face, queerly colorless, heavily lined, with calm, placid eyes like jet and ribbons of scars running across its cheeks, its forehead, its neck and brow, a delicate calligraphy of violence.

Connelly was bellowing before he knew what was going on. He strained forward in his seat and planted his legs and pulled until the cuffs bit into his wrists and his palms were wet with blood. The gray man did not seem to even register it. He let the screams go on until Connelly was gasping for breath. Then he walked around and looked at where the cement floor was spattered with blood from Connelly's wrists. He examined it as though faintly curious and nodded to himself.

"I see," he said, "that you are still alive."

"Fuck you," snarled Connelly.

"You've come a long way since Memphis."

"Fuck you."

"As have I."

Connelly growled and heaved himself at the man. The gray man stood just inches away, looking down on him calmly. This close Connelly could see one scar on his cheek went up into his scalp, cutting his ear in half and nearly splitting half his head. The gray man seemed strangely still. He did not even seem to need to breathe.

"You should not have followed me," he said with a trace of sadness.

"Bastard! Bastard!" Connelly howled. "You killed my daughter! You killed my little girl! My little girl, my little fucking girl!"

"You should not have followed me," said the gray man again.

"I'm going to kill you," snarled Connelly. "I'm going to kill you. Cut your throat, you fucking bastard. Kill you."

"It has been a long time since I have been aware of men," said the gray man. "A man, more specifically. You are all so alike. I can no more tell you apart than I could a drop of water in the ocean."

"Fuck you."

"It's so strange. If I were to take a man from the hills of this country on which we stand," said the gray man, "and then take another from some foreign place — China, perhaps — and if you were then to cut a foot off of each of those men I am certain the noises they would make with their mouths would be similar. Their histories and cultures and names would crumble and they would be the same man then, would they not?"

"Bastard," said Connelly. "Fucking bastard. You sick, sick bastard."

"But you are different," said the gray man. "You and I. I notice you, I even know your name, which is strange in its own right. We are alike in some fashion which I find difficult to perceive."

Connelly screamed and heaved himself forward again. The gray man seemed not to notice. His blank eyes were fixed on Connelly and he might have been blind, seeing but not seeing, staring through everything like all matter and all creatures within his eyesight were immaterial.

Connelly finished screaming. The gray man said, "You don't agree?"

"Goddamn you. Goddamn you to hell. I am not like you, I'm not."

"You have taken lives in getting here. You are willing to take more in the future."

"I don't kill little girls!" howled Connelly.

The gray man considered this, accepted it with a tilt of the head. "No. You do not. Not yet."

"I ain't never going to, neither. I ain't like you and I ain't like the goddamn sheriff. I don't kill, you bastards, I'm no murderer. You're all fucking monsters doing whatever the hell you please, ain't you?"

"The sheriff does as I ask. I see you survived his little poison. I'm somewhat impressed." Then he reached forward and dropped something onto the floor. A pile of twigs and string, horribly mauled. Chewed, almost. "An old magic, and a minor one," he said. "You fed the taint and made it slow and fat. But it would have gotten you in the end, you know, had you not found it."

"I'll kill you both," said Connelly, now almost sobbing. "Kill the both of you. I don't understand why the hell you'd bother to do this."

"The sheriff is a friend of mine," said the gray man. "I have given him something very precious and he does small tasks for me."

"And what the hell could any man ever want from a bastard like you?"

"Life," said the gray man. "Peace. These things are valued, yes?"

"I'm going to kill you," said Connelly. "Maybe not now and maybe not today, but goddamn you, the last thing you see on this earth is going to be my face. Last image your fucked-up brain is going to take in is going to be my face, and I'll say her name. I'll say her name and that'll be the last thing you hear because that's what killed you, the second you touched her you were dead and I'm going to be the one to do it. And you'll die knowing it. You'll die knowing it. I swear."

The gray man listened to that and once more Connelly saw some strange fear work its way into his face. He said, "Mr. Connelly, you should go home."

"Fuck you."

"You should give up now and go home."

"Keep running. I don't care how long it takes. I'll find you."

"You think I am running from you?" said the gray man. "Is that what you think?"

Connelly didn't answer. The gray man bent low. His eyes were huge in his face and his ruined mouth twisted into a snarl. "Dawn is breaking," he whispered. "Night has fallen and the dawn comes. It is on the horizon. Do you not feel it? Each breath this nation and this world takes is one taken in anticipation, for in our future something rears its head, something new and terrible, and the sun shall show it. These past years have been the long night before it, the long midwinter. But now I ask you, what will you see once that dawn breaks? What will it reveal? When the cold gray light washes across the face of this earth, will it be the same earth you fell asleep in? Or will it be something new? Will it be something so great and awesome that it will deny words and dwarf language, something to belittle all the previous creations of man and beast? Can you say for sure?"

"I don't know what the hell you're talking about."

"Do you not? Why not? Does your life matter so little? It is happening out there!" he cried, pointing westward. "Just out there! The years and ages line up and somewhere in those endless flats time itself heaves with pangs of labor, a sick, red cunt that readies to birth a new age! A new era! Do you not understand?"

"You're crazy. You're a fucking loon."

The gray man thought about that and stooped to eye level.

"No," he whispered. "No." He leaned close. "Do you know what I've seen out there?"

Connelly did not answer.

"I have been to the far reaches," said the gray man. "I have walked to the edge where the black vaults swallow creation and I stood on the edge of the world and pissed into nothingness. I've seen the things that hide and dance behind the stars in the sky and I pinned them to the ground and laughed and made them tell me their names one by one, one by one."

The gray man drew himself up to his fullest height, an impossibly tall man, and as he spoke Connelly swore his scars were no longer scars but it was all one mouth, enormous and ragged. His voice grew loud and as it did the light seemed to shrink.

"I have walked in dark places where eyeless things of no mind and no soul gnaw the bottoms of mountains and eat rock and stone the likes of which mankind has never known and will never know. I have watched eons being devoured by crushing waves and as I watched I knew in my heart that I was the sole witness of their existence and their passing. I have stalked the forests that ring the top of this earth where snow is thick and silence has gone undisturbed for centuries, and *lifetimes* may pass before finding a single footprint in the snow. And I have walked toward the center of this vast spinning world, Mr. Connelly, where light has no meaning and all is consumed, and I looked at the great violation that makes this land's heart, that fills it with hunger, and on the sides of that black crack was my name written again and again and again. And again and again and again. Do you hear me, little man? Do you hear me?"

He looked down on Connelly, eyes still blank. "I have done things which your mind cannot possibly comprehend, which you cannot ever approach. I am in all shadows and in no shadow, I am in every atom and I am in every heart. And I will not allow the new day to break. Night everlasting, if it may be so. And you must stop, Mr. Connelly. You *must* stop. You must leave me be and *stop*."

Connelly said, "Then kill me."

The gray man charged forward, his long white hands grasping out, but they stopped inches away from Connelly's neck. He saw the scarred man struggle, face contorted, like he was pulling against an unimaginable force. He shuddered, then withdrew, his chest heaving and a sheen of sweat across his pallid brow.

"I could," said the gray man. "I could. I dearly wish to. But there are *rules*. There is order. Natures which cannot be denied." He stared down on Connelly. "You will die here. If you follow this path you will be destroyed. I know. And if you follow me any further, Mr. Connelly, everyone you know and everyone you trust will find their end here as well. Know that. Know that and do what you will, if you survive the next day."

The gray man turned to walk away. He opened the iron door and as he stood in the hall light he looked like any tramp again, just a tired old tramp with a ruined face.

"I want to know something," said Connelly.

The gray man looked back, his expression inscrutable.

"I want to know why you killed my little girl."

The gray man cocked his head. There was no thought in his face or his posture. He regarded Connelly for a second and said, "So that she would die."

The door shut. Connelly began screaming again. He screamed until the guards came and beat him and threw him back into his cell.

CHAPTER TWENTY-ONE

When they dumped him off Connelly spent the better part of the next hour hurling himself against his cell door. Peachy tried his best to talk him down but Connelly would not listen, could not listen. He raged and flung himself against it until his shoulders were bruised and his ankles ached and it was only when he paused that they realized they could hear another noise.

Screaming. A man somewhere in the jail was crying in fear and pain.

"What is that?" asked Peachy softly.

"Roosevelt," whispered Connelly. "Rosie. He's doing something to him. He's doing something to my friend."

"What do you think he's doing?"

"I don't know."

"Are you scared, Connelly?" asked Peachy.

"Yeah. Yeah. You?"

"Yes. What'd they do to you?"

"Hit me. And..."

"And what?"

"Nothing. They didn't do nothing good, that's for sure."

"You...you think they're going to kill me too, Connelly?"

He looked at the little crack in the wall. Somewhere Roosevelt stopped screaming. "No," said Connelly.

"What makes you say that?"

"I-I don't know. Just don't think about that, Peachy. Just don't."

"You think we should pray?"

"I guess."

"Come on. Pray with me, Connelly."

"All right."

Connelly sat on the floor and put his hands together and bowed his head. It was not until his palms touched that he realized he was trembling. He could not remember the last time he prayed. He listened to Peachy's whispering but he could not understand any formula or any process in it. So he steeled himself and sent a wordless, desperate cry for aid up into the sky, hoping it would pierce the roof of the jail and the mantle of clouds and the net of stars behind that, venturing out beyond to where nothingness had no claim and there might be some consciousness, some intelligence that would listen and understand and sympathize. Something, just something. But it seemed unlikely that anything so vast would notice or care.

He was so small. A little man scrambling across the wilderness, trying to make the cosmos pay attention and make sense. In that midnight belly of the jail, dawn was a memory and the sun was no more than a dream, and hope tasted more of a curse to him than a blessing.

But still he steeled himself, culled those thoughts of higher powers and purpose from his mind, and thought about simpler matters—of getting out of the jail cell, and of tomorrow, and of murder, which appeared simpler by the second.

Then they waited for the executioner's footfall. It seemed like there was something they needed to say. But they could think of nothing.

Three hours had passed when they heard a sound: a rustling, not outside, but somehow below.

"You hear that?" asked Peachy.

"Yeah," said Connelly.

They listened. There were voices whispering, cursing and shushing one another. Connelly stood to his feet and looked down. The voices were right below him. They stopped and he heard a giggle, and then a voice said, "Hey, you."

Connelly shrank back against the wall.

"Aren't you going to say hello?" said the voice.

"H-Hammond?" he said.

"Yeah. It's me. Give me a sec."

Connelly fell to the floor and grabbed at the warped wood, feverishly trying to find some way to pull the planks apart but finding none.

"Get back, you damn fool, we don't want to cut you any."

He stepped back and before him a small saw pierced the bottom of the floor, rising up between the cracks. It wriggled to get a better bite on the wood and then began moving up and down, sawing diagonal across one of the boards. It seemed to take hours to get through the wood. They pushed up on it and Connelly grabbed the severed end and tried to pull it back.

"Not so loud! You'll wake up the whole damn place!" hissed Hammond's voice.

"Connelly?" said Peachy. "What...what's going on?"

"Who the hell is that?" said Hammond.

"Just hold on, Peachy," Connelly said.

"Peachy?" said Hammond, incredulous.

They pried the board up and sawed through a few more and Connelly saw Hammond and Roonie crouched below in a curiously large space, like the jail was not built on any firm foundation but instead was on a basement of some kind. They were covered head to toe in mud and soil.

Roonie stared up at him, mournful and terrified. "You won't believe what we had to dig through." He shook his head. "You won't believe it."

"Shush," said Hammond grimly. "Jesus, Con. You look like shit."

Connelly dropped through the hole in the floor. When his bare feet touched earth he began weeping.

"It's okay," Hammond said. "You've got to...Come on, Con, buck up."

"Peachy," said Connelly. "We got to get Peachy out."

"Who the hell is Peachy?" said Hammond.

"Peachy's my friend."

"We don't have time for this. We still have to get Pike and Rosie out."

"Peachy's my friend," insisted Connelly.

"Damn it all."

They sawed through Peachy's floor in minutes. When the floorboard was pulled away Connelly peered through and looked at the face above.

Connelly blinked. "You're colored," he said to Peachy.

Peachy smiled, white teeth shining bright in his dark face. "Am I? Never noticed."

Connelly considered this and shrugged. "Okay. Come on."

Peachy wriggled through the hole. He was tall and thin and lanky and his beard and hair were overgrown, much like Connelly's.

"I thank you kindly for the exit," he said to Hammond.

"Hell," said Hammond. "We got us a merry band of mother-fuckers now, now don't we?"

"What is this place?" said Connelly.

"A basement," said Hammond, now grim again. "We think. We dug in through the side of the hill and we thought it was going to take weeks. As it turns out, this hill's been hollowed out for some time. And…and he's been doing things down here."

"Who?"

"Your sheriff."

"Awful things," whimpered Roonie. "I don't know what he does to the prisoners here, but…"

"He beats them," said Connelly. "He's got a little room he does it in."

"No," said Hammond. "He does a little more than that."

The floor turned to rough-cut flagstones and Connelly smelled rot and bleach ahead. They moved through a small passage with an earthen ceiling and entered a low chamber. At the far end was a large stone table, almost an altar, and in the center were those strange, red-rust stains he had seen up above in the sheriff's confession room. In the center was a short stone stool, covered in the same stains. A pipe was installed in the ceiling just above it, opening onto the seat, and Connelly had no doubt the pipe led to the drain in the confessional. He envisioned men sitting on that stool, eyes shut and palms up, listening to the cries above and feeling the warm rain baptize them for whatever life they were willing to live.

As they neared Connelly could see there were stars drawn on the roof and walls of the basement, and a symbol was painted above the stone table. It was the snake devouring itself, and its paint was such a color that he could not tell if it was dark red or merely black.

"They think he's their god," said Hammond softly.

Connelly shook his head. "The gods go begging here."

They wound through the sheriff's labyrinth, staring up through the cracks in the floorboards at the inmates. The variety was astonishing. Some were idle drunks, others raving madmen, several seemed dead to the eye or surely would be soon without attention. Quiet sobs and enraged mutterings tumbled from the ceiling like so much dust.

Connelly found Pike and Hammond sawed him out quick as could be. The old man climbed down without so much as a twitch of the eyebrow. He surveyed them, looked at Peachy without surprise, and said, "God takes care of His own." Then he crooked a finger and they followed him through the maze.

They came under one cell and whoever was above it was whimpering constantly, clawing at the walls and the door. Pike looked up at it and said, "And here is Mr. Roosevelt, I think."

Hammond and Connelly shared a look and then began sawing him out as well. Roosevelt shied away from the blade and cried and would not quiet until Hammond stuck his head up. Then he began sobbing and clambered through the hole. When he saw Connelly he collapsed at his feet and pawed at his trousers like an invalid.

"Jesus, Rosie," murmured Hammond. "Jesus."

"What have they done to that boy?" said Peachy.

"I don't know," said Pike. "I was close by and heard. Whatever it was, it was quite bad."

There were no marks on him, though, no wounds or blood of any kind.

"Connelly," whispered Roosevelt. "Connelly. Connelly, are you there?"

"I'm here," said Connelly. "I'm right in front of you."

"He...he came. He was here, just now. Did you know that?"

"Yeah, Rosie. Yeah, I did."

"He came and he spoke to me."

"Okay, Rosie. It's okay."

Roosevelt's eyes grew wide. "Do you know what he showed me?" he whispered slowly.

"We need to get moving," said Pike. "Now, Mr. Hammond. I suggest we leave right now. Where's your tunnel out?"

"This way," said Hammond. "Come on, Rosie. Come on, man, on your feet. Come along, now."

Roosevelt staggered up and with Hammond's support they began to hobble through the passageways. Soon Connelly smelled night air, fresh outdoors air for the first time since his capture. They sped up, desperate to be outside again. Wind howled ahead and a breeze flew through the tunnels, speckling them with grit and forcing them to shield their eyes.

Above them they heard a voice say, "Say, where's that draft coming from? And that damn noise?"

They ran forward, stumbling through the passageways, clay earth crumbling about their ears as they moved. They came to a hole in an old brick wall, barely more than two feet wide. Pike went first, then Hammond, then Peachy, then Rosie and Roonie, and finally Connelly stuffed himself into the earthen gap, wriggling through the clods.

It was tough going. He did not have room enough to work his elbows and he was forced to kick himself forward. More than once dust fell before his face, causing him to cough. He was sure the tunnel would cave in soon. It seemed to last forever and often Roonie would slow down and Connelly would be kicked in the face in the dark. Someone sobbed ahead of him, probably Roosevelt, maybe Roonie.

It was ten long minutes of crawling and struggling. As Roosevelt tumbled out the earth shifted around them and the sides of the tunnel slid down to trap Connelly and Roonie both. Connelly shut his eyes and took a breath as soon as he could and tried to ignore the burning in his sinuses. He felt Roonie fly forward, surely dragged out by the others, and he reached forward blindly, thrusting his hands through the soil. He felt someone's fingertips graze his and disappear. His lungs burned, he pushed forward again. Then someone felt his hand and grasped his wrist and pulled.

He spilled out, gasping and heaving. "Quiet," said Pike's voice.

They were covered in dirt, like some breed of warriors camouflaged for wasteland combat. Connelly brushed it out of his eyes and Hammond whispered, "Come on."

They ran down the hill and as Connelly looked over his shoulder he saw the jailhouse had been stationed on the very top, allowing Hammond to tunnel straight in. At the foot of the hill a wide figure rose and they heard Monk's voice softly call, "You got them all? All of them? They all right?"

"We got them," said Roonie. "Now we got to—"

"Bastards!" called a voice from far up behind them. They turned to look.

Connelly heard the throaty bark of a shotgun and tiny flecks of dirt erupted around them. Hammond dropped to the ground and swore and clutched his ankle. Pike cried, "Run!" just as pistol fire began cackling on the top of the hill.

Connelly looked over his shoulder. He saw torches weaving down after them, both fire and electric. He ran with the others, not caring what direction they went in.

"Split up!" called Hammond. "Spread out!"

A shotgun roared again and Connelly heard someone cry but he could not see who. He dove to his left and grabbed the figure beside him and threw it down. Shot buzzed through the space he had just occupied. The man in his arms cursed and he realized it was Roonie. Connelly lifted his head to look around. He could not see the others. They had run on and taken cover as quickly as they could.

When he thought it was safe they got to their feet and sprinted for the woods, velvet fir trees swaying gently below them, almost indigo in the dark. Halfway there they took cover behind the skeleton of an old Zephyr tumbled in a ditch. They crouched and looked through the spindly remains of the windows. Muzzle flare glowed here and there, the shooters invisible against the backdrop of the hill. He could not tell if it was the sheriff's men or if perhaps Hammond and Monk had armed themselves. Behind the crest of a knoll he saw flames dancing gaily, a small fire eager to grow. Shouts of warning, maybe shouts of rage. The dip and bob of heads and rifle barrels as men scrambled over the gravel. All of them, riding thunder down the mountain.

Nearby a shotgun roared again and buckshot showered the Zephyr, clinking and clanking like hail. Roonie wailed and the two of them ran the rest of the way down to the woods. They crawled through the furry limbs of the pines until the hillside could only be seen through gaps in the treeline. Once there they threw themselves beneath a tree to wait and look.

"You see anything?" asked Roonie softly.

Connelly shushed him. Roonie took a breath, then dove across to another trunk to get a better look. As soon as he did the shotgun went off again and Connelly heard shot biting through the trees. Roonie fell behind the trunk and Connelly thought him dead until he saw the man's face lift up, his cheeks covered in tears, hands shaking uncontrollably. Connelly motioned to get down again and he did.

They stayed still. They heard the crunch of dirt and gravel, a rain of loose earth tumbling down the slope. Nothing for a while. Then Connelly thought he heard soft branches being bent or needles being crushed, the whisper of a footfall. A dove grieved somewhere, but he was not sure if their stalker was calling for aid or if it was as simple as it sounded.

Roonie rose to a crouch across from him. Connelly shook his head no. Roonie nodded, pointing down the slope, and in return Connelly motioned to get back down. The little man shook his head, still trembling.

A branch snapped. Close by, too close, no more than a dozen yards. Something stopped moving and Connelly withdrew farther into the branches.

A gout of yellow-white flame roared up into the air a few feet away and Connelly knew the man had been closer than he had ever guessed. Roonie leapt up, startled like a partridge by the warning shot. As he tried to sprint away the other barrel fired and Connelly saw the little man's side dissolve and his cheek burst open. He tumbled in a heap, thin lines of smoke rising into the air, a puppet whose strings had been abruptly cut. A voice cried out in triumph.

"Hot damn, I got you!" shouted the sheriff's voice. "I got you, you big son of a bitch, I told you I would! I told you I would!"

The sheriff skipped over to the fallen man with the spryness of a child and looked down on the corpse. The mere action of murder made his face more boyish than it had ever been. He smiled and put a foot under it and turned the body over. Then he grunted in surprise.

"What?" he said.

Connelly sprang out from the cover of the tree.

He carried him deep into the forest, a quarter mile at least. It was hard going. The sheriff was not a big man but he was not light either, and the odd times that he resisted slowed Connelly considerably. But he kept on.

Connelly dragged him far away from his town, far away from any roof or hut or home. He did not cry out. Connelly had seen to that, having broken his jaw at the onset. When he judged he had carried the little man into the heart of the forest he sat down and went to work.

He broke his knees, his shins, his feet and hands. He broke his elbows and his wrists and put fractures in his pelvis. Connelly could not say for sure but he felt he broke the little man's eye socket and maybe a few of his ribs.

Bones crushed to dust, grinding in the sockets. The little man writhing under his grasp, unable to strike back. To relish it was an evil thing, he knew, but he found resisting it difficult.

As he worked Connelly whispered, "This is the world I make for you. This right here. This is the world I make for you."

He did not kill him. He would not give the sheriff the dignity of murder.

When he was done Connelly was covered in sweat from his toil and he turned and continued down the gentle slope of the mountain. The sheriff whimpered behind him, his limbs shuffling in the pine needles. Connelly did not look back. Soon the whimpers and noises faded and he could not hear anything at all.

r

CHAPTER TWENTY-TWO

Connelly walked for more than a day. He guessed he could not go back as all the woods close to the jailhouse were probably hunting ground, and besides, he knew if he followed the slope long enough he would eventually find water.

He did not realize how weak he was until three hours in, when he stumbled and fell down a gully. He twisted his ankle and tried to pry a dead branch off a tree for a crutch but found he had lost most of his strength. The starvation and sickness and lack of water had taken their toll and then some.

He saw and heard no animals, no other people. When the dawn rose it wove a silver forest world of mist and gray-green undergrowth. The air was fresh and thin here, perhaps due to the elevation, but Connelly was no longer sure where he was. Perhaps New Mexico, maybe Colorado. Maybe it was no state at all, just an empty land with no allegiance or creed. As all states were, if one walked long enough.

The silence was unbearable and soon the cold matched it. As the day wore on the frost wormed into his bones and his shivering made every step uncertain. He was still barefoot. He had done his best to keep his feet uninjured but now he could barely feel them.

He looked up as he stepped across another small gully and saw a thin, gray stream of smoke rising into the sky. He studied it and guessed the distance and changed his course.

He came to a rocky stream and examined the smoke again and decided they had to be camped next to the river. He stripped and washed himself first and drank deep, the water so cold it stung his lips and face. Then he limped along and saw the smoke was coming from a crumbling chimney whose snout poked above the tops of the trees, just off the river. He heard singing and he looked and saw there was a woman washing clothing in the water. She was old with skin like molasses and her voice warbled like a man playing a saw. She lurched back and forth between the stones, scrubbing down her laundry, and as Connelly approached she glanced up and grinned hugely.

"What you doing there, dead white boy?" she called.

"I'm not dead," said Connelly.

"Sure you are. Just don't know it yet."

"Ain't really a boy, neither."

"Well, what you going to do to prove me wrong? Take your pecker out and wave it at me? That'd raise a few eyebrows, white fella doing that in front of a colored woman, wouldn't it?" She cackled gaily.

Connelly leaned on his crutch and hobbled closer. The old woman stood up and looked him over.

"You seen some shit, white boy," the old woman said.

"I'm…I'm hungry, ma'am. I don't mean to interrupt, but—"

"But you going to anyways." She sighed and clucked her tongue. "Oh, well. Set you on down by the bank there and try not to die anytime soon. I won't have no corpse-water dirtying up my stream. You just set there and wait."

He did so. He looked behind and saw a wide, low cabin hidden back in the trees. Its windows danced with the warmth of a hearth fire and on its porch sat three empty rocking chairs. A winding path led up through the trees to the front door. At the mouth of the path was a pile of loose odds and ends, shoes and fishing poles and even cheap jewelry. He listened to the old woman sing and toss her clothes into a wicker basket. Sometimes she would peer into the stream and dart her hand in and fish out some piece of junk, a shiny bauble that was no more than trash. Then she would caw happily and bring it over to the pile and carefully place it on the mound.

"You live here by yourself?" said Connelly.

"With my sisters," she said. "I'm the only able one, though. They old. They old as hell. You know?"

"Sure."

She laughed. "You don't know."

"Sure."

"Boy, you every woman's dream, agreeing with whatever fall out of her mouth."

"I try."

"Give me a second," she said. "I'll give you something that'll put a spring in your step, maybe your trousers too." She cackled again and shuffled up into the cabin. She returned with an old tin cup, plumes of steam pouring out the top. She handed it to him. "Careful, now. It's hot."

He took it and looked at it. The fluid it held was thick and brown-green and smelled strongly of mint and herbs. "What is it?"

"Pine needle tea. With mint. And wormwood. All sorts of good shit. It's my sister's recipe. Give it a whirl, you been freezing for God knows how long, I can tell. It lets you know you're alive, white boy."

He blew on it and sipped. As it dripped down his throat his insides turned cold and hot all at once. He breathed out and it burned but seemed to burn away the fatigue as well.

"God," he said. "It's . . . it's . . ."

"It's awful," she said cheerfully. "I said it was good for you, I never said it tasted good. Things that's good for you are never fun to swallow. Ain't that the way," she said to herself. "Ain't that the way."

She shuffled back down to the creek and picked up her basket of clothes with a grunt. Connelly rose to help her.

"Oh, sit down," she scolded. "You in worse shape than me. Them clothes are all that's holding you up and there ain't much of those, neither. 'Sides, I need the exercise."

She strung a line from the window of the house to the cedar across from it and draped her clothes over it, humming tunelessly. She stepped back, brushed her hands, and nodded in satisfaction. Then she turned to Connelly and looked at him with a keen eye.

"You been causing some serious trouble, ain't you?" she said.

Connelly did not answer. He readied himself to run if he could and attack if he had to.

"Oh, come on now," scoffed the old woman. "I just served you some damn good tea. Secret recipe, too. I don't waste that on just anyone."

"How did you know?"

"Smoke told me," she said with a grin, and she gestured toward the chimney. "Rose on up into the sky, looked over the mountain and said, 'Say, old Nina, I see a lot of hubbub down south of here and there's a man coming your way carrying a lot of trouble.'" Her grin faded. "A lot of trouble," she repeated solemnly.

"Yeah," said Connelly. "I know."

"That's just it, ain't it? You don't," she said. "Here, come on up to the house, boy. We'll let my clothes dry and we'll get you close to a fire. You can rummage the junk heap too, if you want. Try to find shoes. Come on."

The old woman led the way, clucking whenever Connelly tried to help her up. As she opened her front door she shouted, "Dexy, we got company!"

"Oh?" said a voice even older than Nina's. He rounded the corner. A shrunken old woman sat in an overstuffed chair before a guttering fire. She was so bent double her chin almost touched her chest. In her lap she was doing her best to crochet but her knuckles and wrists were swollen with arthritis. She was blacker even than Nina, her skin like cracked volcanic glass at the edges of her eyes. She stared into Connelly's waist, then grunted and looked up at him. She worked her lips, tonguing her toothless gums, and said, "Good gods, you're a big one. I don't know what they fed you but they fed you too much of it."

"He's been starved, Dexy," said Nina.

"Oh, no."

"Yeah. Wandered on out of the woods like a wild child. Raised by wolves, maybe."

"No. He looks wolfish but he's got a boy's eyes," said Dexy.

Nina grunted noncommittally, like she disagreed but would not argue.

"Here, sit you down, boy," said Dexy. "There ain't a chair here can hold you, but just sit down on the floor if that's all right."

"I've sat and slept on worse," said Connelly.

"That I believe," said Nina.

The cabin was large and shabby but still comfortable. The stone floor was cracking but laid well and the rafters were kept clean of cobwebs. Three chairs sat around the fire, the empty ones on either side of Dexy. Each was made for little old ladies. On the opposite wall were three doors, two open and leading to bedrooms, the third slightly closed and the inside dark.

"Your tea is good," said Connelly. "I had some."

"Oh, flattery," Dexy said, but she smiled. "Flattery. That will get you anything. What do you need, young man?"

"Just, well...I came up, and..."

"Oh, you don't have to say no more," she fussed. "Nina, this boy needs to eat."

"Well. I guess I'll feed him, if that's the way it's going to be," said Nina grudgingly, and went to the kitchen.

"Here," Dexy said to him. She held out a melted lump of wax with a small bit of wick swimming in the center. "Here, take this candle and light it in the fire, if you don't mind. My damn eyes ain't worth a lick anymore."

Connelly did so, using a thin branch as a match. He set it on the table beside her and she fiddled with her crochet halfheartedly.

"I used to be so damn good at this," she said. "Only thing that's worse than a thing that don't work is a thing that almost works." She dropped her needles, sighed, and raised her head up to the ceiling in despair.

"Mind if I ask you a question?" asked Connelly.

"Oh, probably. But go on ahead if you want."

"What are you all doing out here? It must be miles from anything."

She grunted, turning the question over. Then she said, "Knitting."

"Knitting?"

"Yeah. Well, that's alls I do, at least."

"You moved out to the woods to knit?"

"Most days it seems like I've always been here," she said. "But then, it may just be my age."

Nina came out and served him cold chicken and corn-meal. She left to get him a fork and when she returned he had already eaten most of it with his hands.

"Lord, I said you was starving, but I didn't realize you was dead on your feet," she said. She sat on Dexy's right and pulled a shawl about her shoulders.

He took the fork from her. He had not used one in a very long time and it took some remembering.

"Hold it like a pencil," said Nina.

"Been even longer since I held a pencil," said Connelly, but he tried. The two old women watched him eat.

"Boy's been living on the edges a while now, Nina," said Dexy in her frail little voice.

"Ain't that so. Long time."

"He went out there himself and now he don't know where he's going."

"No idea at all. I agree."

Connelly looked up and saw the two old women were watching him, Nina no longer cackling, Dexy's face no longer old and confused anymore. In the firelight they could have been carved from wood.

"What?" said Connelly.

"Hmm. Lookie here," Nina said. "The knight errant, wandering through the forest, a-questing. Olden days he'd be cantering on a white horse. Not no more."

"Not at all," said Dexy. "Things change." They looked him up and down, studying him as though he was some strange anomaly. They did not seem so old now, or so fragile.

"What's going on?" said Connelly.

"You think we don't know your type?" said Dexy. "We seen your type before. If we lined up all the men like you we seen, why, it'd stretch all the way down the river."

"The man on a quest," said Nina almost condescendingly. "Venturing out to slay the beast."

"What monster you hunting, white boy?" Dexy asked. "What demon is it you seek to slay?"

"There is one, ain't there?" asked Nina.

Connelly stared back and forth between them. "You know about the shiver-man?"

That surprised them. Their eyebrows rose up, crinkling the skin of their faces like butcher paper. They did not seem so dismissive anymore.

"Ah," said Nina faintly, and nodded. "That one."

"Who are you?" said Connelly.

"Oh, us?" Nina said, and laughed again. "We just three black bitches sitting by a river, minding our own."

"We're old," said Dexy. "We just been around a while, sugar. We know a thing or two."

"All of us," said Nina.

"All of who? Who else is there?" asked Connelly.

Nina gestured to the shut door behind her. "Our sister, of course. She lies dreaming, as she always does. Always has. Best not to wake her. It's what she likes."

"And you . . . you know about the scarred man?"

"Everyone knows," said Dexy. "Maybe they know in a part of them they don't want to think is there. But they know. We just know a little more."

Connelly shook his head. It was incomprehensible to have this happening, to have stumbled half dead from the jail and wandered here to be met by the same. Weeks ago he would have fought for a scrap of news of the gray man but now he seemed to dominate every patch of earth Connelly walked over.

"No, I-I'm leaving," he said. "I'm going to go. I-I thank you for the dinner but I've had, I have had enough of this."

"You won't go," said Dexy calmly.

"And why's that?"

"Because you want to ask us questions. Because you want to know."

He turned at the door and shook his head again. "No. No, not this, not again. Do you have any . . . Do you know what I've been through? Do you?"

"Yes," said Nina.

"We got an idea, hon," said Dexy.

"No you don't!" he shouted. "Don't you . . . Don't you sit there and tell me that! Just don't!"

There was a noise from the back of the house, a faint thud. Dexy and Nina looked at each other in fear and Nina stood to her feet. "Oh, Lord," she said. "Oh, Lord, he woke her up. Such noise, such *noise* these boys make." She pulled up the hems of her skirt and opened the bedroom door and slipped in, but before it could shut Connelly smelled stale air and the noxious scent of bile and decay. He did not know who slumbered back there but he did not think he wanted to.

"There," said Dexy. "I hope you're happy."

"I'm...I'm sorry."

"Oh, you didn't know. She's just...crabby." She looked balefully at him. "So you done yelling?"

Connelly shrugged, then nodded.

"Hm. You made up your mind, then? You staying or going?"

He watched her for a while, then slowly lowered himself back down to the floor.

"Good," Dexy said. "That's sensible. Very smart of you."

"So what are you going to tell me?"

"What you need to know, I suppose. But give us a second. We ain't all woke up yet. Here, let me get you your tea right quick."

She shuffled off to the kitchen. Connelly sat before her chair and leaned back. He felt comfortable. It was the first time he had been warm since he had camped with the Hopkinses. He watched the flames dance and fight and thought about how mad this all was and soon abandoned that train of thought.

He listened to the fire and his eyelids grew heavy. There almost could have been words in its crackling.

He slept.

Someone touched him on his arm and he woke. Nina was standing over him.

"It's time, boy," she whispered.

He stood and followed her out the back. Night had fallen

and with it a thick fog had crept down from the mountains, gathering around the bases of the trees. She led him through the maze of trunks until they came to a small clearing. In the center a gray mountain ash grew and before that was a small fire. Dexy sat across from it, a small stew cooking on its flames. As he sat she spooned a little into a bowl and took a bite with a tiny spoon.

"Good," she said with a nod. "Nice and spicy. Good to keep the chill out. Care for some?"

Connelly took his share and it was warm and buttery. Nina sat on Dexy's left, each of them on small stone seats, Connelly on the forest floor. To Dexy's left was another stone seat, this one empty.

"Your sister's not here," he said.

"She's here," said Nina. "She just ain't over there."

Connelly shrugged. "So what are you? Witches?"

"Witches, no. Bitches, maybe," said Nina, and she laughed.

"I already had my fortune told," he said.

"And did it answer anything?"

"Not really."

"Well, here's your chance. Just give me a moment," said Nina. "Need to wake things up a little."

With stunning speed she reached into the fire and grabbed a fistful of burning coals and flung them up into the air. Connelly raised his arms to shield himself from their hot rain, but they did not fall. Instead their ascent slowed and they came to a stop, hovering above, and then each of the little sparks began to twitch and move, dancing like fireflies. They spun in little orbits and some left the clearing to explore the woods. Then it felt like the air grew close and nothing existed but the clearing. The trees seemed to grow taller and thicker, hiding the night sky until they were towering giants. It was as though they were in some primeval version of the world they lived in now, some original version whose wildness and savagery had slowly been worn down with age until it was the complacent time they called the present.

"Now it knows," said Dexy softly, looking about. "We got the word out. Now it knows we going to ask, we got troubles on our mind and we going to ask it."

"Ask who?" said Connelly.

"The night. Everything. Eat some more stew."

He did. He coughed, as its spice seemed to have increased now. The forest's colors seemed painfully bright, liquid browns and violent blacks, and once again the sisters no longer looked like people so much as carven statues.

"What's in this stew?" he asked.

"Good shit," said Nina, and grinned.

"Stuff from the earth's heart," Dexy said. "Bit of root, bit of mud. Bit of blood of things that live down there, things that listen. Earth knows everything. Bones under your feet, they know everything. You want to know the truth of things? You got to take a bit of the earth's heart and put it in you. Then you ask."

Nina was still grinning, now looking like some squat, wicked shaman, some priestess of rituals that happened far from the eyes of men. "So go on, little white boy," she said. "Ask."

Connelly looked at them a while and said, "Who is he? The shiver-man. You know him. Who is he?"

Dexy laughed. "You mean you traveled all this way and you don't know?"

"The farther I go the less I understand."

"You know," said Nina. "Don't be fooling yourself, little white boy. Everyone know who he is. You known all along."

"You been in his wake all this time, so what's he left behind?" said Dexy. "Each place you go to that he been, what's there waiting? Why would he show up in the country in these famished times?" She chuckled, exasperated. "Boy, what has he marked you with and every other soul he meets?"

Connelly stared into the fire and thought. Thought about Molly, dancing and laughing. About Roonie and Jake and Ernie and every other soul lost along the road, and those blank, black eyes and the joyless grin.

"He's Death, isn't he," said Connelly.

"Death," snorted Nina. "That just a word. Might as well be writing in the sea or the sand, for who can name nothing? Should you try it would surely eat that word as well."

"He has a thousand names and each one catches but a part of him," Dexy said.

"He is the Harvester, the Sickle Man," said Nina.

"The Night Walker and That Which Devours."

"The Skullsie Man, the Star Reaper, the Grinning Bone Dancer."

"He is the Black Rider, the great beast below all and beyond all."

"Fenrir Wolf-End, the Sightless Hunter, Forest Stalker and Singer of Ends."

"The Red Axis, the Forgotten Plowman, Destroyer of Worlds."

"Pale Conqueror, the Crownless King."

"Death?" Dexy scoffed. "Death is but a term. To say he is Death is to call night a mere shadow. He bears a dread weapon in his hands, that thing we call nothing, and he brings it down as a blade. Cuts under all, plows it all up, turns it over. That is what he is."

"But you knew that, didn't you, boy?" Nina asked him. "You knew it all along."

Connelly thought about it. "Yeah," he said. "Yeah, I think I did."

"'Course you did. You're slow, but you ain't stupid."

Connelly looked down and set the bowl aside. He stared into the fire a great long while.

"Can I kill him?" he asked.

Nina and Dexy looked to the blank seat, then up at the sky.

"To kill death," said Nina. "Ain't that a thing man's hungered for since he looked about and saw where he was."

"Could death be so great a thing that death itself could die?" asked Dexy.

"And were it to come about, what would follow? More death? More suffering? Perhaps. Who can say save he himself that has seen the deaths of thousands, of millions, the deaths of all?"

"Well?" said Connelly. "Can I?"

"Yes," said Dexy. "Yes, he can be killed. But not easily. With great effort and sacrifice, it may be done."

"I sacrificed plenty already," said Connelly. "Little more won't matter much. But he can die?"

"Yeah. But you knew that already, too, didn't you?" said Nina. "Otherwise you wouldn't been chasing him at all."

"I guess so. I saw him scared. Scared of me. Don't know why, but . . . He looked like a man who knew he could die."

"And he can," said Nina. "Listen — he weakens now, before

the new dawn. He races to stop it. He knows it is driving him back, driving him down, ending the old and bringing in the new. He fears it. More than anything, he fears it, and the birth it brings."

"All right," said Connelly.

"But consider your actions, white boy," Nina said. "Consider what you doing. Why you doing this, first of all? For everyone? For yourself?"

"Not for me," said Connelly. "For my little girl. It wasn't right. I got to make it right. And if the world refuses to be right then you just have to force it. You have to make it. Beat it until it listens."

"Death will always be a part of this world, though," Dexy said softly. "One way or another. I can't say how but it's always going to be here. Remember that."

"It defines all men," said Nina. "Starts it. Ends it. What defines a country or a civilization ain't how it lives life, but how it ends it. How it conquers and controls. How it reaps what it needs. He going to be there for that. He going to be there. You know?"

"I do," said Connelly. "And I don't care. Anything's better than him. Folks shouldn't go the way they do out here. Shot down in the night, cut in half by trains. Scared and alone. It ain't right."

The sisters nodded to themselves.

"I asked him something," said Connelly quietly. "I asked him something last I saw him. I asked him why he took my little girl. And he just said so she'd die. Which wasn't any kind of answer at all. So I'm going to ask you. Why did he kill my little girl?"

"Boy," said Nina, "do you not know where you are? Are

you but a year old? What fool looks Death in the face and asks 'why?' and expects an answer? Perhaps even Death does not know why he comes to those who die. Perhaps there is no motivation, no driving force, no intent."

"If he cannot say, surely we cannot either," Dexy said. "Certain questions can never have answers."

"Dammit," said Connelly softly. "Goddamn it. Goddamn it all."

A breeze blew through the little clearing, pulling the flames this way and that. Dexy and Nina looked at the blank seat once more. Then Nina scowled as though having heard some foolishness and Dexy shook her head.

"Well, Lord, Lord," Dexy said. "First time for everything." She turned back to Connelly. "Ask another."

"What?" said Connelly.

"Ask another," said Nina. "Ask another question. First time in a long age since we were asked beyond the three. But we couldn't answer the last, and so you can give us another."

Connelly thought about it for a long while. Considered what he was doing, perhaps for the first time. Considered his life after death and the lives of others.

"What's going to happen if I win?" he asked.

Dexy peered into the fire, her eyes sifting through the flames, and said, "The same thing that always happens after death. Rebirth."

"The wounded and injured and dead rise again, fully healed," said Nina. "That which came before rises up and goes on. Whole. As it was before. Perhaps greater."

"And I'll go home, right?" said Connelly. "Then I can go on home. And rest."

"Maybe," said Dexy. "But if not, white boy... If what was

lost never could return, would you still do this? Would you still hunt this creature down?"

"In a heartbeat," said Connelly. "Without a second's thought."

"All right, then," said Nina. "All right. Your mind's made up."

Dexy glanced at the empty seat and tilted her head as though listening. Then she said, "Are you certain of what you want to do, boy? Understand that you are not merely attempting to kill a man, or even a god, but a thing that perhaps holds the endings of men and gods in his hand."

"He looks like just a man to me," Connelly insisted.

"And so he is, in a way. I suppose that is his weakness. I suppose that's what gives you a chance to succeed as well as what makes you so sure." She sighed and the clearing seemed to grow and the trees to shrink. The dark was no longer so close, nor did he feel so little.

"All right," said Nina. "Enough of this. We're done. I'm tired."

"I got what I wanted," Connelly said.

"You like things simple, don't you, boy?" Dexy asked.

Connelly shrugged.

"Well," she said. "They ain't going to be for long."

Nina spat through her teeth, the glob of saliva arcing out through a gap and landing yards away. She sniffed and said, "It's cold as hell out here. Get on back up to the house, boy. We got some talking to do and you look like you could use a year of sleep."

Connelly rose and did as she asked. When he looked back the women were gone, but he thought he saw their figures moving into the trees, and unless his fatigue was playing with his eyes he thought there were three of them.

He slept before the hearth and in the morning Dexy awoke him with breakfast. She served him chicken once more, now with rye bread. Neither of them spoke. Nina rose and went to the third room to tend to the last one's waking.

"I suppose I'll get going," said Connelly once she came out.

"Yeah," she said.

He went to the junk heap out front and picked through it. He found two old boots worn raw with age and a thick black coat, streaked with gray mud. He washed it off in the stream and let it dry before putting it on and going out. They packed him a small bag of dry foods and a canteen of water, its punctured skin roughly patched with old bandages. He slung it over his shoulder and walked out front.

The mist had receded. Sunlight sparkled on the crinkled waters of the stream. Dexy and Nina came to watch his departure and he was not sure but he thought he spotted a dark shape move in the far window.

"I thank you for your hospitality, and for your advice," he said.

"Didn't give you no advice," said Nina. "Just told you how it was going to be."

"Well. I thank you anyways."

"Wasn't anything."

"I hope I see you again," he said.

"You won't," Dexy said. "Boys like you are always running

off chasing one thing or another. They never know when to sit still."

"Maybe."

They bid their farewells and he walked upstream and turned north through a passage of hills. Each time he turned around he expected to see the stream of smoke was suddenly gone. But it was always there, threading up into the sky. Watching him, perhaps, and frowning.

CHAPTER TWENTY-THREE

Wandering days came then, drifting days. He learned he was in Colorado from a passing motorist who then gave him a ride to Hawtache and provided directions to Willison. His travels became quick, desperate jaunts between towns. Each time he reached the next his resources were exhausted and his belly empty. He bought food when he could and lived off of garbage when he had to, stayed in the little Hoovers that grew in the backlots like so much fungus and slept in ditches and alleys when he could not find these. Children thought him a boogey man, a great, shambling shaman, wandering backroads and scavenging whatever he could find.

The sheriff's town had been called Marion, Connelly learned. He made a crude map of charcoal and newspaper and began scouting the areas around the town of his capture. He heard no news of the gray man but he did catch wind of some wounded men making their way north, men with bad business on their mind. People could only guess at their numbers. Some said four, others five or three. Connelly wondered how many of his companions were still alive.

He kept to their backtrail, following the followers. He learned to survive. Taught himself how to trap and kill small animals and through trial and error he learned how to gut and cook them. It was a messy process and sometimes he was tempted to eat them raw.

By necessity he was drawn back to the rail, but not to ride. Hobo jungles offered the most protection and news, no matter the size, and he knew his companions would have slept there if it came to it.

He met a great many strange people in the Hoovers. In one encampment he ate a strange, stringy meat for the first time and did not find it unpalatable. A grime-covered man came and sat down by him as he ate and confided, "They's fought over it."

"What?" said Connelly.

"They's fought when we killed it. Fought over it and ate his body."

"Whose?"

"Dog's," said the man, and nodded at the leg in Connelly's hand. "His pack. We killed him and cooked him and when we was done his brothers fought over the pickings. Ate it up." He grinned wickedly. "Ate it all up," he said, and laughed.

Connelly looked at the meat in his hand. Turned it over. Then he finished it and tossed the bone away.

In one shanty Connelly watched a man build a lute out of a coffee can and sit playing it and whistling songs, to the great delight of everyone. In another he fought and beat a drunk senseless while the rest of the jungle watched and clapped.

When he was done his opponent left the clutch of foul homes, weeping like a child. And in yet another he awoke one morning to find all the others crowded around one woman who would never wake again, having succumbed to some infection or addiction. They did not know her name but buried her under stones and sang for her regardless.

One evening he came upon a jungle that was no more than a collection of tents and rags. He spotted a young man with an eye patch and a bandaged hand sitting guard before a fire. Connelly approached slowly as he always did, showing that he was unarmed. The young man stood and said, "What do you want?"

"Calling in. Just rest and a bit of talk."

"Well, I'm not in a talkative mood. Look elsewhere."

"I got some food on me."

"Whoopte-doo. I don't care. We don't want you here."

"You sure are unfriendly. All the other places have been okay."

"Well, all the other places aren't here. I—" The young man stopped and peered at him. "Holy hell, Connelly?"

"Yeah?" He looked closer. "Hammond?"

Hammond crowed laughter. "Hot damn, I knew you hadn't kicked the bucket! I damn knew it!" He threw his arms around him and they spun around. "Where you been?"

"All over. I was in the woods a while. Been moving from town to town. I almost didn't recognize you, you look...Well..."

"Yeah," said Hammond. "I got kind of roughed up getting you all out of jail. You lost some weight, Connelly, Jesus. You're skinny as a rail."

"Not too much."

Pike and Peachy emerged from tents behind Hammond.

Pike grinned humorlessly. "Of course!" he said. "Of course, it's Mr. Connelly. A man such as you doesn't die easy, Mr. Connelly, if he dies at all."

Peachy ambled over and shook his hand, pumping it up and down. "Oh, damn, I thought you were dead. I really did. I thought that'd be a shame, you getting busted out and dying just after."

"Sorry to disappoint. Why are you still sticking with these bums?"

"These boys broke me out. I'm indebted to them. Got to do good by those who done you a decent thing." He smiled. His bright teeth shone in the night, his dark skin making the rest of him almost invisible. "I am glad to see you, I must say. Seems odd us talking all the time and not seeing each other."

"I'm glad to see you, too. Good to match a voice with a face."

"Yes," said Pike. "Though it's been no easy thing traveling with a colored, we're happy to have him along. It's useful having someone healthy around."

Hammond glanced at Peachy, but Peachy's eyes were fixed on the ground.

"Where's Rosie?" asked Connelly.

"In the tent in the back," Pike said. "He has weakened since your run from the jail. We worry about him, but I think he's doing better."

"And Monk?"

"Gone," said Pike. "Decided he did not want to keep with us much further." Hammond frowned behind him but still did not speak.

"Oh," said Connelly. "What happened at the jail? Did you all get away all right?"

"Easily enough," he said glibly. "Scratches and bruises here and there. But we survived."

"And Roonie?" Hammond asked.

Connelly shook his head.

"Damn," Hammond whispered.

"The way is hard," Pike said, and sat before the fire with a grunt. "The Lord is testing us, perhaps. One should not complain if He beats us, for surely He is beating us to serve as some great tool, like iron in the fire."

Connelly sat beside him. The rest followed suit and rain began to lightly fall. They set out cups to catch the drops to later funnel into their canteens.

"I heard one or two things while I was wandering," Connelly told them. "I ran into some folk who knew a thing or two about Shivers."

"How?" asked Hammond.

"I didn't ask. They were nice but sort of strange. I listened and when that was done I left."

"What did they say, Mr. Connelly?" Pike asked. "What news did they give you?"

He told them.

They were not all that surprised, he thought. Then again, the idea was not new to them. They had imagined the gray man as a monster for so long that labels and names became pointless.

"So," said Pike. "We hunt Death itself, do we?"

"It would seem," Connelly said.

He stared into the fire. "I would call that a worthy cause."

"Folks been having trouble with Mr. Death since forever, though," said Peachy. "Why are we different?"

"Change is in the wind," Pike said.

"Yes," Connelly said. "Things are changing. Shifting. He knows he's weak and he's slowing down."

"His time is over," Pike added. "And he fears you, does he not, Mr. Connelly?"

Peachy nodded glumly. "If you say so."

"I'd take a run at that," Hammond said. "Yes sir, I would." He rubbed his mouth and toyed with his makeshift eyepatch, his face hungrier than Connelly had ever seen.

"And when we're done we can rest," said Connelly. "We can rest and go home."

"Wishing is bad," said a muffled voice.

"What?" said Connelly.

They turned. Roosevelt crawled out of a tent and sat in the dirt, looking confused. His eyes were little and unfocused. "Wishing is bad," he said again. "It makes you hurt. Makes all the missing parts hurt, makes them open up new and makes them bleed."

"Rosie, go back to bed," Hammond said.

"You take out a part of you," Roosevelt murmured. "Take it out and blow on it and toss it to the winds like dust, and you say, 'Find all the missing parts of me. Go out among the world and find the missing parts of me.' But instead of getting back what you lost you just lose more. Wishing is bad. Wish long enough and there won't be any of you left."

"Go back to bed, Mr. Roosevelt," Pike said sternly. "Go back and rest. You need it."

Roosevelt played with his bottom lip, then crawled back into his tent. He did not seem aware of anything around him at all.

"He's gotten worse," Pike explained. "He mutters often.

Whatever the gray man did to him, there does not seem to be any repair."

Connelly looked at Roosevelt's tent. Remembered the screaming he had heard in the jail and the way his friend had pawed at his knees like an animal. He pulled his coat tight.

"We have heard some strange news ourselves, Mr. Connelly," Pike said to him. "Though it was by no means as stunning as yours."

"What was it?"

"Apparently our quarry traveled through Marion before. I suspect it was a safe haven for him where the sheriff could offer protection, or perhaps it was just an entertaining trap to toy with us."

"I had heard that, too," said Connelly, frowning at Pike.

"You may have been right to have believed that man so long ago," admitted Pike. "Korsher? Was that him?"

"Yeah."

"Yes. I-I wanted so badly to...to be able to hurt this man that I was not willing to listen." He rubbed his beard, took off his cap, then replaced it. He said, "But I listen now, as should you — there was a young man Hammond met not more than a week ago who had heard a story from his grandmother. A story about another group of men who had come through these very towns and cities, looking for a man with revenge on their minds. The boy could not recall if the man they searched for was scarred or not, or if he was the same thing as we hunt now, but I feel it is. He told us they were all found dead," he said flatly. "All of them killed, up in the mountains. Found by a mining team. Well, all but one. There was one they never found. A young blond man, they never did find his corpse. But the rest died in their attempt."

"How long ago was this?" asked Connelly.

"Sixty years. Seventy. Maybe even a hundred. It's a story, the boy said, just a story... But out here, tales and stories don't seem like playthings. It feels as though time sits and stagnates and ferments in some spots out here. It's a feeling you get." He looked down at the fire. "The road is not like other places."

"What do you mean? It's just a road," said Peachy. "Just a road, I think."

"Do you? I think everyone's seen a few strange things along it, yes, but... but sometimes the road goes through places that are... not normal." He scratched his face and said, "The road is more than just dirt. Or stone. It's bigger than that. And where it's bigger it goes into other places. That or these places cling to the road. They cling to it as mistletoe clings to the tree branch, desperate to be seen by those walking by. Perhaps desperate to lure someone away from the road, and draw them in."

"We've been there," said Connelly. "We've been in those places. Yes."

"And seen the truth of things," Pike said.

"This has happened before," Hammond said softly.

"Yes," said Pike. "But your news gives us heart, Mr. Connelly. This thing can be killed, you say, and I believe you. You said it could not be done easily. I agree. And yet I feel that all of us, *all* of us here, have enough strength to do it. More strength than those who failed before."

"I think I understand, a little," said Connelly. "This... this man and the world he walks in. They're twined together. He's its Death, the end of everything alive in it. But look at what the world has become. Old and broken and dying. And there's him. Crazy and mad. An animal. A wild thing. He's winding down and so it's winding down. The world is dying and so is he." Connelly licked his lips. "If we kill the Death of this world, well. Maybe we change it."

"But what comes next?" said Hammond.

Connelly shrugged. "Anything's better than this. Anything."

The rain increased. They moved the fire beneath a tree stick by stick, but once there Pike shook his head and said, "Enough of this. I'm tired as it is. I'm going to my tent and I advise all of you to do the same." He stood up and entered his shelter and was quiet.

"How are you doing?" said Hammond once he was gone. "I mean, really."

"Okay, I guess."

"Monk didn't just leave," he said softly.

"What?"

"Monk didn't just leave. Or at least, I don't think he did."

"What happened?"

"After the fight at the jail we was all shook up," said Hammond. "I lost a finger and an eye but I've gotten along all right. Monk took one in the arm, Pike got grazed. We had guns we had bought or stolen from a few places and we shot back, maybe killed a few, I don't know. We got away and recovered once they couldn't find the sheriff. When we had healed up Monk said he didn't want to go any further. Said he should have gone with Lottie. Said this wasn't worth it anymore and he was giving up and he encouraged all of us to do the same."

"And?"

"Pike said he and him should have a talk. Talk about this like learned gentlemen, he said. So they went off and did. They were gone a long while. Only Pike came back and he said they discussed it and he gave Monk his blessing and sent him on the road. Said Monk felt so guilty he didn't want to say goodbye or take any of our food. But Pike was all out of breath. All out of breath and he had hurt his hand. I don't know where Monk is now but I don't think he's on the road and I don't think he's looking for Lottie, neither."

"Pike is a strong man," said Peachy quietly. "But he's a frightful man, too."

"Yeah," Hammond said.

"Maybe we need frightening men to fight other scary men, but it just don't sit right with me, Connelly. It just don't."

"I know," said Connelly. "Are you armed?"

Hammond nodded.

"Where's it at?"

"Two. In the bindlestick. Both loaded." He pointed to the satchel.

"Okay," said Connelly.

They looked at the two tents. Neither Pike nor Roosevelt stirred. Then Hammond and Peachy went to bed and Connelly slept beneath the tree.

They went north again the next day. Roosevelt had to be led, like an old man.

"We know he went this way, Mr. Connelly," said Pike, striding along with his walking stick. He did not seem nearly so tired or beaten as all the rest. "You are right, he is weakening. Slowing. We will prevail, don't you worry."

"Let's hope," said Hammond, more to himself than anyone. He limped slightly but his face did not show any pain, or at least what remained of it.

Connelly dropped back to speak to Peachy. "You don't have to come with us, you know."

Peachy smiled. "I know."

"This is dangerous stuff."

"Know that, too."

"I appreciate you keeping me up and going in jail but, hell, that isn't worth this. You don't have to do this."

Peachy laughed. "It ain't about worth. We're not bargaining, keeping a ledger or nothing. I just figure, well, you folks need help. Seems like you all have a rough road ahead, but... Well, these fellas believe in what they're doing. They believe it's right. And I think it may be, though it scares me. Besides," he said, and lifted his face to the sun, "you got to keep to those who keep to you. If I'm not good, then who will be?"

"Well," said Connelly. "Okay, then."

"There used to be a town close to here," said Rosie, and he sounded more lucid than normal.

"Did there, Mr. Roosevelt?" Pike said.

"Yeah. Real nice town. Everyone there was nice and if you were coming through they'd give you a bed and coffee and a nice warm bit of sup. I was there when I was a boy. Real churchy town. Everyone there was nice."

"I didn't know you were out here as a boy, Rosie," Hammond said.

Roosevelt looked briefly confused, like he forgot where he was. Then his face went slack and he said, "Father traveled through there with me. Before we went up to Chicago. I think we should go there. I think we should go up to that nice little town."

"It would be nice to get some rest and some real food," admitted Hammond.

"Yeah," said Connelly. "What do you say, Pike?"

"Where is it, Roosevelt?" Pike asked.

"Oh," he said faintly. "Oh, it's a bit northwest of here, I think. I think. I remember it had a nice white steeple and big old oaks. Mountains rising up behind it. Yes, it's just a little northwest of here, an old dirt road running beside the mountains, big white steeple. I remember."

"What's its name?" said Hammond.

"Gurry," said Roosevelt quietly. "Gurry."

"Hm. Well. It's along our way, a little. And we are hurting, hurting something fierce." He twirled his walking stick absentmindedly. "Certainly. A little rest and Christian aid for our ills could be what we need before the final run."

Evening fell softly. The gently clouded sky swam past the mountains, dappling the hillsides with violet spots and streaks. As they followed the road they came by a dance taking place in a field. Lanterns and torches bobbed up and down and sousaphones and trombones played a civilized waltz. They listened and followed the music.

They crested a small knoll and looked out on the field and saw young men and women laughing and dancing, the women in ghostly white, the men in dour brown. They wheeled and waltzed and held one another while their friends clapped and looked on. Small children aped them with an air far more serious than their elders, bowing like dignitaries at a ball. Then the waltz slowed and couples drew close and swayed back and forth in the freshly mown grass.

Connelly's stomach rumbled. He swigged water to dull it.

Someone whooped in the night and a young man hefted a woman up and spun her around and brought her back down, laughing. Drew her hips close to his and kissed her deeply and placed her head on his shoulder.

Pike watched them, still as stone. He said, "It must be a very easy life indeed where love is your only concern."

They walked back down to the road and continued on. The sounds of the band died soon enough and they were glad of it.

They found a small abandoned church and stayed the night there. Its short white steeple stabbed the sky, and inside the broken windows let light fall on the lacquered pews so they gleamed like guns on the rack. Pike made bed up at the pulpit. He sat before the big white cross and muttered to himself for hours before falling silent. He might have fallen asleep but none wanted to check.

Peachy and Hammond sat in the corner, sipping whisky and talking of women. They ate cured squirrel meat they had prepared along the road, no more than a handful. As the temperature dropped Connelly wound a dusty blanket around himself and kicked a pile of leaves from underneath the pews and lay down between them.

When his eyes shut he saw the desert once more.

Still the wild blue sky, still the bleached-bone sands. He was standing in the middle of the basin from before, barefoot and nude, and when he looked at himself he saw scars crisscrossing his body like a roadmap. Some he knew—the blow from the man on the train, the beatings from the sheriff, the gouges from all the fences and ditches and forests he had crawled through. Others he did not know. A white puckered scar from what was surely a gunshot shone at him from his shoulder.

He looked up. On the lip of the basin he saw the pale young man sitting cross-legged. Connelly called to him but he did not answer. It may have been the distance but to Connelly's eye the young man was weeping.

CHAPTER TWENTY-FOUR

They found the town the next morning. They were nearing the mountains now. Roosevelt led them without watching where he was going, his head bowed like a cripple. He became distracted by many things in the road. He spent minutes staring at a dead field mouse, his gaze fixed on its stiff little body, and with childish glee he began grinding its skull beneath the heel of his shoe. Pike reprimanded him severely and Rosie laughed gently, like he had done no more than strike the head of a daisy from its stem.

"Boy ain't right," said Peachy.

"No," said Connelly.

Then they wound about a group of tall firs and before them they saw a small, quaint little village nestled in the hills, and all the surrounding area was the greenest and healthiest any of them had seen in months. Dry scrub washed against verdant green like two different oceans crashing together. A little

white church sat at the center, small cottages radiating out-
ward. Cheery smoke tumbled up from their chimneys. Connelly felt he had never seen a happier place in his life.

"This is it," said Roosevelt faintly. "This is my little safe
haven."

They came into the little village and made for the church.
A festival of some kind was going on. Green and yellow
streamers hung from the streetlights and somewhere someone was playing a flute. They walked through the streets until
they came to the front of the church where a large crowd was
arrayed on the city block. They could not see much of what
was going on but at the center was a dead gray tree, yellow
and green streamers hanging from its limbs. At the tips of the
limbs green boughs from other trees had been tied on.

They stayed at the fringes until they were spotted by a
churchman. Though they expected him to be wary and dis-
trustful like all other folk they had seen he instead walked over
and politely asked, "May I help you?"

Before they could speak Roosevelt said, "I see you make the
dead tree live. May it live long and lasting, should you water
its earth well."

The churchman's eyebrows rose and he looked at Connelly
and the others with surprise.

"You'll have to excuse our friend," said Pike. "He is a little
addled. He has recently had an accident so at times he is not
unlike a child."

"You all have been traveling long?" asked the churchman.

"Yes. Very long. Very long indeed. Our friend stayed here
once as a child and . . . and we thought it would do him some
good if he came back."

The churchman looked at Rosie a long while and he seemed

to find something in his face. "Ah, yes. I-I do recognize him here. It's in his eyes, yes. I see him there." He beamed at Connelly and the others. "Here. Here, you all look hungry and troubled."

"Yes," said Hammond. "Don't mean to cause any commotion, but it's been a while since our last meal."

"Oh, well then, we're just about to have a dinner of our own, and we'd be more than happy to serve you as well. It's a holiday for us, and I'd be ashamed to turn away hungry guests," he said. "I'm Pastor Leo."

They walked through the crowd of people. Connelly noticed that all who turned and looked at them smiled widely and waved.

"What celebration is this?" asked Connelly.

"We celebrate the close of the fall months," said the churchman. "Winter comes. Harvest. We have a lot to harvest and lot to be thankful for."

"I notice this land seems healthier than most," said Pike.

"It's because of the way the rain catches on the hill," said the churchman. "We manage to get just enough to keep ourselves growing no matter what state the rest of the nation is in."

Peachy looked at the slopes about them. "That don't seem right," he said to Connelly. "This seems to be the dry side, 'less I'm mistaken."

Connelly shrugged and they continued on. The pastor said his hellos to those he walked by and each time the people would greet Pike and the others as well, welcoming them to their town and touching them upon the shoulders. They had not been so warmly greeted by anyone in weeks, months, perhaps years. Hammond was so overwhelmed he stopped and turned away and rubbed the mist from his eyes.

"Dear boy, are you all right?" said Leo. "Oh, I can't imagine what you've seen out upon the road."

"I'm fine," mumbled Hammond.

"Don't you worry. Don't you fret any at all. All that's over now, now you just come on with me and I'll see you right."

The pastor led them toward the church and down into the back where there was a small gathering room. Long tables lined each of the walls, all of them laden with crock pots and dishes and platters, all steaming. People in church clothes moved from dish to dish, chatting and drinking before moving out into the courtyard. The rich scent of butter and cheese and baked bread filled the air. Roast pork and casserole and steamed vegetables and soups. The room was so laden with the promise of succor that it was nearly painful.

The pastor sensed their discomfort with the crowd and filled a basket and led them to the corner of the courtyard where they could sit alone in the shade. They undid the cloth covering and took rolls and cheese and ate. The very taste of each was so strong it hurt. Hammond began weeping again.

"This is so nice," he said. "This is so nice."

Connelly did not say anything. He was watching a small girl in a green dress dancing across the courtyard. She carried a short stick with a little toy blade at the end. It resembled an axe or perhaps a scythe of some sort. More streamers ran from its top, and she twirled it like a baton and sang, "Reap day, reap day." Then she saw Connelly and the others. She grinned but there was no mirth in it, no joy. Her eyes shone like black buttons and she laughed and Connelly was reminded of Roosevelt grinding the mouse's head into the road.

"They all got long sleeves," said Peachy.

"What?" said Pike.

"They all got long sleeves on," he said again. "It's hot out. Just seems odd."

"These are formal people. Might I also remind you that we wear long sleeves as well?"

"Yeah. But the clothes we got is all we got, so the more the better, yeah?"

"Yeah," said Hammond.

Roosevelt said, "Water the earth. Water it deep. Wake the roots that sleep in sunless places. And eaters all up their strange fruits that are growings. All the dead that slept before, the roots eatings them up good and plenties and growings them up again."

"Jesus, Rosie," said Hammond. "Knock it off."

"Waterings it deepenings," murmured Roosevelt. He became enraptured by a fly and caught it in his hat. Then he buried his face in his hat and giggled.

The pastor came to them again when the afternoon wore on and led them to a small room in the church where other men in suits waited. Other churchmen, deacons of this little parish, perhaps. This little slice of paradise buried in the toes of the mountains.

"These are men of my church," said the pastor. "They noticed you and were moved by your state and wished to see you."

"We don't get many drifters here," explained one of them. "Nor do we hear much news."

"We don't know much news," said Pike.

They laughed. "You know more than us, I bet. We don't even get telegraph out here. Used to, once. Line broke down a whiles back."

"What news I know isn't the type I'd like to share," said Pike. "I'd no more infect a man with typhoid. You are happy here, I'd not spoil that."

"Please, sir," said the pastor. "We just want to know."

Pike shook his head. "Well," he said, "I suppose I could try."

Pike told them the best he could. He spoke of the desperation that ran wild just beyond the borders of this town. Of Hoovers bigger than even this village, stretched along fresh water or whatever resource could be found. Rumblings of war in strange places. Children with arms and legs like twigs and stomachs swollen with hunger. States that had not seen rain in months and so were half blown away by now, dissolved by the furious winds. A broken world of wandering and refuse.

He spoke of the now. Of this moment which they all now felt was penultimate. They lived in a dead and dying age. Already they were but memories for the future.

The pastor and his men became very grave. He nodded. "Change is here," he said.

"Well, I hope it's change," said Pike.

"We all do," Hammond said.

The pastor considered something. He said, "I suppose in times like these a man must do whatever he can to survive. To keep his family and those he loves going."

"No one could disagree with that," said Pike.

"They could. Somewhere someone out there is robbing another man for a day's survival. That man who is robbed, that victim, he would disagree."

"He would take if he could. Rob and steal. If he could get away with it."

The pastor nodded. "I believe so. It makes me feel better to hear you say that. It makes me feel better."

"Why?" said Connelly. "Do you know someone who has stolen to survive?"

Leo blinked, startled. "Me? No. No, not at all. We are blessed here. Whatever sickness that has taken this nation has passed us by. We live in peace. I would do whatever was necessary to . . . to keep it that way, yes, but . . . but that time is not now." His eye twitched and he glanced out the window up into the mountains. "I hope Christ and God almighty will forgive all of us in the future for what we do in the present."

"I am sure He will," Pike said. "I once taught the Word myself. I have seen the most desperate places of this blessed nation and there the Word still lives."

"Yes," said the pastor. "Lives."

He and Pike continued conversing. Connelly and the others soon tired of it and asked for a washroom. There was one in the church and they cleaned themselves, the first soap and combs they had seen in months. A wife of one of the men offered them fresh clothes but they could not accept, already unnerved by the hospitality. Then they went back out to the town square to enjoy the rest of the day, accompanied by two of the other churchmen.

They looked up at the gray peaks rising up into the sky before them.

"I have never seen the mountains," Hammond said. "Not really. Just plains and plains and plains. I never knew the earth could be so tall."

"Tall and dangerous," said one of the churchmen. "I don't know where you boys are going next, but it shouldn't be up there."

"Why?" asked Connelly.

"Wolves. We've had lots of trouble with them. They rove in packs up there. Makes hell for the livestock."

"Wolves?" said Peachy. "There are wolves around here?"

"Yes."

Connelly peered up at the slopes. He stood and shaded his eyes. "There's something up there," he said.

"What?" said one of the men. He sounded startled.

"I see a little roof up there. Just a little higher than here. See?" he pointed.

"Oh. That's the old farm. It's abandoned. It was abandoned because of the wolves."

"Oh," said Connelly.

The two other men scratched their arms awkwardly, then bid Connelly good day and walked off to the other celebrations. He watched them go. Two little boys ran by carrying the toy axes or scythes, twirling them about and singing about the harvest. The two men shushed them. The little boys halted, abashed, then glanced at Connelly and the others and scampered off.

As evening came the pastor and the other churchmen took them to a small barn at the edge of town where they sat on stools and drank cool ale in the shade. Connelly and the others smiled and were happy but the churchmen stayed somber. They sipped from their dusty glasses and stared at their feet and spoke little. Soon Hammond and Peachy were talking of women yet again and Pike was pounding his fist into his palm and speaking of God and righteousness, all of them red-faced and laughing. Only Roosevelt did not drink. He sat in the corner and stared at his fingers and traced lines on his face. Connelly approached, stumbling.

"What you doing, Rosie?" he asked.

Roosevelt looked up at him. "A green day. A water day."

"What?"

"What would you give for a water day?"

"A water day?"

"Yes. For home?"

"Home. Shit. I don't know. A lot. Everything."

"Everything you have?"

"Yeah."

"What about everything someone else has?"

Connelly could not think to answer.

Roosevelt nodded. "Yes," he said. "Yes."

When night fell they were roaring drunk and wild-eyed. The churchmen laughed but it sounded flat and anxious. They led Connelly and the others into the hay to sleep and they tossed themselves down and were soon snoring.

Connelly awoke deep in the night. His head still throbbed with drink but his stomach would not quiet. It was not nausea, but some anxiety he could not name. Again, the animal thing. That strange, wheedling sense that something was not right.

He stood up and walked outside. The moon was just cresting the peaks, like a pearl mounted on an immense black stand. He looked back at the cottages of the town. They were dead and quiet, almost abandoned. The odd window glowed among their ranks, a drop of honey among jet. He rubbed his belly and walked away toward an old tree to piss. While there he looked and saw the tallest copse of trees he had ever seen in his life rising at the foot of the hills, less than a quarter mile away. He studied them and looked back at the town. He could not say why but certain things seemed to line up between the two. Rocks and stones and some shrubberies, the gentle rise and swirl of the landscape — they all aligned themselves like some path leading from one to the other.

He buttoned up and walked to the copse. The trees were enormous, all firs at least a hundred feet tall, each of them a green so dark they were nearly purple. There had to be at least a dozen of them. He walked into their center. Stones and lumps of earth lay scattered in the little clearing. He stood in the center and looked about and noticed there was a gap in the trees that opened on the side of the mountain, and through it he could just make out the roof of the abandoned farm.

He was about to leave when he noticed a marking on one of the trees. A circle with two parallel arrows, gouged in the bark. Connelly ran his fingers over it and looked at the stones and the small mounds and then up at the farmhouse above. Then he turned back and studied the town for a long, long while.

"What are you doing, Connelly?" said a voice.

He spun around. Roosevelt was sitting beside one of the trees.

"Rosie?"

"You should be asleep," Roosevelt said.

"So should you."

"I am asleep."

"You should go back and sleep in the barn, though."

"No. I wanted to be where everyone else was sleeping."

"What?" said Connelly.

"Everyone's sleeping," said Roosevelt, and gestured into the trees. "Everyone sleeps." He smiled and looked back at Connelly. "You should sleep, too, Connelly. It would be better."

"I will," he said. "Just once I get something figured out, I will. Stay here, will you, Rosie? Just stay right there."

Connelly walked quickly to the barn to rouse Pike. He prodded him with his foot until the old man's eyes snapped open.

"What?" Pike muttered.

"Something you should see."

"Why? What is it?"

"Don't know yet."

Pike stood to his feet. "Should we wake Hammond?"

There was a quiet moan. "I'm already awake," said Hammond's voice. He sat up in the hay and smacked his lips. "What are you doing stomping around in the middle of the night, Con?"

"Found something," he said. "Follow me if you want." He thought and added, "Bring your guns."

Pike and Hammond shared a glance but did as he asked.

"Christ, I got a headache," Hammond said as they stumbled out the door. "My head pounds like no tomorrow. There's no waking Peachy, he's snoring away."

"Roosevelt was up," said Connelly. "Saw him not more than a minute ago."

"Roosevelt doesn't sleep anymore, I think," Pike said. "What's this you want to show me?"

"Some markings. Thought you may know them. Over there, in the trees."

He led them to the glen. Roosevelt was nowhere to be

found. Connelly searched for the markings again and showed them to Pike. He grunted and went down on one knee before them.

"This is hobo code," Pike said, tracing them with a finger.

"Markings?" said Hammond.

"Yes. Markings in chalk or scrawled in wood, left behind for other hobos. They can mean all sorts of things. Cross means this house serves food to hobos after a party. Triangles on a line like teeth means a dog. Cat means a nice old lady lives there. You see?"

"And these?" said Connelly.

He rubbed them with a thumb. "These mean get out fast. Danger."

"Danger from what?" said Hammond.

"I cannot say." Pike got to his feet and looked around. "It'd be something close. Something for us to notice. Here." He stood in front of where the man who drew the markings would have been and looked around. He leaned to the right and to the left and waved. "I don't know. Something over there?"

They looked with him. There was nothing there but the stones and the small mounds of earth.

"Come here," said Connelly to Hammond. "Get your knife out."

"Why?" said Hammond.

"Just do it and give it here."

He handed Connelly his buck knife and Connelly knelt beside one of the small mounds. He ran his fingers over the grass and began digging with the knife, pulling up stones and rich black earth.

"What are you doing? You're going to ruin the blade," said Hammond, but Pike shushed him.

The knife struck something small and hard. Connelly dug it out and brushed it off and held it up to the light.

"What is that?" said Hammond.

Connelly examined it. It was gray, its ends hard knobs, its center rough like sandpaper.

"A finger," he said. "Or at least it used to be. Long ago."

They leaned in to see and then turned to the other mounds. Hammond reached down and touched one and withdrew his hand as though burned. Connelly walked over to another and plunged the knife in and wrenched it around in a circle. He reached in and pulled the mound apart, the grass thick and the soil dark and fragrant. He thrust his hand in and clutched at what he felt there and tugged it out. He cupped his hands to his chest and blew the dirt away from his find.

Rib bones. Curled and smooth. They looked strange jumbled together, no longer adhering to the structured, concentric arcs of human anatomy.

"What is going on here?" said Pike softly.

Connelly threw the bones away. "Peachy."

"What?"

"We got to get Peachy out. We got to get out of here. Now. Right now."

They got low and crept back to the barn but found that there were men there already, at least a dozen figures lurking in the shadow of the building. A few took a long board and blocked the door with it and jogged away. Connelly could see something shining in the moonlight, something metal. Rifle of some sort. Maybe a shotgun.

"What are they doing?" whispered Hammond.

"Get down," said Pike.

"Peachy," Connelly murmured. "What are they doing to Peachy?"

One figure's hands lit up bright, then another's. They stepped back and before Connelly could move or cry he saw bottles with flaming rags in their hands. They lobbed the twirling bombs through the open windows up above in the barn.

There was a tremendous thud as air was split and pulled back together, then a wash of fire dancing bright and begging to lick the roof. A hoarse cry escaped from Connelly's throat but no one heard. Two more men lit ragged fuses and hurled the bottles in. The faces of the men were strangely lit by the fire but even from there Connelly could see they were the very churchmen who had been friends earlier.

Connelly got to his feet but Pike jumped forward and wrapped up around his legs. They grappled but the old man was stronger than Connelly would have ever believed and he pinned him to the ground.

"Listen to me!" Pike whispered into his ear. "Listen! You run out there now and you're dead. You try and do anything and you're dead. They'll shoot you down like a mad dog and not think again on it. Do you hear me?"

Connelly gasped and choked as he struggled to stand. Behind him the barn began to collapse. They heard no screams. It seemed a terribly unfair thing that Peachy should be killed in such a cowardly fashion and his killers would not even hear his cries. They would not know the pain they had inflicted, have no notion of what they had done.

"What the hell is this?" Hammond said. "What the hell are they doing?"

"Mr. Hammond, have you ever wondered how a town on

the dry side of a mountain could stay more lush and more safe than any other place in the country?" asked Pike as he released Connelly.

"N-No..."

"Because they made a trade," growled Connelly from where he lay. He lifted his head to see the remains of the barn. "Because they did what they had to to keep to their own."

"Yes," said Pike.

They sat hidden in the glen, watching the fire burn low. The men began to depart, leaving only a few to make sure the fire did not spread. Hammond said he had wondered why the barn was so far out from the rest of the town. Pike and Connelly sat so still they might not have heard.

"You still got that knife?" asked Connelly.

"Yeah," said Hammond.

"And the guns?"

"Yeah. Why? What do you have planned?"

"Trouble," said Connelly, and wiped his hands on his pants. "Lot of it."

They went around the outskirts of the town like wolves on the prowl and crept up through the lanes in shadow. They draped rags over their guns and the knife so they would not glint in the light, spoke with hand gestures and glances. Hammond picked the lock of the church with ease and they moved through the halls silent as ghosts, eyes dead, shoulders hunched.

They found the pastor's bedroom and moved in quietly and gathered around his bed. He sensed them and awoke but before he could speak Connelly said, "Shut your fucking mouth."

"What's goi—"

Pike struck him on the temple with the base of the knife and his eyes went dull. They picked him up and bound him and carried him to the glen. There they tossed him down roughly and undid his gag and Connelly cut off his right sleeve. On the inside of his forearm was the mark they had seen on the sheriff's arm weeks before, the crude symbol of the serpent madly devouring itself.

"My friend was in that barn," Connelly told him softly.

"Wh-what are you going to do to me?" Leo asked.

"Don't know. What'd you do to all those folk back there who're being eaten up by the trees?"

Leo looked behind them. His face went ashen and he said, "You don't understand."

"I understand plenty. This is his town, isn't it? It explains the sleeves. There's a deal with him. Scarred man in black and gray. He said he can keep things green and growing. Keep everyone in this town healthy. Longer lives, even. Is that it?"

"How... how do you know?"

"I met a sheriff who was almost a hundred but didn't look older than fifty. He had the same setup. And you don't want to know what he lived on top of but I'm willing to bet you got a guess. Because see, I've figured it out," he said, and hefted the knife in his hands. "Something's always got to die. Always. If something's going to live there's something else out there that's got to die. If it's something small that's got to live then a little thing's got to die. But a whole town? Hell. That'd be something. So what goes under the knife? Who's out here? Drifters? Criminals? All out here under this strange little altar?"

Leo said nothing.

"How many of them know?" asked Connelly.

He didn't answer. Connelly took the knife and pushed it a quarter inch into his sternum. He squealed and tried to wriggle away, a thin trickle of red running down his chest.

Connelly removed the knife. "How many?"

"All of them!" he cried. "The entire town! All of them."

"Christ," said Hammond. "Jesus goddamn Christ."

"Reap day," said Connelly softly. "Reap day. And what does he get in return? Safe haven? A place to stay when he needs it? Where is he? Where's the scarred man, Pastor? You've been feeding him all this time, so you got to know where he is."

"I thought you a man of God, Pastor," Pike said over his shoulder. "Do you know what I would like to do to men who claim the name of the Lord and then do acts such as these?"

"You've seen what's out there," Leo snarled. "You've seen how hungry this world can be. Wouldn't you do everything you could to keep what you loved fresh and alive? Wouldn't you? We haven't had a child or a mother die in labor in thirty years. No more sickness, no more accidents. The guns we have are all older than their owners, near enough. The youngest death we've had has been seventy-six, in bed. And in return for what? Drunks? Criminals? Thugs and vagrants? Tell me you wouldn't do the same."

"Maybe," said Connelly. "That doesn't matter anymore. You killed my friend. Tried to kill us. Makes things pretty simple, doesn't it?"

Leo bowed his head and tried not to sob. "God... You're not... not going to..."

"Where is he, Pastor? Where's he at?" asked Connelly. "Or do I even need to ask? He's up in that farm up there, ain't he? Where the wolves are supposed to be? Where it's not safe to go, yet it looks down on this very town right here?"

"You can't go up there," said the pastor. "You can't. H-He's getting ready. You don't know what's happening up there."

"When'd he come in?"

"Two days ago. He was falling apart. You're killing him, you know."

"Yeah," said Connelly. "Yeah, we know. And he said to get rid of us, didn't he? Said some boys would be hot on his trail and wouldn't it be nice if they wound up dead. Right?"

The pastor nodded.

"Right. Okay," said Connelly. "Okay, then. I want to know one more thing. Where's some kerosene?"

"Kerosene?" he asked.

"Yeah. Where?"

"I don't know. There's a garage over where you all came in."

"Okay. Fair enough."

The pastor shuddered. "I-I have a wife. Children. A little girl—"

The knife flashed forward and Connelly buried it up to the hilt in the pastor's neck. Warm red sprayed from his collarbone and his eyes went wide and he coughed and soon it dribbled from his mouth and nose. Connelly twisted the knife in his neck until there was a thick red river running down his shirt and the man quivered and pissed himself.

"I had one, too," Connelly said to him as the man died.

He lay still. Connelly wiped his hands and the knife on the dead man's nightgown and stood.

"What are we going to do?" asked Hammond.

Connelly put the knife back in its sheath. "Show them what they're worshipping."

*   *   *

They found a drum of kerosene in the garage and they filled up three tanks with it and divided a box of matches between them all. Then they split up, each working the outskirts of town, splashing the houses and the fields and the church and the barns. They moved quietly, carefully rationing out the foul-smelling fluid.

Connelly carried a shovel with him, digging small trenches to carry the kerosene, running under porches and bushes. He made a crude sort of irrigation that might or might not really work, he was not sure. He labored quickly but carefully. The town seemed deserted. After they had killed the fire in the barn they must have gone home to peaceful slumber.

"Everyone sleeps here," he murmured to himself. "Bastards. All of them. Bastards."

He was dousing a trellis of one house when he heard a voice say, "What are you doing?"

There was a young girl at the side of the house, no older than Hammond. She leaned around the corner and then took a few steps out to see. She wore a white nightgown and her hair was gold and her features sharp and childlike. Her eyes were as green as the hills around her, like sunlight filtering through leaves. When Connelly turned to see her she took a step back.

"You!" she said. "You're the drifter-man. You ain't supposed to be out here."

"Go back to bed," said Connelly.

"You're supposed to be dead," she whispered. "Dead and gone."

"Don't you...Don't you cry out or damn you, I'll beat you raw," Connelly said.

She smiled. "You wouldn't. You ain't the sort of person to hit a girl."

"I would."

"No you wouldn't. You're just a big softy. Just a big old softy."

Connelly stood up to his full height. "Don't you do nothing," he said quietly, "or I swear...I swear to God..."

"Swear what? That you'll kill me?" She laughed. An angelic sound. "You ain't the type. Why, I bet I could open my mouth right now and holler bloody murder and they'd come running, wouldn't they?"

Connelly did not move.

"Sure they would. And you wouldn't do nothing. They'd find you and cut you to ribbons," she said, and smiled wide.

Cold green button eyes, mean and merciless. Flat and shallow like a muddy pool.

"Watch," said the girl, and took a deep breath.

The shovel bit deep into her skull under her right eye and the force of the blow sent the eye flying out, spiraling away and down onto her cheek. A gout of blood poured from her mouth and nose and she fell to the ground and began madly twitching and a ribbon of black began seeping from her exposed sinus. In the moonlight her crumpled head made her look far from human, some twisted, mindless inversion, and Connelly stood over her and brought the shovel down again and again on her neck. Soon she stopped twitching and he was glad. It was as though in decapitating her he made her human and recognizable again.

He stood over the slain girl and dumped the kerosene out

and lit a match and tossed it behind him. Then he started to run.

Exactly when it happened he could not say. He saw the firelight flickering on the trees ahead and felt the heat on his back, but it was not until he heard the guttural burp and the shrieking roar that he knew it had really caught. He turned and backpedaled and saw jets of fire shooting into the night. Twin blazes were on his left and right and he knew somewhere Hammond and Pike were making for the woods.

He ran into the hills of the mountain and climbed a ways. Then he heard the screams. Maybe a man, maybe a woman. A child, perhaps. Then more. He turned and looked out on the inferno he had left in his wake, the crumbling cottages and the blackening church, the thick pillar of black smoke that reached up into the sky. He tried to silence the dreadful part of his heart that sang and danced joyfully at the sight of his hellish wreckage but found he could not.

"Look at that," said a voice.

He turned back around. Roosevelt was sitting on a stone, smiling at the fire.

"You made the sun come up, Connelly," he said. "You made the sun come up."

CHAPTER TWENTY-FIVE

They headed for the farm and on the way there they came upon Pike and Hammond struggling through the brush. Hammond grinned at him wickedly, his face sooty and mad.

"Show those bastards," he panted. "Show those bastards how to do a burning."

"Roosevelt?" said Pike. "Where have you been?"

"Walking," Rosie said. "Walking and seeing."

Pike looked at him mistrustfully and Connelly knew they shared the same thought.

"If we're going we need to go," said Hammond. He looked behind at the column of smoke. "The whole place can't burn. Whoever's left is going to lay hands on guns quick."

"How long do we have until dawn?" Connelly asked as they started their way up.

"Three hours," said Pike. "More."

"Let's make use of it, then."

The slope became nearly vertical. They wrapped their hands in rags from their shirts and gripped roots and stones to hoist themselves up the damp hills. The stink of the fire was still in their nostrils but as they mounted the air became thin and clean. They found a ravine and crawled when they had to and leapt to solid ground when they could.

Roosevelt no longer needed to be led. He seemed to have an easier time of it than the others. He jumped to one stone and smiled down at it, pleased. "La," he said, and laughed.

Connelly and Pike glanced at each other and continued climbing.

They came to a small landing in the hills. Cedars and furs dotted it in rings and they crept their way through the little maze, guns drawn. Then Hammond held up a hand and whispered, "Look."

They saw the roof of the farmhouse a few hundred yards away. Weeds rose up higher than the waist and shielded part of it from view. They worked their way around and farther up the slope so as to get a better angle.

It was an old place, all the color and darkness of the wood long since washed away from years of rain. It seemed to be made of nothing but splinters, everything cracked and white and leaning, all the angles askew. The windows were dark and Connelly imagined black eyes watching them from behind each misplaced board. The house was paired with another barn, queerly placed in the small stretch of barely usable pasture. Decaying fenceposts ran along the slope. To their eyes each segment resembled the shattered spine of some long-decayed creature lying askew in the field.

They watched for any motion. They saw none. They checked the rounds in their guns and moved down through the weeds and over the fence and up to the porch, leaving Roosevelt sitting behind in the trees.

Everything creaked, leaving no chance of stealth if the fire had left any. There was no inch of the farmhouse that was solid. Each time the wind blew the house filled with a chorus of groans. Pike and Hammond checked the windows and shook their heads and Connelly looked in the door. The front hall stretched away, roof bulging down and the walls awry. He squinted into the dark and waved in and they entered.

It was as though they were in the belly of some monster. The house muttered and squalled and some parts of it dripped. They could hear the scutter of insects and rodents from somewhere in its walls. A strange scent was in the air.

"Something's dead here," whispered Hammond.

"Yeah," Connelly said.

They found nothing in the house. The kitchen and living room were filled with the scattered remains of old furniture. A child's chair. A soiled rag that had once been a linen tablecloth. They paced through it and exited on the other side. There the previous owners had once kept a playground of sorts. A ragged swing hung from an ancient tree and shattered glass and old toys glittered in the weeds. Some sort of foundation was on the ground, cracked and broken, shards rising from the turf like a rocky shore among the sea.

Pike pointed. There was a stone shed on the side of the house. Bricks and stones were missing from its entry and its front passageway was far longer than they had expected. They walked to it and looked in and though it was dark they knew they faced a tomb.

The reek was worse here, pungent and sour. Connelly remembered the house from long, long ago, the winding stairs that had led down to the basement, the wave of flies and the stench of decay. He knew the sensation of walking where the dead had once lain, but something far worse waited inside. He did not know and did not want to know what the gray man had kept in that place, but there in his hallowed ground he surely kept something special, something that went beyond any sickness mere men could ever know.

What was in there? What did the passageway hold? Connelly had turned away before and refused that grim knowledge, but he was not sure if he could do so again.

The wind blew across the mouth of the shed and it moaned. Hammond took a step forward, almost hypnotized. Connelly awoke and threw his arm out to stop him and whispered, "No. No."

Hammond glanced at him, perplexed, and they struggled. Hammond tried to push past to enter but Connelly refused to let him go.

Then Pike held up a hand and motioned toward the barn. "There," he hissed. "There, you damn fools. There."

There was movement in the barn. They turned away from the shed and crouched down around the corner of the house and waited. Pike cocked his gun, then Hammond did the same. As the creature in the barn came out into the weeds a ray of moonlight broke through the clouds and fell upon the small field, illuminating it until it was a translucent silver.

It was a bull, enormous and white. How it had gotten up so far in the mountains they could not say, but there it was. It would have been a stately animal had it been cared for, but one horn was cracked and its coat was ragged and its backside spattered with dried shit. Flies buzzed around it in a thick cloud and it lowed as it made its way toward the center of the field.

Movement came from the opposite end. The leafless trees twitched and rustled and then the gray man emerged, shuffling out, his eyes fixed on the bull. He stood at the edge of the grass and he looked more tired and worn than they had ever seen him before, like he barely had the energy to lift his head. Yet when he stepped into the light he straightened, almost growing taller, and he breathed deep and opened his eyes. He flexed his limbs, testing them. Stretched his back and took a firm step forward. Then he looked down on the bull across from him like a king examining his subjects. The bull lifted its head at his arrival and stepped forward.

Connelly and the others did not fire. They did not shout or attack. Instead they sat frozen, aware that they were witnessing some ancient rite, a thing so old it had no name. It preceded language. Preceded any knowledge of the world at all save that those who watched it turn around them were fading from it even as they looked on.

The gray man and the bull circled each other. The animal dipped its head and swung its broken horns but the gray man did not flinch. It dug one hoof into the mottled earth and lifted its head and lowed again, warning him, yet the gray man still took no notice. Instead he reached inside his coat and took out a small silver knife. It glittered greedily in the moonlight. He breathed out, a cloud of frost forming and evaporating. Then the bull charged.

It was a short space but the animal's speed was still immense. The gray man flickered away, dodging like he could walk on air, and the bull flew by him harmlessly. He scored a mark in the bull's side as it passed, tongues of blood running down its white coat, and it lowed again and whipped its head but the gray man was already moving away, dancing over the ragged grass. They both turned at the perimeter of the small field, facing one another again, judging their weaknesses and strengths and waiting for the next strike.

The bull charged again. This time the gray man stood perfectly still, hands at his side as he looked down on the animal barreling toward him. When the bull neared he leaned to one side and his hand flicked out and grabbed hold of the horn. He spun himself around onto the bull's side and put his knee into the back of its neck. It collapsed and slid to a halt, its massive legs lashing out and gouging lines in the grass. The gray man held his knife high and plunged it into the side of the animal's neck. It bellowed in anger and blood sprayed from its throat, dotting the head and shoulders of the gray man and soaking the ground around it.

The gray man kept the knife in place until the bull lay still, its sides heaving with breath, and then he dipped his head down to the wound. What he did there they could not see but when he lifted his head it was smeared with blood, black-red and glistening. He shut his eyes and moaned softly as though pained, then brought his hands to his face, trembling. He touched the red on his forehead and rubbed madly at it like it either pained or exhilarated him. He pushed his fingers into his mouth and then when he seemed on the verge of tears he spread his arms wide and lifted his face to the sky and screamed, long and loud.

They had never heard a scream like it. There was fury in it, terrifying rage, a cry of dominance and power that could not be ignored. But there was also sadness in it, a sense of futility, like he was a lone man screaming his curses at a sky that would not listen. His scars appeared to open wide until they were no longer a disfigurement but instead were a part of his enormous mouth, a jaw that stretched to such a size that it could swallow the world. He held out his hands as though beckoning the stars to come and hear his plea. For a second Connelly believed there were invisible strings that ran from the ends of his fingers to every star, and though he felt there was a great tension there he could not tell who was pulling whom.

The gray man howled again, holding his bloody hands before him, and then dropped them to his sides. A cloud passed over the moon and the field darkened again, like a curtain covering a stage. He stood still for a moment, drawing his strength. Then he snapped his head around and stared right at them. Connelly felt that the man's eyes were for him alone but before he could be sure the gray man turned and sprinted into the trees with a speed they never knew he had.

The spell broke. "Goddamn it all," said Hammond, and they began trudging through the field after him, no longer sure why they had sat still at all.

As they entered the scrub Connelly heard a snap somewhere and something buzzed by him. He leapt and tackled Pike and Hammond and dragged them to the ground. Hammond began to curse him but Connelly held his hand over his mouth.

There was another crack and something whizzed through the tall grass. Connelly motioned across the clearing toward the barn and pointed at the black smoke from the town burning below. Pike and Hammond looked back across the scrap of pasture. Someone was moving in the far trees.

Connelly pointed at himself and Pike, then at the path of the gray man. He pointed at Hammond and then pointed to the trees and mimed firing. Hammond nodded. They got to a crouch and silently counted one, two, three.

Connelly and Pike raced up the hill while Hammond opened up on the moving shadows on the side of the clearing. No more than three shots, carefully placed, then he turned and began running as well.

"You sons of bitches!" screamed an anguished voice. "You goddamn sons of bitches!"

Crystal-white flashes lit up across from them and shot and bullets rained here and there. Connelly and Pike threw themselves behind a large outcropping and Hammond knelt down behind a tree, arm carefully poised, his aim steady. Their surroundings snapped and popped and whined but they did not move.

There was a gap in the shots and one man awkwardly stumbled out of the treeline and made for the cover of the barn. Hammond squeezed the trigger and the man spun around and fell. More furious screams from the trees. Another hail of shots. Hammond smiled grimly as he reloaded and sucked his fingers when they burned.

Pike took out his revolver and took aim. Connelly counted again, one, two, three, and he and Hammond scrambled up the rocks while Pike fired across the field.

"How many do you think are there?" said Hammond as they ran.

"Five or six," said Connelly. "Few rifles, one or two pistols. One shotgun, from what I heard."

Hammond laughed harshly and took cover behind a boulder. "Goddamn townies," he said.

A shot whined by and Connelly felt a heat in his shoulder. He ignored it until Hammond said, "You've been hit."

"What?" he said.

"They hit you."

He looked at his shoulder and at the spreading blotch of red. He pushed the torn clothing apart and saw a nick on the mass of his shoulder, about an inch long. He clucked his tongue and rolled his sleeve up to stanch the bleeding.

"You good?" said Hammond.

"Yeah," Connelly said.

By the time they protected Pike's retreat they were well up the hill. The mountain started honestly a little over a quarter mile away. Connelly and Pike climbed up over the bluff and Connelly called to Hammond to come on. He emptied his pistol and turned and began to follow, grabbing stones and heaving himself up.

Behind him the townspeople broke cover and began to run after them. Pike raised his gun and squeezed off three shots, hitting one in the neck. His target clapped a hand to his collarbone but his partner took a knee and fired.

Hammond cried out from below. Connelly moved to look. He saw Hammond leaning against the rock face, a dark red patch growing just beside his spine. He pawed at it uselessly, unable to bend his shoulder. Someone whooped happily and Pike fired his gun empty and began to reload.

"Shot!" cried Hammond. "I've been shot! Goddamn... goddamn townies sh-shot me." He choked and made a sob, rolled over to look at his wound. "Connelly?"

"I'm here," he said.

"They shot me."

"I know."

"Right in the back."

"I know."

Pike began firing again, letting shots fly wherever. They rained on the pasture and one of them found a home in the back of the dead bull.

Connelly said, "You got to get up, Hammond. You got to get up and climb up."

"My God, Connelly!" he shrieked. "I can see my insides! I can see them!"

"You've got to get up and climb up to us, Hammond! Just get up and we'll help you!"

He heard shuddering breaths from below. Pike fired another round and someone squawked.

"Hammond?" called Connelly.

"I'm... I'm trying."

Connelly rolled to look below. Hammond was extending one deathly white hand toward a tree root. His fingers clutched at it but could not grab hold. "I'm trying," he said softly. "Going to pull myself up. Pull me up. Far as I can go."

"Come on, Hammond."

The boy's head lolled into his upper arm. He coughed. A bullet caromed off of a stone above him.

"Connelly?" he said.

"Yeah?"

"I'm dying."

"I know."

"I'm dying here, Connelly."

"I know, Hammond."

"This... this is an awful place to do it in."

"Yeah." He stared down at the boy. Rubbed the sweat from his head with his coat. "We'll get him for you, Hammond," he called down.

"Get who?"

"Shivers. We'll get him."

"Oh," he said weakly.

"It's his fault. Bastard trails death behind him, and... and..." He left off. All words of justification and purpose sounded pathetic against the silence of the boy dying below.

"Connelly?"

"Yeah?"

"I want to go home."

Connelly did not answer.

"I want to go home, Connelly," Hammond whimpered. His voice was terribly soft now. "I should have never come out here." He coughed again. "I want to go home," he said, louder. Then he shrieked, "I want to go home! I want... I want..."

His voice faded. Connelly looked below. The boy was rubbing at his wound, his eyes glazed and almost dark. "Connelly?" he whispered. "There's... there's..." Then the movement stopped and he lay still.

"Don't," said Pike.

"Don't what?"

"Don't go get the gun," he said.

"What... what the hell do you mean?"

"I mean don't go get it. It's too dangerous. It's not worth it."

"I wasn't going to, anyways."

"They aren't chasing us anymore. Whatever spine they had we took out of them, shot for shot."

"Shut up," said Connelly.

"What?"

"Just…just shut up. For once. I mean…" Connelly shook his head.

Pike turned his blank face back to the woods, waited a moment, then stood and started on the trail again. Connelly stayed for a second and then followed.

CHAPTER TWENTY-SIX

They staggered through the bends and gullies of the mountain, fighting the dry cold. Pike tried to follow the gray man by bent leaves and broken twigs but eventually said he wasn't sure what the hell he was looking at anymore and they limped along in silence. They walked until the sky was white with morning light.

"I'm thirsty," said Connelly.

"I am, too."

They sat down on the side of a steep embankment and drained their canteens. Connelly tossed his over the edge and listened to it clanking and rattling as it tumbled below. He could not see where it landed.

"You shouldn't have done that," said Pike.

"There isn't going to be any water up here."

"You don't know that."

"Yeah I do."

Pike looked at his canteen and then hurled it over. They listened to it crash and stood up and dusted themselves off and started walking again.

"We should have asked those goddamn bastards for more food," said Connelly.

Pike laughed. It was a nasty, grating sound. Connelly was not sure if he had ever heard him laugh before.

"Did I ever tell you about my friend?" Pike asked, shivering. "My friend, Jonas?"

"No."

"He was my friend. Back in Georgia. I was a preacher and he was one of my flock." Pike was quiet for a long time. "He was a beautiful boy. Most beautiful boy I ever saw. I-I was young then. At least...I think I was."

Connelly took measure of the terrain and stepped over a wide ditch. Pike followed.

"He cut his throat," said Pike. "I remember that. Cut it ear to ear, for no reason I can understand. You have to remember those things. Keeps you going."

"I remember my daughter's eyes," said Connelly. "She had the most beautiful brown eyes. Eyes like...like molasses." He stopped. "At least...I think they were brown." He reached for his wallet but found it was gone. He could not recall when he had lost it.

"What happened to her mother?"

"She's waiting for me."

"Oh. I remember now."

"She's waiting for me. I'm going to go home. I'm going to go back home once this is done and everything's going to be the way it was. Just the way it was."

They heard something and stopped. It was whistling. They

followed it and found Roosevelt sitting upon a stone, look-ing down a cliff at the fog, kicking his legs like a boy on a church pew. He heard them coming and looked and beamed at them.

"Hello, boys," he said. "Hello. Morning. I think it's morning."

Connelly and Pike glanced at each other.

"Where did you go, Mr. Roosevelt?" asked Pike.

"I went here, of course. Walked right here. Just a stroll."

"Are you sure no one told you to go and sit there?"

"No. No one told me. I just thought, well, there's got to be a nice seat up there, I bet. I'd like to sit up there. Sit and look. So here I am."

"I see," said Pike. "What's your name?"

"What?"

"Your name. What is it?"

Roosevelt faltered. "I…Something. It's something," he murmured. "I know I have one. I'll remember it," he said, and smiled again. "Don't you worry."

Pike nodded. "Well, stay here for a moment longer, sir. Just stay there while we talk." He motioned to Connelly to follow. They walked a few yards away.

Pike said, "Roosevelt is not himself."

"I know."

"He led us to that town. When he first saw the pastor he said something. It was a code, or a message. Then the pastor looked at us and knew he had to kill us. Did you see?"

"Yeah."

"The shiver-man did something to him in that jail. I don't know what, but I have an idea. I think he told Roosevelt to lead us here. I think he tortured it into him. Like he wrote his orders in Rosie's skin or on the inside of his skull."

"I know. The pastor looked in his eyes and said, 'There he is.' He recognized the gray man had changed him. Somehow."

"All right. Who's going to do it, then?"

"I don't want to kill him."

"And I don't mean to," Pike said tonelessly. "At least, not yet. If the shiver-man told him one thing he might have told him others. We may not have his devilry but there are ways we can ask Roosevelt all the right questions and get him to answer."

Connelly looked at Pike. Then he looked at Roosevelt, just beyond. Rosie was holding a small stone and cooing at it and telling it to wake up and give him water. Connelly watched him for a long time.

"I don't want to do it," he said.

"At least help me bind him."

"Goddamn it, Pike."

"Do you want this or not?"

Connelly took a breath. "All right, then."

They walked back over to him. "Mr. Roosevelt!" called Pike. "Here. Let me help you."

"Help me with what?" asked Rosie, curious.

"Help you with your hands," he said, and he took off his belt and handed his gun to Connelly.

"All right," Roosevelt said, and smiled and held them out.

"No, no. No, no. Behind. Behind you."

"Behind me?" asked Roosevelt, now confused. Connelly walked around him.

"Yes. Behind you. It's good for you, you see."

"Oh," he said. "Did you see where I left my rock?" he asked as Connelly tied his wrists.

"No, I'm afraid I didn't," said Pike. He tore off part of his sleeve and began tying Roosevelt's ankles.

"That was my special rock. I was going to get water from it. Poke a hole in it and make it give me drink."

"Were you?"

"Yes." He whimpered. "That's tight," he said, wriggling his arms. "That hurts."

"Yes, yes," said Pike. "Now sit."

"Listen," said Roosevelt as he sat. "Listen. Listen to me."

"We're listening," said Pike. He secured the binds at Rosie's feet.

"Listen—take a man," said Rosie. "Take any man. Lawyer-man. Preacher-man. A man of law and civilization, the highest in the land. Take that man and put him before a desert and march him across that desert with naught but the clothes on his back and a thimble of water a day—"

Pike nodded. "He's been changed, all right."

Rosie's voice grew stronger. "—march him across that vast dry expanse with no contact and no food, no meat nor grain, and by the time he reaches the other side he will have been whittled down to his darkest heart—"

"Do you want to stay or go?" Pike asked Connelly.

"—and his eyes will see no love nor comfort nor compassion in the arms of others—"

"I'll go," said Connelly.

"—but his hands will sing with the great red song that they have been waiting to sing their whole life."

"Then go," said Pike. "But give me the knife."

"He will be as he was meant. The knife he has carried in his heart, the weapon that he is, it will find use —"

Connelly took the knife out and looked at it. Watched the edge gleam with the morning sun. Then he held the hilt out to Pike. Pike took it, nodding like he was listening to Roosevelt's words.

"—he will find the bright cold use among his brothers and among the beasts of this world and he will find joy in it. He will find joy in it. He will find joy in it."

Connelly began walking away. He heard Roosevelt say, "What's going on?" in a quieter voice. "What's going on?"

Connelly heard Pike say, "Hush now. We're playing a little game," and Connelly walked to the other side of the cliff and moved behind a stone and sat.

He was still for a second but then shifted uncomfortably. He reached behind and into his pocket and took out what was digging at him. It was a small crescent wrench. He could not remember where he got it. He tossed it away and looked up at the sky and wondered if it was going to rain. Then the shouting began.

There were words to the exchange but he did not listen for them. A question, calmly asked. An answer, given in panic. The question came again, whatever it was. A protest, again and again, no, no, not me, I don't know, no. Then the mountain quiet was pierced by hysterical cries and maddened wailing. He heard Pike ask something again, calm and low, but the screams did not answer, just intensified. Then the voice choked and coughed and Pike said something once again.

Connelly listened for what felt like a long time, for hours or perhaps minutes. In that place time no longer functioned. Its purpose was moot, perhaps forgotten. When he could bear no more he stood up. He walked back down the path and paused behind a rocky outcropping, listening to what was happening on the other side. Then he steeled himself and looked out.

It was only the briefest glance, but it was enough. First he saw Pike crouched before something, something twitching and supine against the rock. He did not immediately recognize it as Roosevelt, could not even recognize it as a person, but then he saw a mouth and eyes in it, vague human features adrift among all the writhing redness. Pike sidled up before Roosevelt, back and legs taut, knife clutched low like the ovipositor of some foul insect. He whispered something to him, a priest delivering some depraved last rites, eyes small and muddy and empty and his fingers testing the hilt of the knife. Then the blade began to move back in and a burbling sound came from deep within whatever was left of Roosevelt, a sound that steadily grew to a scream.

Connelly withdrew and walked back up the path as the screams went on. He looked back. Thought. Then knelt beside a stone. He took out the last gun and counted the rounds in it.

"Bastard," he said softly to himself. "Bastards the world over. Ever since I met you. Bastard."

There were five rounds left. He did not know if there was any other ammunition. He rolled the cylinder and snapped it shut and stuffed it in the waist of his pants. Then he waited, listening. Trying to see if Pike had any more questions and hoping it was done with and he would see no more of it.

When he judged it was time Connelly got up and returned

to where Pike and Roosevelt sat. He saw the two men ahead, piled on each other in the mist. Pike calmly digging at something in Roosevelt. Moving with the lapidary care of a master craftsman, eager to see his work done right. He was not asking any questions. Connelly could tell all his questions had come and gone.

"Stop," said Connelly. "Jesus Christ, stop."

Pike looked at him, startled, and stood. His knees and hands and front were stained with gore. "Mr. Connelly," he said. "What are you doing here? I'm ... I'm not yet finished."

Connelly looked at Rosie. Looked at the lines in his scalp, his toes at sick angles on one shoeless foot. Below his chest he was a mass of redness. Connelly could still see his little soft eyes among the wreckage of his face, lids fluttering, struggling to stay conscious. He was curled around the rock beside him like he was trying to anchor himself to the earth and a few more seconds, even if they were spent in agony.

Connelly took out his pistol. He lifted it and looked away as he put the little soft eyes under his sights.

"No!" said Pike. "No, no!"

He pulled the trigger. The report seemed to sound from far, far away. When he turned back there was a gaping wound in Roosevelt's breast, drooling blood. His back warped against the stone in his last throes, spasms racking him as the bullet drifted through his body. Then his back went slack and he was still, his face mercifully away from them.

"Damn you!" shouted Pike. "What ... what did you do that for? I wasn't ... I wasn't done."

Connelly swallowed and tried to slow his breath. "What did he say?"

310 Robert Jackson Bennett

"I wasn't done. I wasn't done at all. Not at all."

"What did he say, damn it? Did you ask any questions at all?"

"I did," Pike said, indignant. "I most certainly did."

"Then what?"

Pike considered him. Then looked back at Rosie and studied his work. "He said the scarred man was looking for a cave. A cave somewhere in the mountains."

"Where?"

"In a fault," he said. "A fault that ran between two peaks. One short, the other tall, rising up like one's leaping on the other."

"What's he doing in there?"

"He said he was looking for something," Pike said. "Looking for...for rebirth. To make himself anew." Then he crouched before Roosevelt and reached out and touched the man's cheek. He put one finger to his chin and tilted the dead man's face toward him. Looked into his eyes. Stroked his bloody temple with one knuckle. Then he patted Roosevelt on the shoulder as though bidding goodbye to an old friend. "Well. He's gone," Pike said, standing. "He'll be of no more trouble to us. Eh?"

He turned to Connelly and smiled. Connelly lifted the gun again and pointed it at Pike's face and cocked it.

Pike's brow furrowed as he saw the gun. He looked at Connelly, confused.

"I never liked you," said Connelly, and fired.

A red eye opened on Pike's cheek and his head snapped back and he fell in a heap. He stared up at the gray sky, forever perplexed at the way the world was developing. Smoke drifted out of his nose and mouth and the eye above the bullet hole sank in and filled with blood. One hand twitched as the wiring in his damaged brain fought to process information before giving up and going dark.

Connelly looked at both of them, then checked the rounds in the gun. He put the gun back in the waist of his pants and then stripped them both of their coats and put them on. Then he continued up the trail.

CHAPTER TWENTY-SEVEN

He climbed around little peaks and through little valleys. His feet were wet in his shoes, perhaps from burst blisters or maybe from blood. He stripped his coat and shirt to rags to keep his hands bandaged and insulated. When his breath became visible he deliriously considered trying to trap some of it in his hands to hold on to it in case he needed it.

Over stone and brush and wood. Far above the world. There on the points of the craggy teeth that snapped at the heavens Connelly wondered if the land below was real. Were he to venture down he was not sure if he would recognize anything.

He knew now it was not real. Not at its heart. Before this all he had thought he was journeying out, heading to the fringes and forgotten lands, but now he knew otherwise. With each step he had taken he had moved away from torpid slumber, from the complacent dream-world of home, and instead had approached the visceral savagery whose wax and wane formed the heartbeat of creation. This place in the mountain, the ruins of the village below. Tar shacks and shanties in the desert, lit by guttering fires. Rootless and wild and hungry. They were the real. The other way was a willful lie and having awoken he would not return. Could not even if he wanted to. There was a grim joy in it and he savored its taste and thought it beautiful.

Tattered wanderer, these are hollow countries, hallowed lands. See them arranged here at your feet, broken ruins of people long forgotten, ancient in their silent rage. See this. See this and know it to be your home.

Every fifty yards he would stop and look for the mountains. One big, one small, right behind one another. Leaping on top as though one attempted to subdue another. And perhaps they did. Even in this barren place conflict seemed inescapable.

Each time he stopped he would reach behind and take out the gun and check the rounds. It was his ritual. His method of remembrance and prayer. He tried to count how many times he stopped but gave up at fourteen.

When he saw the two mountains he did not believe it at first. He peered at them against the sky, suspecting some trick, but then relented and checked the gun again and began walking toward them. He nodded from fatigue as he walked and it was in waking from one of these relapses that he spotted a red-black streak on the stony path. He knelt and touched it.

Blood. It was sticky. Fairly fresh. Fresh enough, at least.

Connelly began following him again. His eyes roved back and forth for more drops, tracking a wounded creature and waiting for that doorway he'd find in the mountain.

A crevice. Crack in the world. Breaks down deep to where

things don't forget. Where things still remember what can never be forgotten no matter how much we try.

"Kill you," said Connelly, and kept walking.

He came to the feet of the two mountains and saw the gouge before them, cavernous and crooked like some giant had carved a lightning bolt in the ground. He stopped again and checked for blood. He himself was bleeding from his hands and so he kept them behind his back to avoid muddying the trail. He found a few splotches on a bit of mossy stone. He looked at the earth around the stone and examined the tracks and guessed the scarred man had sat there. Sat there to catch his breath or to look for Connelly or maybe just to sit. Connelly studied the scene and picked out his quarry's next direction and continued. He took out the gun and kept it out.

The trail led to the edge of the cliff and he leaned out and looked down. It might have been the way the sunlight made the shadows but the fault appeared endless. He turned back to the trail and saw it led along the edge in a straight line. The man had not tired yet. Connelly would not expect him to.

Death is tireless, he said to himself. That's okay. I don't tire easy, either.

Then he came upon a path, leading down into the chasm. It was so gentle and so firm that it had to have been constructed, and well constructed. He began down it, gun still out, eyes still searching. He walked down until the light was a thin line above and the edges of the cliff yawned about him. He wondered if this place had actually been carved. A primitive sanctuary, bored down into the earth to greet and remember one's forebears. He wondered if this had once been the culminating point for some savage pilgrimage and debated whether or not he was such a pilgrim himself.

Halfway down the cliff he came upon the cave. It was not large, no more than four feet high. He did not see any blood before its entrance but he did not need to to know that this was where the scarred man had fled.

Connelly reached into his pockets and felt around and pulled out his box of matches. He took off his shirt and wound it around a nearby branch and lit the end. It was a delicate fire, slow and smoking. He would have to move slowly, otherwise he would be moving by matchlight. He let it catch better and walked into the cave.

The passageway wound through the rock, widening and twisting. He walked with his head bowed and his knees bent and the torch thrust ahead, the gun trained on the dead center of the passage. Behind him the mouth of the tunnel moaned and grieved but he paid it no mind. His eyes grew used to the darkness and patches of moisture winked and glittered at him. He could not say how far he walked but if a mountain had a heart he felt he had to be near this one's.

Then he heard a sound from far away in the tunnel.

"Connelly," said a voice.

He stopped. Waited. Then began creeping ahead.

"You came," said the voice. It sounded as though the speaker had been weeping. "I knew you would."

He came to a wide atrium in the tunnel and saw vaults of rock stretching out above and beside him. Crystals burst into radiant prisms as the firelight found them and he believed for a second that all the night heavens were inlaid in the walls, like someone had pulled the sky down to this room. He scanned the room with the torchlight but saw nothing except another passageway on the far side.

"I tried to stop it, you see," said the voice from far ahead. "I thought I could. I thought I could come back and stop it."

Connelly began walking toward the next entry, still moving slowly.

"But I don't believe I can," the voice whispered.

He stepped to the side of the entryway and looked in, leading with the gun. He saw nothing. The tunnel turned away below.

"It's leaving me," said the voice. "Can you feel it? It's abandoning me. In a way I am glad but I weep at the same time. Because what will come after me? What will be next? I do not know. And I fear it."

Connelly began walking down the passageway. It curved in a long spiral and he could not fathom how deep below the earth they were. Miles, if anything. But he felt somehow that this place was not a part of the earth in any way he knew. He had never been in a place older than this. It was so old it was below everything, below all things. Below time. Below knowledge.

"Death will not die," warned the voice. "It will not. You must know that."

Connelly did not answer. He kept the torch ahead of him, wiped sweat from his brow, tried to ignore the sting of smoke in his eyes and his nostrils. The torch was fading fast and he was not sure how far away the scarred man was. Two more turns? One? Three?

"It will not die," said the voice, and this time it sounded stronger, stranger. "It will come back. Stronger. Wilder. Harder."

Connelly cocked the gun. The voice was very near now. He could hear it whimpering nearby. Light dappled the far stone wall, coming from some source around the next bend. He studied it and took a breath.

He turned the corner and saw the scarred man sitting on the floor of the cave before another large passageway, his head bowed in his lap and his shoulders shaking. Before him was an old lantern, the flame dancing slowly in the waxy glass. The silver knife was still clutched in his fingers. Bones littered the floor around him, eye sockets flickering with the torchlight, rib cages arced and poised like hands ready to pray. Among them were weapons but weapons like nothing Connelly had ever seen before. A long musket with a wooden stock and a flint hammer. A thin rapier with a silver hilt. A broadsword easily three feet long. Even stone weapons, chiseled blades crudely lashed to sticks, spears carved from wood, pieces of stone hacked to resemble maces.

Connelly's eye moved to the figure on the stone floor. The scarred man, sitting in the center of it all, weeping silently.

Connelly raised the gun. The gray man lifted his head to look at him, scars burning white, eyes dead and hollow. Shark eyes. Eyes that had seen the rise and fall of civilizations, and did not care.

The man's face twisted in fury. Gray needle-teeth flashed in the firelight. "No!" he screamed. "I will not let you do this! I will not let you do this!"

He leapt to his feet and Connelly fired, but it was too late. The shot went wide and punched through the scarred man's coat. Clay and bones burst behind him as the bullet struck the cave floor. The silver knife surged forward in the man's hand and Connelly lifted his arm to block it but it dipped up and in, biting into his side and raking his ribs. He screamed and the scarred man reached under to try to push it up and into his chest, but Connelly pulled the scarred man in and butted him in the face. A dozen tiny stars of pain came to life on his scalp where his forehead met the man's jagged maw. Then he shoved the scarred man back, hand held to the wound at his side, knuckles already dripping.

The scarred man melted away to dart back in again and drag the knife over Connelly's shoulder and across his neck and cheek. He seemed to be made of nothing but cloak and teeth and knives. Connelly felt lines of pain light up in his wrist and in his knee. He stumbled back and saw the icy point of the dagger glide by him once more, hissing through the air. He fired again without thinking, gunflash casting shadows on the cave wall, and the scarred man gasped and clutched his leg. Then he growled and feinted to the side and pounced forward again and Connelly felt bright blinding pain in his leg. He fell to a kneel as the leg died underneath him and he struggled to stay upright, left arm held close and winglike, a thousand wounds blossoming on his body. The scarred man seemed shaken by the last shot but he gathered his strength and leapt upon Connelly, snarling like a beast. As Connelly's back met the stone floor he pushed the nose of the gun barrel up and fired.

Then silence. He waited for the knife to come home, to worm its way into his rib cage and ravage his heart until it lay cold. But it did not come. There was nothing but the scent of burning powder in the air and the pain in his legs and side. The gun lay on his belly, hot and heavy. Somewhere in the room someone exhaled slowly.

Connelly opened his eyes and saw the scarred man sitting

on the floor again, the silver knife now on the ground. The man clutched his belly, breathing gently, then drew his hand away and looked at the smooth stain on his palm.

Dark red. Red enough to be black.

"Got you," said Connelly softly. "Got you, finally."

The scarred man shook his head. His mouth worked open and shut like a fish dying on a mudbank, suffocated by the air. "Fool," he said softly. "Useless. Useless fool." Then he started to try to stand up. He failed once and kicked the lantern over and the muddy glass bled fire onto the earthen floor. Then he fought to his feet and staggered back uncertainly until he leaned against the brick wall, hand still clutched to his stomach.

"You goddamn fool," he gasped.

"I got you, you bastard," Connelly said.

"You wouldn't listen," he said. "You just wouldn't."

The pool of fire spread. As it did the light in the chamber changed. Then for one instant Connelly thought he saw the young blond man standing in the cave with him in place of Shivers. The young blond man from his dreams. Then the light changed once more and he was Shivers again, and yet somewhere beneath all the years of scars and fury Connelly could still make out that sad young face, that brow anointed with red...

"Did you... Did you really think you were first?" said the scarred man. Breath whistled from down in his chest. He coughed and his teeth gleamed redly. "Or I? Look...look around you. Look at them. Did you...How could you..." Then he coughed again and rolled sideways. He stumbled into the chamber beyond and was swallowed by the darkness.

"No!" said Connelly. "No!"

Connelly gathered his ragged body together and stood and stepped forward over the pool of fire. He looked at the ancient corpses that lay around the cavern's entrance and stared into the entry ahead. He could see nothing but he knew something waited there. Something was watching. He dropped the gun and walked into the cave.

Endless dark. No walls, no ceiling. If he ran on stone his feet did not feel it and he was not even sure if he breathed air.

"Where are you?" he asked. He walked farther ahead, one hand out in front, stumbling like he was blind.

"Where are you? Where are you!" he screamed.

His scream echoed on, yet as it faded he became aware of a second sound. A faint trickle, the muted laugh of a stream or brook somewhere in the cavern. Connelly stumbled toward it until his fingers met slick rocks and the cool caress of water. He huddled by the waters, clinging to the only concrete thing in this darkness, and then he realized the tiny stream was faintly luminescent. Some spectral blue light, seeping up from within the brook. He let his eyes adjust to its light. Focused until he saw it trickling out of the small aperture in the rock wall, then weaving away until it made a staggered arc on the cavern floor.

Something coughed in the darkness. He squinted and saw the form of a man, lying on the riverbank on the far side of the cavern. Connelly wrestled himself to his feet one last time and stumbled over, wiping the sweat and filth from his eyes.

The scarred man lay with his arms and part of his head submerged in the waters of the river. The stream gently curled and foamed around his elbow and his scalp and the black stones around him. Connelly stood over him and the scarred man tried to look at him with one staring eye, unable to lift his head, panicking like a felled deer. His mouth still opened and closed uselessly. Ghostly streamers of red ran from his chest and down the riverwater.

Connelly looked down at him for a minute or more. Then he stooped and picked up one of the black stones. As he did he heard the scarred man say, "No. Don't."

"Shut up."

"No..."

"You shut the hell up."

"Look," the man whispered. "Look." He moved one hand and tried to point into the waters.

Connelly knelt at the bank. Then he looked into the brook and saw something. Flickering images, trapped within the waters like rays of light within a prism. Then they swelled and grew until he could not look away.

Screaming. A great fire, a city burning. The sky rained daggers and knives and up in the clouds he heard the roar of engines and the bellow of explosions. He watched as some twisted black wreck swam smoking to the earth and erupted as it touched the ground. Great, hulking machines toiled across miles of mud, pausing only to spout fire that arced across the country. The seas boiled with vast iron ships that spat long spears to rove through the waves and bury themselves in the sides of crafts the size of islands.

Someone wept. He was in a forest of barbed wire and he saw a crowd of people shuddering beneath blankets thin as paper, their arms like twigs and their faces like skulls. Rivers of blood rolled through the gutters and he heard the barking of dogs and the howl of commands and somewhere there was gunfire and gasping. Then the horizon lit up as though it had been kissed by the sun and he watched as the sky boiled and the atmosphere evaporated. A wave of fire so hot it was invisible swept across a city that crumbled into dust.

The world went dark. Died. Then lit up.

Cold illumination, blue and bland. He saw cities grow cement tendrils and heave themselves up from red earth, glass towers growing from their centers to touch the very clouds. Chrome and red stars swarmed through the cities and lights flickered on and before his eyes the buildings rose and fell, each time outdoing the last until all was dwarfed by their construction. The glass obelisks glared down upon him and he felt tiny and meaningless at their feet. The cities belched poison into the rivers and seas and immense chimneys arose far in the distance and from their crowns came pillars of smoke thicker than any mountain. Then the bases of the towers filled with fumes and fire and he watched as several rose up into the sky like fireworks and disappeared behind the penumbra of moisture that made the roof of the world.

A millions voices droned. A billion. More. Metal stars wheeled above, whispering along. Everything speaking all at once. A crowded world delivered in tremendous violence, a world that sipped war's offering and was fueled by its captures and casualties to ascend to heights that Connelly had never guessed existed.

A dawn. A rebirth. Bought with terrible sacrifice, a great suffering to drown out all others. But one that would give birth to a new age.

And for that age, a new Death. Something that had been forged in desperation and beaten hard until it was inured to all pleas and did not know the meaning of mercy. Something that would bring this suffering without hesitation and so usher in the future.

Connelly looked up. Something stood across the river from them. Something familiar. It gestured to him, calling him.

"Don't," whispered the scarred man at his feet. "Don't do it."

Connelly looked back down at the thing on the riverbank. He lifted the stone in his hands and took a breath.

"It'll be worse," the scarred man said softly. "So much . . . So much worse."

"Bastard," said Connelly.

"Just die. Just die and leave it. Don't go across to it. Let it be."

"Fucking bastard," said Connelly. He lifted the stone higher.

"No," said Shivers. Blood sputtered from his mouth and lips. Connelly saw a wild fear in his eyes, the same fear he had seen a lifetime ago in Memphis when Death had seen him and perhaps had seen the future as well. "No," Shivers said again. "No, don't. Don't!"

Connelly brought the stone down. It struck the scarred man on the eyebrow and his head snapped back and his eyes went sightless. Then Connelly lifted the stone again and brought it down again and again. And again and again.

All other things fell away. The sound of the stone on blood and flesh echoed into the chamber and the mindless action seemed simple and crude and glorious. Connelly thought there was a song in it, wild and primal. And somewhere in it was the rhythm of the world.

Savage and perfect. Hungry. Endless.

He kept hitting him long after he was dead. He could never be dead enough. Not ever.

Finally he stopped. The stone clattered to the ground beside his feet. He wiped his brow and held his hands before his eyes and watched them tremble with joy and exhaustion. Then he looked back at the thing across the river.

It beckoned to him again, calmly waiting. Patient enough to wait out ages. Connelly looked into its black eyes and over its scars. Looked at its thick beard and long black hair. Then he imagined he saw something under all of it. Under all of the scars there was a face he knew. A face like his.

A predecessor slain, a mantle won. A torch and sword to bear among the coming billions, passed down as it had been before.

The figure extended its hand to him.

Connelly nodded. "All right," he said softly. "All right."

And he waded across the river.

EPILOGUE

Dawn falls across the country.

The sun's warming fingers reach down into the plains. What little growth there is stretches to its touch but goes ignored by the shifting thread of people that wanders by it, heads bowed. They have traveled far but will travel farther, maundering the edges of these cracked lands as they search for a place that can sustain them for a little while longer.

The people are many and know countless countries and many creeds. They know no nation and no course, no government and no law. They navigate by hunger alone and in doing so survive another day. They are pilgrims and nomads, drifters and wanderers, bound to nothing more than whatever fruits the earth is willing to offer. From the Great Lakes to the Pacific. From where the Rocky Mountains form their long wall to where the Atlantic swirls its muddy waters. They have walked there and called these places home and made their names and then moved on.

They have seen much and they will see more. They have been here before. Have always been here. Will always be here until the world fails and only then will they be truly homeless and pass on.

From somewhere among them comes word. Rumors of the scarred man who still moves among their ranks, bringing with him his coat of night and his grim smile. We have seen him, some say. We have seen him treading the very ground we tread now. He's come back. Come again.

The whispers grow as the dawn rolls across the land. He comes from the west, they say. Comes striding from the west, eyes forever fixed on the east. A great, tall man with wild hair and a thick black beard, scarred from head to toe. But he is different now. Not half so wicked, not half so savage. He has grown to be a huge thing, blank and dour, his face expressionless yet grim. He is a new man who walks in a different way and so leaves something different in his wake.

From a cabbie comes word that with each step he takes one can hear the footfalls of thousands falling in line, an army marching somewhere in the shadows behind him. When he sets up camp and starts his fire the smoke forms shapes in the air that suggest a crowd of people huddling with him, millions of them, gray and cold and hopeless. The gypsy-folk whisper that when he slumbers in the fields his chest makes sounds of screaming steel and from his nose and mouth comes a thick black smoke, like burning oil. And a street-preacher claims that when the scarred man passed through St. Louis the entire city was struck with nightmares, envisioning a great fire, and that fire spread and consumed the blind eye that made the world.

They say that in his pockets he does not hold the fates of single men but the fates of cities, of countries, of the world. To him we are as ants, scuttling around the face of our hill. With a wave of his hand he scorches the sky and merely by closing his eyes a whole city may perish. He brings the new way. He brings the new world. He brings tomorrow, and so we grieve.

Others listen. The word spreads. Soon it is among all of them, all the drifters, all the travelers. It seeps into towns and bleeds into the cities. Jumps among ports and swims down rivers. And as the story spreads they become aware of a growing darkness, a sense of deep dread as the ground beneath them moves and revolves and twists itself into a new form.

Things are changing, they say. Time is moving on and leaving us behind.

They quiet and for the first time they stop walking. They stop shifting all at once and stand where they are and lift their heads. The people in the cities and the people in the farms, those at work and those at rest, men and women, young and old, they all stop and turn to the horizon, to the east and to the west, toward what is brewing there and what hides behind the next second or month or year.

Something is close, they whisper as the clouds darken above them. Something is near.

Listen. Listen. Do you hear it? Listen.

ACKNOWLEDGMENTS

A thousand and one thanks to Carrie, Carla, Ashlee, Jameson, Josh the ever-ready cameraman, my astoundingly patient family, Cameron and DongWon for taking a gamble and giving me a shot, and anyone else who tolerated me, even when I was pretty much intolerable.

1/10